A Spy in the Family

The bestselling author of THE LOOM OF
YOUTH, ISLAND IN THE SUN, FUEL
FOR THE FLAME, etc. describes this book as
an erotic comedy. It is the amazing story of a
respectable Treasury official, Victor Trail, and
his wife Myra, whose marriage has lost its
flavour, owing to Victor's clock-work
schedule and Myra's bland acceptance of it.
The unexpected revelation that Victor has
suspiciously altered his routine rouses Myra
out of her complacency, and her jealousy
rapidly changes the shape of their lives.
It leads her into a series of quite extraordinary
adventures and demi-monde activities which are
altogether astonishing in a respectable married
woman.
Her discomfiture is made all the more
excruciating by her new-found intimacy with
Victor, who apparently knows nothing about
her illegal actions and amazing amatory
diversions – or does he?
The reader of this novel of sex and
international intrigue is in for a number of
surprises. The only unsurprising thing about it
is that it is a marvellous piece of entertainment
by a master of that art.

Alec Waugh

A Spy in the Family

An erotic comedy

MAYFLOWER
GRANADA PUBLISHING
London Toronto Sydney New York

Published by Granada Publishing Limited
in Mayflower Books 1972
Reprinted 1973, 1975, 1977, 1979

ISBN 0 583 12033 4

First published in Great Britain by
W H Allen and Co Ltd 1970
Copyright © Alec Waugh 1970

Granada Publishing Limited
Frogmore, St Albans, Herts AL2 2NF
and
3 Upper James Street, London W1R 4BP
1221 Avenue of the Americas, New York, NY10020, USA
117 York Street, Sydney, NSW 2000, Australia
100 Skyway Avenue, Toronto, Ontario, Canada M9W 3A6
110 Northpark Centre, 2193 Johannesburg, South Africa
CML Centre, Queen & Wyndham, Auckland 1, New Zealand

Made and printed in Great Britain by
C. Nicholls & Company Ltd
The Philips Park Press, Manchester
Set in Intertype Times

Granada Publishing ®

A Spy in the Family

1

That's curious, she thought. That's very curious.

She stared perplexed at the telephone receiver she had just replaced. Five minutes earlier it had rung. "Please can I speak to Mrs. Trail? Oh, but that is you, Myra; yes, of course it is. Naturally I recognised the voice; but it *is* long, so very long too long. It's Kitty here. Kitty Severod. When did we meet last? The Carringtons? That's a year ago."

"It's thirty months!"

"It can't be. Really. Yes, I suppose it is. That's what's so awful about London. So rushed, so driven, no time for anything; never seeing one's friends, one's real friends. Yet when one gets to the end of the year, one asks oneself what it's all been about. Doing so much, but what? That's what I keep telling Martin. We're losing touch with all the people that we care for. So that this afternoon when I saw Victor ..."

"You saw Victor!"

"Yes, in the Brompton Road."

"The Brompton Road?"

"From the top of a bus. I'd been lunching with Marjorie Fitzgeorge. You know her? Oh, but you must. The dearest person, you'd love her, with the loveliest flat; in Chelsea. That new block just off Tite Street; with a wonderful *au pair* girl from Vienna making the most scrumptious pastry. You can't think about calories when you lunch with her. I must see that you meet. All the same I *have* only known them for six months; that's not the same thing as someone you've known all your life. Which is exactly what I was saying to myself as I came away. There wasn't a taxi in the whole Brompton Road; there never is, is there, when one really wants one, so I caught a 14 bus and there I was sitting on the top deck, thinking of all the people I never seem to see these days, when lo and behold right down below me, on the pavement, just where the old tube station used to be ..."

"No ... no ... you must be mistaken. Victor couldn't possibly be there in mid-afternoon."

She knew her husband's movements too well to have any doubt upon that score. Victor was a Treasury official; and there was no one in Whitehall whose routine moved more smoothly to a clockwork rhythm. At half past nine every morning he was at his desk; at a quarter to one he would walk up Whitehall to his club, the Athenaeum. He would lunch frugally, for his figure's sake, though he would enliven his meal with a small carafe of wine, or divide with a friend a half bottle of better wine. When his hair needed trimming, he would have that done for him at the Athenaeum. Every other Friday he would be manicured at Simpson's, three minutes' walk from Piccadilly Circus. At Simpson's, he would make any personal purchase he might need. His tailor was a hundred yards to the north in Savile Row. Day after day, week after week, year after year, his movements in London between 9.15 in the morning and 5.45 at night were contained within the circumference of a circle, its centre in Piccadilly Circus and a radius of a quarter of a mile. He could not possibly have been in the Brompton Road at three o'clock in the afternoon.

"You must be mistaken," she insisted.

"Oh, no, how could I be? Victor! That guardee look, the black hat slightly tilted, the gloves, the rolled umbrella and that dark, short overcoat with the black velvet collar – another half inch and he'd be a hippie. I couldn't mistake Victor. The moment I saw him I thought, Now, isn't that just what I was saying to myself? I never see the people whom I'm fondest of. Myra and Victor ... when did I see them last, and is there anyone I'm fonder of than Myra? Myra whom I learned skiing with. I've got to do something about them right away. Then I remembered ... Friday. The Jacksons, the Eric Jacksons, you must remember them; they're dining with us. Couldn't you come too? We're eight at present, but ten is a much better number. You can have the host and the hostess at each end. It's terribly short notice, but can't you manage it?"

"Unless Victor's got something fixed."

"Is he likely to?"

"It's most unlikely."

Most, most unlikely. Victor never made arrangements on his own. He was completely predictable. The standardised civil servant. Winchester his school; a scholarship at New College. One of the top men of his year at Oxford, but with successes exclusively scholastic. He had never made the headlines. From the start he had been destined for the Treasury. As he had begun, so had he gone on. Completely organised. He never wasted time. That was why he was able to do so much. He belonged to a couple of masculine dining-clubs. The Omar Khayyam and the Odde Volumes, which met eight times a year on the fourth Tuesday of the month. Wine was one of his hobbies. He was a member of the Wine and Food Society. Occasionally he went to tastings; as often as not he took her with him. They were usually in cellars, in the City. Far from the Brompton Road. He was on the Wine Committee at the Athenaeum. Once every six weeks or so, the committee would meet to discuss additions to the cellar. He had been a useful cricketer; he had now given up the game, but often on Saturdays in the summer he would go up to Lord's, and he would always take the day off for the first morning of the Test match. On an average, she supposed, he had a masculine dinner of some kind every other week; as did most Englishmen of his taste and training. But everything he did fitted into a pattern. At the start of every year, he would know roughly what he would be doing on every single day of it. What could he have been doing at three o'clock on a March afternoon in the Brompton Road?

"That's settled then, isn't it?" said Kitty. "Eight o'clock, black tie."

From the hall below she heard the sound of a door opening. It was ten past six. He would have walked from Whitehall to the Charing Cross tube station. Seven minutes. The Northern line would have got him to Hampstead station in twenty minutes. Six minutes' walk down hill, past the parish church to their house in Holly Place, a synchronised piece of clockwork. His black hat was laid on the hall chest beside his gloves and his umbrella. He was taking off the short dark overcoat with the black velvet collar. He was unmistakable. He was wearing a black, pin-stripe suit, double-breasted, a black and white striped shirt with a starched white collar, and a black and white polka-dot tie. She drew a long, slow breath. He was good-looking; and he would stay good-looking, for a long, long time. Friends had said to her when she was engaged, "How wise to marry someone quite a little older than yourself, someone who knows his mind." But though he may have known

9

his mind, he had not been that much older – twenty-six to her twenty. But he had looked thirty-five. Now, five years later, he still looked thirty-five, while she, the mother of two children, was starting to catch up. In the middle thirties they would look contemporaries. At forty she might look the elder. I'll have to be on my guard then, she had warned herself. Young girls will be setting their caps at him. I'll seem to them exceedingly autumnal.

"Had a good day?" she asked.

"Like all my days."

"No high affairs of state?"

"Not on my humble level."

He hung his coat upon a hanger. He came up the stairs with a light bouyant stride, two steps at a time. He put an arm round her shoulders. He drew her close against him; his cheek against hers was a little rough, but though he was dark, he did not look quarter-shaven, and there was about him a fresh air of soap and toilet water.

"Kitty Severod rang up," she said.

"She did? What was on her mind?"

"She wanted us to dine on Friday."

"And can we?"

"Unless you've anything arranged."

"Me, on a Friday? What an idea. The Severods. That'll be fun. It's a long time since we've met."

"That was what she said."

She almost added: "She saw you from the top of a bus this afternoon. That's what made her think of us." She did not though. Something held her back. She was wondering whether he would tell her on his own account what project had taken him two miles from his desk and telephone.

He was carrying two parcels, one small and one large and flat. He handed her the large one. "A record that I thought you'd like; the other one's for Jerry."

Jerry was their daughter, four years old. Their son Frank would be two next month. "Let's go up," he said.

Their house was three-storeyed; the nursery quarters were on the second and third floors. They had had the good fortune to find two Swedish *au pair* girls, who looked after the children and ran the house, leaving Myra to do the cooking. "It's

10

all too good to last," Myra kept saying. But it had lasted for two years, and the girls seemed happy. They were cheerful, healthy creatures who liked bicycling over the Heath. They did not seem to have any boy friends. "I've an idea," said Victor, "that they're more interested in their own sex than the other."

Jerry jumped to her feet as they came in. She ran towards her father, arms spread wide. "Dadsey man, Dadsey man," she cried. His return every night was the big moment of her day. As often as not he brought her back a present, something appropriately fragile and inexpensive that would amuse her for ten minutes and next morning be forgotten. He handed her the packet. She tore it open. It was a toy he had bought her in the street, an ostrich that you wound and that darted its head forward as it walked. "Dadsey, I love it. Thank you, thank you, thank you."

Her father went down on his knees beside her. He had hitched up his trousers before kneeling down, but there was no sign of guardee starchiness as he assisted his daughter's effort to control the toy that pranced uncertainly across the carpet. "What a clumsy fellow," he exclaimed. "We'd better send him to a dancing class." Myra smiled fondly. What a father he's going to be, she thought.

She turned to the far corner where Frank, before being put to bed, was being fed his final bottle. Lena, the younger of the two Swedish girls, was cradling him against her shoulder, murmuring softly in his ear. She was blonde and slim and tall, with a clean, clear complexion. She was barely twenty-one. She adored Frank. She was very feminine, the kind of girl any man would go for. Was it really true what Victor had suggested? Myra looked across the room at the other girl. She knew from her passport that Anna was only twenty-six. But she looked thirty. She was blonde too, almost flaxen, but she was less tall. She had a firm, almost protuberant jaw and heavy haunches. Her eyes were very blue; and she had the complexion that is known as typically Swedish. She would have been a strikingly handsome man. Even as it was, Myra could imagine some men falling for her. She had a commanding presence, but her smile was welcoming. She gave the impression that she found life fun, something to be enjoyed, that she was eager to have others enjoy it with her.

11

It must have been easy for Lena, who was younger not only in years but in experience, to fall under her influence. But surely, at base, Lena was completely feminine. She was certain to shake out of it, to find her true nature, her true destiny through a man. And Anna ... what happened to Anna then?. .. Move on to another Lena?

Myra looked across the room to Anna. Anna seemed so relaxed, so self-fulfilled. She had accepted her particular, her peculiar destiny, had come to realise that the Lenas of the world moved on, that there were always other Lenas; until one became old oneself, but then wasn't that the human lot ... had not the psalmist said just that? We are old who once were young . . .

Myra mentally shook herself. What on earth was she doing, following this sultry daydream! She looked from Anna to Lena and then back again. Was it true what Victor had suggested? She tried to picture them together ... the attempt sent a spasm of prurient curiosity along her nerves. What was it *precisely* that they did together?

The Trails dined alone three or four nights a week. This night was one of them. After they had said goodnight to the children, Victor mixed a martini. Usually while they drank it, they would put on records. Music was very special for them. After their cocktail, Myra would prepare dinner while he bathed and changed. "What was that record you brought back?" she asked.

"Aaron Copeland's latest. I think you'll like it."

She did; but she found it difficult to concentrate her attention on it. She was still curious about the afternoon. It was too late now to question him. She had been stupid perhaps not to have told him at the start, but she rather enjoyed knowing something about him that he did not know she knew.

It was a short record, a bare seven minutes. Ordinarily she would have asked him to put on another. But she was still fretted by uncertainty.

"You remember that novelist we met the other evening at the Strouds," she said.

"Of course. Ralph Symons. I picked up one of his novels in the Athenaeum the other day. It looked entertaining. I wished I had had time to read it."

"I always read him. I asked him why so many of his characters were in jobs that had to do with writing, advertising, publishing, the BBC or films. He said it was the only kind of job that he knew anything about. 'It's a problem,' he said. 'One of my greatest problems. I wish I didn't have to write about that kind of person. I'm always afraid that because my heroes are alike, my books will seem alike. Perhaps they are. I wish I could write about stockbrokers and chartered accountants. But I don't know anything about them.'

" 'But you must,' I said, 'know some stockbrokers and accountants.'

" 'Of course, naturally...'

" 'Can't you ask them?' I said. He shook his head. 'I do, but the answers that they give don't help me. They say it would all sound boring. Routine stuff, they say. "It isn't boring to us because our lives depend on it; you have to be a part of it to understand." And that, of course, is what one needs to be if one's going to put a character into a novel; one has to be a part of his life, to see it from the inside. I can't do that. I have to be devious. In the novel I'm writing now, my chief character is an underwriter at Lloyd's and I'm going to try to make his problems real by showing them through his wife's eyes. She'll be wondering about him. As she's arranging the flowers in the drawing room, she'll be saying to herself. "It's ten o'clock. He'll have finished going through his mail. What kind of a mail was it? He told me that he was worried about the insurance of that new estate; will there be any answer about that?" You see the kind of thing I mean. I'll make him real because he's so real to her. Yet I don't know about him basically, nor does she. You see my point?' Of course I saw it and what do you think I said to him?"

"You tell me what you said to him."

"I said, 'That's exactly how I feel about my husband. I've no idea what it is that he's doing in that office of his. I hardly ever see any of the men he works with. Half the wives I know are expected to entertain their husbands' business friends. In America a firm insists on seeing an applicant's wife before it takes him on. It wants to know whether she'll be a liability or an asset. It isn't like that in England, at least not in the high echelons of the Civil Service. 'Keep your home and your office separate,' Victor says. 'I don't want to see in the evening the people I've been with all day long. You can choose your friends, after all. You can't choose your opposite number in a ministry.' Isn't that what you do say, Victor?"

He laughed. She was speaking lightly in the teasing way that she knew he found attractive. She assumed the role of the irresponsible female. The directrice of her finishing school in Switzerland had described her once as *papillon*, a bird-brain. It made her a good foil for him.

"What else could I say?" he answered. "That is the way it is."

"And if I were to ask you exactly what you had been doing today, hour by hour, there wouldn't be anything in the whole day worth recounting. Just another day like any other."

"Exactly."

Exactly. But it couldn't have been a day like any other. If he had made a practice of going out to the Brompton Road he would certainly have mentioned it, at some time or another before now. But he never had.

She finished her martini, then stood up. "Time I was getting along with that sole Amandine."

In the kitchen she thought, Something is going on that he doesn't tell me. For the first time in five years of marriage she had a presentiment of trouble.

2

They arrived at the Severods' on Friday after eight. Myra would have preferred to get there punctually, but Victor with his invincible respect for protocol was insistent that one should never be less than five or more than fifteen minutes late. In consequence four of the guests were already there. That left very little opportunity for the conversation between Victor and his hostess that would with any luck refer to that glimpse of him from the top of a 14 bus.

Kitty rushed forward with outstretched arms. "My dears, am I glad to see you. It has been so long. How have we come to miss each other all this time, with all the friends we have in common? No spare time, yet I don't know what I'm doing with my time. I was saying all this to Myra on the telephone, and you wouldn't be here this evening but for chance . . ."

Ah, now it comes, thought Myra. She could hear Kitty talking about that glimpse from the top of the 14 bus. Would Victor blush? She had never seen him blush. She had never seen him discomposed. What would happen then? Would he let it pass, accept as the most natural thing in the world that he should be walking down the Brompton Road at three o'clock on a March afternoon? Probably he would. But what would he say afterwards to her? With her he couldn't let it pass, or could he? Make no reference to it; ignore it. If he did, that left it up to her. Do *I* then let it pass? How can I, after all I've said?

"The purest chance," Kitty was hurrying on. "I couldn't have been more surprised —" Now here it comes, thought Myra. But the sentence was never finished. Again the door was opened. The last couple was coming forward. Kitty had broken away. Once again her arms were flung out wide. "Darlings, how glad I am to see you."

The moment had passed. Myra was reminded of a play by J. B. Priestley called *Dangerous Corner*. It had shown how a happy family that included several couples suddenly stumbled upon a secret that ruined all their lives. Everything was brought into the open. Nothing could be the same again. The hero committed suicide. Just before the curtain fell one of the characters said, If that secret had never come out, we'd all have gone on quietly with our lives. We'd have lived through our problems, accepted the compromises that have been forced on us. It wouldn't have been perfect but we'd have stayed together, ignorant about the things that we wouldn't have had the strength to take. So many things are better hidden.

To the audience, that had seemed the message of the play, the play was over. Then to everyone's surprise the curtain went up again. The action returned to the first act, with the women coming into the drawing room after dinner. The same action identically, except that it was compressed. Within a few minutes it had reached the point when the process of revelation had begun. It had concerned a cigarette box that one of the women recognised. Another woman had said, How could you have seen it, when, where, how? That had started the fatal interrogation which once embarked upon could not be abandoned, which had to run its course to its disastrous conclusion.

Once again in this retake, that decisive moment had been

reached; the woman had recognised the box, but before she could speak, there was a burst of music. The play had been written in the early days of radio; one of the characters had been fiddling with a recalcitrant set. His efforts suddenly succeeded. A fox trot blared across the room. 'Come on, let's dance,' he said. The play had been written in the days when one rolled back carpets. The two women stood staring at each other, defiantly, distrustfully; but already one of them had been claimed by a partner. General talk was ended. The dangerous corner had been turned, been passed forever.

Was this such a moment, Myra wondered. Would she in time to come think: "thank heavens Victor was spared being put to embarrassment – to more than embarrassment maybe; to being exposed in public"? Or would she later come to think: "if only there had been that exposure then ... if only we could have cleared the air. Oughtn't I to have told him right away? Why was I secretive and so coy?"

She closed her eyes. She shook her head. She was out of her depth, suddenly. . . .

The Severods were members of the Wine and Food Society. That was their main link with Victor, and there was always a good deal of talking about wine at their dinner parties. Myra made the best of it. Very dry martinis were what she really liked. She actually preferred drinking before meals. She enjoyed gourmet food, and she had noticed that wine connoisseurs were on the whole indifferent to what they ate, provided it did not interfere with the pleasure of their wine. They seemed to think the perfect dinner was turtle soup, roast beef, and a cheese soufflé. But she enjoyed a glass or two of wine; and so that she could share Victor's hobby with him, she had made herself reasonably knowledgeable. She was not bored when Victor and his friends began to talk about years and vintages.

As always at the Severods', the red wines had been decanted and there were two different types of glass so that one wine could be tasted against another. With the fish course – a prawn cocktail – there had been, to prepare the way, a light white wine of no particular quality. Now on each plate a small plump piece of steak reposed on a piece of toast that had been spread with pâté. Two decanters of red wine went around the table. "Now we get down to business," the host said. "Let's

16

first take the wine in the right-hand glass. Victor, what would you say this was?"

Victor went through the ritual. The glass was two-thirds full. He lifted it against the light; he rotated the wine so that minute drops ran down the inner side. He lifted the glass beneath his nostrils. He took a long sniff. He closed his eyes ruminantly, lowered the glass again, then raised it to his lips. The sip he took was quite a big one. He held the wine in his mouth. He gave the impression that he was rinsing his teeth with it. Then he put the glass back on to the table. "It's excellent," he said.

"No one, I hope, is going to contradict you there. But what would you say it is?"

Once again Victor went through the ritual. He shook his head. "This is just a guess. I'd say it was a Burgundy. A fairly young one, a '62 perhaps and a rather light one. Not as big as a Côte de Nuits. A Santenay perhaps."

Severod laughed. "That's what I hoped you'd say. It's not a bad shot and it is a '62; but as a matter of fact it isn't a Burgundy at all. It's a Bordeaux – a St. Emilion, which as I don't need to tell you, can be very like a Burgundy in a hot summer. We've most of us heard our fathers talk about that incredibly hot summer of '21."

"When the Australian bowlers spread such havoc on those fast wickets."

"Exactly. People talk about the Yquem '21, and there is still a little of it left; but in the thirties the Cheval Blanc '21 was fetching higher prices than Margaux and Latour. It was as rich and heavy as a Burgundy."

"What was this St. Emilion by the way?"

"Something you may not have heard of ... a Château Canon."

"Oddly enough, I came across a bottle a few weeks ago." Myra's attention was alerted; "a few weeks ago." When could that have been? She did not remember that there had been talk about such a wine at any of the dinners they had attended. Surely she would have remembered if there had; she always took note of what was said at dinner, refreshing her memory afterwards. Château Canon, St. Emilion. It must, she supposed, have been at one of his tastings at the Athenaeum. But had there been a tasting recently? A week ago she would have let

17

the moment pass. How could she be expected to know when and where her husband drank what with whom? But now she was on her guard. There was something in her husband's life she did not know about. Something he did not want her to know about.

Don't be an ass, she told herself. It could have happened in so many ways. How easy for two or three other members of a club to say over a lunch table: "I'm told that there's an excellent St. Emilion on the list. Why not have a bottle up and try?" Of course that's how it had happened. All the same, she vowed, I'm going to have a look at that Athenaeum wine list.

Her chance came the following week. They were giving a small lunch party in the Ladies' Annexe, as was their custom once a month or so. It was an easy way of returning hospitality. It had been Victor's idea. Without a cook, it was difficult for Myra to have more than another couple to dine to Hampstead. "Serving a dinner for six means your being in the kitchen all the time," he said. "If people are going to drag themselves all the way to Hampstead, they want to see their hostess."

Myra arrived at the club a quarter of an hour early. Victor always ordered the meal and the wines himself, but she had been there now so often that she had got to know the staff.

"I wonder," she asked the barman, "if I could see the wine list." She looked down the row of clarets. No, no Château Canon. But then she reminded herself this was the abbreviated Annexe list. "I don't want to be a nuisance," she said, "but I wonder if I could see the full club list. There's something that I'd like to ask my husband."

The full list was five times as big as the Annexe one. But there was no Château Canon there. She closed her eyes. Keep your head now, she adjured herself, you are being ridiculous. There was a play by a man called Shakespeare about a jealous Moor.

The sky was blue. The sun was warm upon her cheeks but the air had a keen spring bite. It would be nice on the Heath this afternoon. She would take Jerry out there after tea. But as she paused for a lorry to pass at the corner of Pall Mall, she noticed a westbound No. 14 bus swinging around the curve of the Haymarket. There was a bus stop twenty yards to her

18

left. It must be three years since she had been down the Brompton Road. London changed so fast. There might well be a reason now why a Treasury official should be walking down it on a weekday, at three o'clock. It was worth trying anyhow; anything was worth trying that might allay this worry.

To her left, Sloane Street stretched straight and broad towards the start of the King's Road. The bus swung to the right, through the Knightsbridge traffic jam. On the left was the imposing red brick façade of Harrods, dominating the scene just as it had when she was a girl, and on the other side there was the raised pavement, so that its succession of small smart boutiques could stand upon the level, before the groun sloped up its gentle rise to the top of Montpelier Square. Beyond and above the gracious Georgian lines of Brompton Square was the dome of the Oratory and, in between, the red glazed tiles that proved that a tube station had once stood there. Her father had pointed it out to her many years ago. "All over London you'll see red tiles like that, particularly on the Piccadilly line. One station has had to do the work of two, so instead of Dover Street, Down Street, Park Lane, Brompton Road, you have Green Park and Knightsbridge, and South Kensington. That's what we call progress."

She had always remembered his saying that. She had ever since been on the lookout for red glazed tiles. How little had she thought then that she would be remembering it, fifteen years later, as a married woman with a fierce dread niggling at her. She had pictured herself then as being married, with a child or two and a handsome husband who came back each evening from the office with the papers under his arm – just as her father had. With herself just as her mother was, contented and fulfilled. She had not pictured any other future. And two weeks ago it had seemed that that very picture was in focus, but now, but now . . .

She got down from the bus. She walked slowly up the street on the west side. Yes, it must be over five years since she had been here. There was no occasion. She had friends in Kensington and friends in Chelsea, but coming down from Hampstead, her needs when she came by tube were served by Knightsbridge and South Kensington. She might have been driven through it in a taxi, not noticing such changes as there were.

19

But she had certainly never walked down here. There were several new restaurants on the opposite side. They looked good and far from cheap. Was it in one of those that Victor had encountered Château Canon? The small boutiques on the raised pavement had probably changed their owners, but there was no apparent difference; and behind them was the same cluster of quiet streets that led into Montpelier Square. She turned up Montpelier Street. This part of London had always had a glamour for her, because of *The Forsyte Saga*. Soames and Irene had made their home here. Soames had been very happy at the start, till Bosinney had come, till Irene had realised that she needed more than Soames could offer her. Montpelier Square had not changed since Galsworthy had set his story there. For all the reconstruction that was being carried on elsewhere, the spirit of London reigned in this quiet square, just as in spite of the discoveries of science, the same dramas were being evolved between individual Londoners. The perpetual triangle. What else but another woman could have brought Victor here at such a time?

At the head of the street, left of the Hyde Park Hotel was a succession of large rectangular buildings. There was a similar succession of buildings on the south side. Some of them, the majority of them probably, were offices, but there must be many flats. How simple it would be for Victor to lunch with one of the residents of those flats at one of those elegantly discreet restaurants. It was a typical situation out of *The Forsyte Saga*. There had been so many references to "unhallowed" lovers"; but in Galsworthy, they had remained "unhallowed." The career of a man like Victor would have been ruined by a divorce. It would not be today. And in those days, the other woman was resigned to being in the background of a man's life – what was that novel . . . *Back Street* – she would not be today. Myra shivered mentally. A cold wind was blowing.

She had planned originally to get home in time to take Jerry for a walk, but nursery tea was at four. It had been cleared away by the time she was back and Lena had already gone out with Jerry and the baby. Anna was alone, reading beside the fire.

"They went out half an hour ago," she said. "They should be back within twenty minutes." Anna had vowed on her arrival that she would rid herself of her Swedish accent before her assignment was completed. She had almost but not quite succeeded. The slight northern inflection gave her voice a lilt that Myra found attractive.

"Do you mind if I sit down?" she asked.

"But of course not, please."

"I hardly ever seem to see you."

Anna smiled. "Isn't that the way it is in families, always being with people but never really seeing them? It's what my sister says about her marriage. Her husband makes his own breakfast, then rushes off to work. He gets back late in the evening, exchanges half a dozen words with her, then either they have guests or they go out to friends; at parties husband and wife are never allowed to sit or stand next to each other. When they are home, at the end of it he remembers that he has to get up early the next morning and goes straight to bed."

"That's something I've been on my guard against. We try not to go out more than four times a week."

"You've been very wise."

That was what she had thought. But had she been? Perhaps Victor was bored, coming back evening after evening to the same armchair, the LP records with his martini, the TV afterwards.

"Though we never have a chance of talking," Myra said, "I do hope that you realise how much we both appreciate what you are doing for the children."

"It's easy to be helpful for such charming children."

She smiled as she said that. She had a warm, open smile.

"You are going to be a wonderful mother to some children some day."

Anna smiled again. It was still a friendly smile, but it was a rather different one. Myra felt that they were suddenly on another level of communication. "Something tells me," Anna said, "that I shan't ever be a mother." She said it as though there were a hidden meaning behind her words.

"Whatever makes you say that? A young girl as nice to look at as you are."

"Thank you for that." Anna looked at Myra steadily. "I've an idea," she said, "that the kind of man to whom I am attracted – and it's only to one particular type of man that I *am* attracted – would not be very desirable as a father, even if he would want to be one."

21

Anna was still smiling but her smile was a half smile now. Myra felt oddly tense. Something extremely intimate had been said to her. Yet though she felt tense, she had a sense of being surprisingly relaxed.

"Why must you think that?" she said. "You love children. You're wonderful with children. Couldn't you find a man who, though he did not attract you quite so much, would be a good father to your children?"

Anna shook her head. "I wouldn't be a good wife to that kind of man. And it isn't fair to one's children to give them the kind of father to whom one can't be a good wife." She paused. Her smile had become almost tender. Myra found herself thinking, She really likes me. How had this conversation come about? Had her own problem, her own confusion made her more human, more approachable? "I know myself too well," said Anna. "I guess that that's my problem. I know myself far too well."

Victor returned at the exact moment he was expected. He was in excellent spirits. "That was a delightful lunch, a real success. Don't you think so? They thoroughly enjoyed themselves. You handled everything so well, as you always do. That's what makes our parties such fun for me, the knowledge that you'll do everything as it should be done. So many men must always be uncertain of whether their wives are going to make some ghastly *gaffe* and spoil the party. Once I've ordered the meal and chosen the guests, I can let myself be a guest at my own party. And it's all due to you. Do I take you for granted? I hope I don't. But how can I help it sometimes, when you are so perfect?"

She had risen as he came into the room. He put his arm round her shoulders, drawing her close against him. She could see, reflected in the mirror above the mantelpiece, the perfect young married couple. He was just the right amount taller than she was, four inches when she was in high heels. He looked so elegant, not dapper but well produced, with his creaseless clothes and his close-cut hair; he was one of the few men whom a short clipped moustache genuinely suited. And she, no one could say that she was not considerably more than adequate as a foil for him. She had never thought of herself as a raving beauty; she was not particularly photogenic. But she was unquestionably nice to look at, with her fresh colouring, her short straight nose and her full mouth. There was a wave in her light sandy-coloured hair; she had a trim figure and slim, straight legs. She looked right for him. Whenever, as now, she caught a glimpse of herself in a mirror at his side, she felt a warm stir of pride. They looked good together. They set each other off. Or was it merely, she now asked herself in a mood of doubt, that he set her off, that she made a mark in life because she had him with her? He was her justification to the world. She was the woman who had annexed this handsome, effective man. She was what she was because of him.

What had she been, after all, when she had met him in the very first weeks of her first season, at the Queen Charlotte Ball, which now that débutantes no longer "made their bob" at court was the equivalent of a presentation. She had been one of a hundred other girls, no one in particular, the daughter of solid parents, living in Wessex, well enough known in their own part of the country; her father, a solicitor, had as a Rugby footballer been capped for Somerset, but he was unheard of outside his own area of school and county. It was through Victor that she had come to take her place in the big world of London; through him she had become a wife, a hostess, and a mother. What in return had she done for him? Was she anything but an appendage, a flower to be worn in his buttonhole? If she had married someone else, she would have led a completely different life, while he would have led precisely the same life no matter whom he had married; anyone adequate would have done for him. He paid her compliments about the way that she made his parties go, but nothing surely could be easier than to make oneself gracious to one's husband's friends at a meal for the preparation of which one had no personal responsibility. She could not picture her life without him; through him she had everything that she had imagined for herself when she left that finishing school in Switzerland. What had she done for him? Had she completed his life? Was there something lacking in it? Was that the explanation of those visits to the Brompton Road?

Looking at their reflection in the glass, he caught her eye. He smiled. It was a fond and reassuring smile. It must be all right. Of course it must. If their marriage was so right for her, surely it must be right for him.

23

"By the way," he said, "I was only just remembering as I came home this evening. Your birthday's on Wednesday week. How would you like to celebrate?"

Her birthday. She had forgotten too. Her birthday ... a rescuing wave of hope lifted her from the rocks. Might he not have gone to the Brompton Road to find a present for her, in one of those small boutiques off Montpelier Square? Someone might have recommended one. Or Harrods. That was the kind of store to which Victor went. A birthday present. What a fool she had been. What a ridiculous, suspicious fool.

They decided to go to a cinema for her birthday, to a six o'clock performance. Then they would have dinner afterwards. "It's much more fun that way," he said. "You don't have to hurry over your dinner, and there's not the same temptation to fall asleep during the film; besides, the cinemas are less crowded then." They also decided to go on the night before so that he could wish her a happy birthday when the clock chimed twelve.

They got back to Hampstead soon after eleven. "I've a small bottle of champagne on ice," he said.

Her heart was warm, aglow with expectation as she waited in the drawing room while he busied himself with the glasses and the wine. It had been a happy evening. They had seen *The Graduate*, and that somehow had provided the right stimulus for their mood. It was a wanton film and a romantic film, the kind of film that put you in the right mood for lovemaking. They had dined in Soho, at the Jardin des Gourmets. He had held her hand as they sat together on the banquette seat. What was I worrying about, she thought. How one imagines things.

He brought up the champagne and glasses. He eased the cork out slowly, gently, millimetre by millimetre. It exploded with a lively "pop". "That's a good augury for the year," he said. "The last year was a good one, I can't think of a year being better. May the next one be as good." He raised his glass, clinked it against hers, then sipped. It was clean and fragrant, with a fresh sparkle on the palate. He put his glass back upon the table. He moved beside her. He took her face between his hands; he lifted it to his. It was a long slow kiss, his lips lingering upon hers. She closed her eyes. Her toes curled inside her shoes. As he moved back to his chair, she picked up her glass and drained it quickly. She looked at the clock. It was barely half past the hour. "Would you like your presents now?" he asked.

She shook her head. "I like having them all together on the breakfast table. I've been holding all my letters back for the last three days." She did not want to dawdle over the half bottle. The message of *The Graduate* was thudding through her veins. Quickly, quickly. She was impatient, restless, eager to have her doubts set at rest.

Victor had a small bed in his dressing room. She slept in a wide double bed with a high canopy above it. She put on a nightgown that had a Third Empire look. It was very long and creamy pink, with a ribbon that tied across it, high, just below her breasts. The neck was cut low, and the silk was pleated. It had very short frilled sleeves. She poured a drop of scent into the palms of her hands and rubbed it behind her ears and over her breasts. She sat up among the pillows, waiting.

There was a tap on the door. "Come in," she called. The minute hand of her bedside clock had just that second passed the twelve.

"Happy birthday," he said. He crossed the room, bent over her, and kissed her forehead. "May I tuck you up?" he asked.

"I think you should, shouldn't you, on my birthday?"

He slipped off his dressing gown. He switched off the light. On her dressing table was a candle and he lit it. He had left the light on in his room, and though the door was closed, a line of light above the carpet added to the candle's glow. He slipped in beside her, on her right-hand side. He took her in his arms; gently, gently, he began to caress her shoulders. They had acquired over the years a routine of courtship; turning onto his left side, he slid his right ankle over hers, drawing it towards him, opening her thighs. She laughed, a low, light laugh. "Oh, that professional gesture." It had become, after their honeymoon, one of their secret jokes. "That's how you used to seduce all those poor college girls," she said. His right hand moved along her shin, slowly, caressingly, over her knees, upwards, upwards. "Darling, I can't wait," she said.

25

Myra and Victor breakfasted apart. He had a continental meal – orange juice, corn flakes, toast, and coffee. He made it for himself. He liked to read his letters and his newspapers alone. Myra had her breakfast in the nursery. She made a meal of it. She did not usually go up till the front door had closed on Victor. She enjoyed dawdling in bed. On her birthday morning, he let her sleep on late – as an additional birthday present, he proposed to tell her when he came back that evening. He had left his present for her on the library table.

Her eyes grew eager at the sight of it. She had never looked forward to a birthday present more. In the memory of a night of love that package would be a doorway opening on to an unclouded year. She picked it up. It was soft, some sort of material. She turned it over, her fingers itched to open it. But she wanted to savour the pleasure of delay, in the way that a child leaves the best cake till last. In the drawer of her desk she had kept the letters and presents that she had received during the last few days; there were three birthday cards and two packets. She knew that Jerry would have something for her. She collected her spoils and went upstairs.

As she had known there would be, a warm welcome awaited her. The Swedes made a big thing of birthdays. Jerry had been well briefed. She clapped her hands; she sang, "Happy Birthday to You." A small sugared cake had been adorned with a coloured candle. There was also on her plate, beside a very small present a picture drawn by Jerry.

"Oh, how spoiled I am," cried Myra. The package was from Anna and Lena. It contained a painted china egg-cup. "That's dear of you, that really is," she said. She spread out her other presents.

"Let's see what you've got," said Jerry. "Let's see what Dadsey's given you."

"No, breakfast first," said Myra.

"No, no, presents first."

Jerry was as excited about the presents as though they were her own. "Now which is Dadsey's? Let's have it first.'

"No, no, let's have it last. It's bound to be the best; always keep the best till last."

Lingering over each one, Myra opened them slowly, painstakingly; knotting a scarf round her neck, examining herself in a mirror to see how it suited her. At last there was only the one big packet left. Jerry pounced on it. "That's Dadsey's. I'm going to open it myself."

"No, no," Anna expostulated. "Your mother must open that herself. It's her very special one."

"All right. Let her do it. I'll enjoy seeing the wrappings go."

It had been skilfully gift-wrapped and the wrappings were highly decorative. Jerry could not resist examining them. It all took quite a while. But at last Myra reached the tissue paper; it tore easily.

"It's lovely. Oh, isn't it?" Jerry exclaimed.

Yes, it was lovely – a twin-set in primrose-coloured cashmere. It was something that she had hankered for. But her heart was cold. It had been wrapped by Simpson's, Piccadilly.

3

The Trails' family doctor was a man of fifty-five named Forest Clarke. Victor had been his patient for twenty years. Dr. Clarke's father had looked after Victor's father. Dr. Clarke had brought both Myra's children into the world. When Myra telephoned for an appointment, he assumed that his father's old friend was to be blessed with another grandchild. But Myra shook her head. "Nothing as dramatic as that, alas. I want some sleeping pills."

"There shouldn't be any trouble about that." He looked at her thoughtfully. This was for him a case full of potentialities. Many men assert that they were unlucky in their birthday. That is their favourite alibi. They were born at the wrong time, they argue. They were too young for the first war, too old or too young for the second. Their education was interrupted, cut across. In one way or another, they were side-tracked. Dr. Clarke, on the other hand, asserted that he had been born in exactly the right year, 1913. He had practically no memories of the first war. His father, a respected Hampstead doctor with a large private practice, had been excused military service, but for services gratuitously rendered in military hospitals had been accorded, at the end of the war, the bonus of an O.B.E. His son had not therefore been deprived of his father's care during his early childhood.

From the beginning, Forest Clarke had followed his father's

footsteps. He had taken his degree from Guy's in 1938. That meant that there was no break in his career on the outbreak of war. He applied for and received at once a commission in the R.A.M.C. For six years he served as a doctor on several of the various fronts on which British infantry were in action. "That was," he would maintain, "my greatest piece of luck. I might, had there been no war and being something of a high-brow, have decided to go into psychiatry, which was the fashion then, to cure illness through the mind; but after the years of dealing with wounds and the kinds of malady that troops acquire, I felt that there was a great need for the man who can alleviate specific and immediate physical distress; for that you need the man who can cauterise a septic sore. I decided to remain a general practitioner." Yet since he had grown up in the hour when the world was beginning to recognise how much the mind was responsible for physical distress, Myra Trail could have very easily found a worse consultant.

He drew a pad towards him. He scribbled a prescription on it.

"All the same," he said, "I would be grateful if you could explain to me why you need these pills. You are young. You are healthy. As far as I know you have no problems. How long have you not been sleeping?"

"For about a month."

"When you say that you don't sleep, what exactly do you mean by that? Do you find it difficult to fall asleep?"

"Sometimes."

"When you wake up in the night, do you have difficulty in getting off to sleep again?"

"Yes."

"Do you sleep in the same bed as your husband?"

She flushed.

"I have a double bed; Victor has a small bed in his dressing room."

"Does he often spend the whole night with you?"

"What do you call often?"

"More often than not?"

"I wouldn't say that."

"What I was getting at is this: are you disturbed by having Victor in the same bed as you?"

28

"Oh no; no. I can't say that."

"Because, you know, it does often happen that a husband interferes with a wife's sleep and vice versa. The one goes off to sleep right away and the other doesn't. There are many who like to read themselves to sleep, and they can't because they'll disturb their partner. Then again there are those who when they wake up in the night like to read themselves back to sleep; they can't switch on the light because it would disturb the other. But that isn't your problem, is it? It's not that you want to read and can't because Victor's there."

"No, it isn't that."

"You haven't, in the past, made a practice of reading yourself back to sleep?"

"In the past I've never been troubled by not sleeping. No, I've never had to read myself back to sleep."

"It's one of the best ways. It's what I always do myself. I can strongly recommend it."

"I suppose I could try that." But she sounded unconvinced.

He asked her if she had headaches.

"Only if I've been awake for a long time and then ... but no, I don't really think I know what a headache is."

"You don't have any pains, no aches, so that if you stay in one position for more than a few minutes you feel uncomfortable?"

"No, it's not that."

"You do see, don't you, what I'm getting at? There may be some physical condition that is at the root of this trouble. If that's the case, sleeping pills won't do you any good. They alleviate the results of trouble, but they don't take away the cause. I'm wondering if you shouldn't have a general check-up."

She shook her head. "There's nothing wrong with me. I'm very sure of that. I've never been ill. You gave me a checkup before my children were born; sound as a bell, you said."

He looked at her thoughtfully. She looked well enough, a thoroughly healthy creature; perhaps because he had been consulted about these sleepless nights he could detect a look of tiredness around the eyes. But would he have noticed that unless he had been consulted? Anyone meeting her casually at a party would have thought. There's someone thoroughly wholesome and attractive. She must have something on her mind.

'You don't feel any discomfort, any pain then, as you lie awake?"

"No."

"Do you have difficulty in getting off to sleep or do you wake up after you've been asleep a little?"

"It's both."

"And then you lie there brooding."

"That's it."

"Brooding about what?"

"About everything."

"About cheerful things?"

"Not always."

"What have you got to brood about that isn't cheerful?"

"Oh, this and that."

"Such as?"

She shrugged. "We all have our problems, don't we?"

"Not all of us. Or only a few problems. You in particular I would have thought didn't have too many. Money isn't one of them."

"No, I'm lucky that way."

"And there's nothing the matter with your children."

"I'm lucky that way too."

"Most of my patients have servant worries, or lack of servant worries. But you've got those two excellent Swedish girls."

Myra laughed. "I'm lucky every way, it seems."

"And I expect that most of your friends envy you your husband."

"I shouldn't be surprised."

"Then really I don't know what these grey thoughts are that keep you brooding when you ought to be asleep."

"That's what I tell myself. I'm an idiot. I imagine things."

"What kind of things?"

"Oh, you know."

"No, I don't."

She shrugged. "It's quite ridiculous. I know it is. I get these fancies, and once I've got them, I can't get rid of them."

"Yes, but what fancies? You haven't told me what."

"It's nothing. It's just foolishness."

30

She has something on her mind. Something that she couldn't bring herself to reveal. Should he, he wondered, continue to indulge her, to pry and needle, till at last her reluctance to confess gave way? That was one method. But there was another. He had been told as a medical student that a patient on the verge of hysteria could be brought to her senses by a sudden shock, a slap maybe or a glassful of cold water flung in her face. There were mental equivalents for that slap. It was worth trying, once at least.

He rose to his feet. He picked up the prescription and gave it to her. "Perhaps it's only foolishness. If it is, then maybe you are right; this is the cure. If you remove the result, then the cause, the root of the trouble will disappear. We doctors talk a lot, but we've no real knowledge yet of the causes of mental worry. Try these, and if they don't work, come again."

His voice was brusque. There was a note of dismissal in it. He took a step towards the door. She looked up startled. She had expected the interrogation to continue for a little longer. She had been enjoying it. It was agreeable and refreshing to talk about oneself. Roman Catholics had realised that several centuries ago, and psychoanalysts were now cashing in on the contemporary world's lack of faith. Myra looked aggrieved. He was delighted. He had guessed right. His abrupt leave-taking was the equivalent of a slap across the face. It had brought her to her senses. He held out his hand. But she did not take it.

"I'm not so sure that it is all foolishness. I tell myself that it's only fancies, but I can't convince myself."

Ah, now we're getting there, he thought. He sat down again; he waited and in a rush it came. She told him her whole story from the start.

He listened with alert attention, interjecting a comment or a query every now and then. "You've no evidence that would convince a court," he said. "The only solid thing is that he was in the Brompton Road for no good reason at three o'clock in the afternoon."

"I am convinced that he was there for some reason that he doesn't want to give me."

"Why don't you ask him?"

"That's what I ask myself. But I've left it too late. I should have asked him at the time. If I ask him now, I'll make myself

31

ridiculous. He'll think of me as a jealous, suspicious ass. It might spoil everything. He'd feel I didn't trust him."

"And he'd be right."

"I daresay, but I don't want to have him thinking that. And if he really was up to something, I'd prefer him not to know that he'd been caught. He'd feel resentful. The person who is in the wrong always does. I know now that I should have spoken right away, but I didn't and that's all there is to it."

"You've had nothing else to make you feel suspicious except that bottle of wine?"

"That's quite a big 'except'."

"There are so many possible ways in which he could have had that bottle."

"I daresay, but it adds up."

"Have there been any other things that added up?"

"One or two. For instance, he mentioned the other day that there was an exhibition of Laura Knight's pictures at the Royal Academy. How did he know that?"

"In a dozen different ways. He could have seen an advertisement, or he could have read a review. He could have heard someone talk about it in his club."

"He's much more likely to have seen the posters outside the Royal Academy; and the Royal Academy isn't on his beat. When he goes to his tailor, he walks up Sackville Street."

"Is that all?"

"Not absolutely all. He had heard that one of our friends was going to have a baby. I asked him how he knew. He said that someone had told him but he couldn't remember who. I don't believe that. It's not the kind of thing that he would forget. He said he had forgotten because he didn't want me to know that he'd met the particular person from whom he'd heard it."

"But if he had wanted to keep it from you, he'd not have mentioned the fact in the first place."

"We all make mistakes. We can't be on our guard all the time."

"But it seems to me that you'll be driving yourself off your head if you look for such extravagant interpretations of incidents for which there must be the most innocent explanation."

"I know. That's what's worrying me. I feel I am going off

32

my head. I'm watching him all the time, trying to catch him out in something I can't explain. That's why I don't sleep. Each night I go over and over everything that's happened during the day. Was *that* odd? I ask myself. Was *that*? I can't relax with him any more, I'm watching him so closely, waiting on every word, listening for different intonations."

"You've got to snap out of this."

"I know I have. That's why I've come to you. I've got to sleep. If I can only sleep, then I may stop worrying."

She was beginning once again to go around in circles. It was time for him to administer another shock. This time a minor one.

"Let's suppose," he said, "that there is something in his life which he wants to keep secret from you, how can you be sure that it's a woman?"

"What else could it be?"

To that he could find no answer. What else indeed?

"Well, let's assume there is a woman, though I'm not conceding that there is; what do you propose to do about it?"

"What do you mean what do I propose to do?"

"Whatever the crisis is, we have to have some general plan of defence or of attack. We have our general strategy; then we make our tactical moves, as the situation develops. Let's assume Victor is interested in someone. We don't know how far he is interested, we don't know the nature of his interest; in other words, we don't know how far it's gone. But there, let us assume, the situation is. What do you propose to do about it?"

"I hadn't thought. I was ... well, there was so much else on my mind."

"But you should have thought. You must be on your guard. Now let's get this straight. You don't want to break up your marriage?"

"Heavens, no."

"You're happy with Victor?"

"Yes."

"Or you were until this trouble started."

"Yes, oh yes."

"Your children are well looked after; Victor's a good father, isn't he?"

"He's wonderful with Jerry. He will be with Frankie later."

33

"In that case I want you to look at this thing from Victor's point of view. Ask yourself what he's getting out of this."

"He's getting a love affair, I presume."

"Yes, but what kind of love affair? How much can he see this woman?"

"They can lunch together as often as they want."

"And then they can go back to her flat, provided that she has a flat and that she's alone. It isn't always as easy as that, you know. If she has a flat of her own, and is alone in it, then they can have picnics there, but how much time does that give them? How long can he stay away from his office? An hour and a half, not more. That doesn't give them very much time together, does it?"

"I hadn't thought of that."

"I thought you hadn't. And it is only at lunch that they can meet. You have told me that you know what Victor is doing every night. You know on which evenings the Sette of Odde Volumes holds its meetings. He talks to you about the dinners, doesn't he? He brings back the menu. These wine tastings at the Athenaeum now; of course he could once in a while cut one of those meetings short, but only once in a while. He has very little liberty. I have listened to a great many confessions and I can assure you that nothing is more difficult to organ- ise, even in London where everything seems so free, than a love affair when one of the parties is officially attached. I don't really think that Victor, if he is involved in this way, is par- ticularly an object for our envy."

He smiled; it was a gentle, paternal smile. "And it's just because he is not an object of our envy," he went on, "that we should be on our guard. We must be careful not to make him desperate, not to put him in a mood where he will do something rash. If he is in the position that you think he is, and I am not agreeing with you that he is, he is worried and frustrated. Can you imagine anything more tantalising than to be in love with someone, to have them in love with you, and to be able to see them only for odd half hours? It's one of those cases where half a loaf is not better than no bread. It's a situa- tion which makes a man say, 'This is more than I can stand. We've got to be alone, really alone together.' You can see that, can't you?"

"Yes, when you put it that way."

34

"When a man is in that position, he's ready to cut and run. And if he is, quite often the woman is ready to encourage him; if she's unattached or if she's unhappily married, that is to say."

"I hadn't thought of it that way."

"I'm not saying that it is that way, but it may be; and if it is, then you must prevent its getting desperate."

"How?"

"By making it possible for them to see each other, in the way they want, with all the time to spare."

"How do I do that?"

"By going away alone for a long holiday."

"How could I manage that?"

"Nothing could be easier. You can explain to Victor that you need a change, that I have told you that you need it. I'll tell him myself; doctor's orders. Victor's a very sensible man. He'll take my advice."

"What good would that do?"

"It is one of the sad conditions of the human lot that once we have got a thing, we cease to want it. When we have once realised an ambition, we raise our sights. We are hungry. We are ravenous for food. A banquet is set before us. We gorge ourselves and don't want to think of food again for several hours. If Victor and this lady have their three weeks together, a sense of lassitude, of disenchantment, is very likely to arise, a feeling of, Well, is that all there was to it?"

"Surely that can't always happen?"

"Not in the grand passion, not in 'the real thing' maybe, and in marriage there are so many other things besides the personal relationship to maintain, to strengthen, deepen, and defend the personal relationship. But affairs rarely last, and why? I'll tell you; they become too much bother, once that first, fierce, all-demanding urge is satisfied. When you return from your holiday, Victor's honeymoon will end; and he'll have to revert to the routine of snatched half hours. He'll begin to wonder if it's worth it. He'll think, We've had the best; why spoil the memory of that with this? He'll have had his lesson."

"And you expect me to sit quietly by some beach somewhere, knowing that Victor is . . . well, I'll use your simile, enjoying a sumptuous banquet?"

He laughed. "You haven't lost your sense of humour. Don't think of Victor's banquet. Think of how glad he'll be to see you back, particularly if, as I believe, there's really no basis for your suspicions." He paused. He looked at her, thoughtfully. "I suppose you've never been on a holiday by yourself?"

"How could I have? I was engaged in my first season."

"Then I'm not sure that I don't rather envy your going off alone. May I recommend Malta? A lovely climate, delightful people, and it's in the sterling area. You'll still have your holiday allowance untouched for your holiday later in the year with Victor."

The moment that she had left the room, he called his secretary. "Could you please get me Victor Trail, at the Treasury. I don't know his number." He was rung back within three minutes. As often in the past, he noticed how quickly one got through to busy and influential people and how long one was kept waiting by self-important underlings. "It's Dr. Clarke here, Victor; Myra's been to see me. Did she tell you that she was coming?"

"No."

"Well, it's nothing serious, nothing to worry about. But she hasn't been sleeping well. She wanted a prescription for some pills. I gave her one, but I'd as soon she didn't use them. It's a bad habit to get into. What she really needs is a change. She's in a nervous state, without realising it. She wants a clear break, in a new place, in the sun. Somewhere like Malta."

"But I couldn't get away right now. I've booked our holiday for August."

"There's no need for you to go. In fact it would be much better if you didn't. She wants a clean break from everything, even you and the children."

"Right. That's settled."

The conversation had not lasted ninety seconds. That was why people like Victor were never in a hurry. They did not waste their time. He wished he could have seen Victor's face when he learned that he was to have three weeks alone in London. Had a look of relief crossed it? There had been no change in his voice. But then there wouldn't be. Victor had acquired through upbringing and training the marmoreal composure of the diplomat. He would never betray his feelings.

Not that Dr. Clarke believed that Victor had any to conceal. If he had, he might not have given Myra that advice. There was in every love affair, at the dawn of every love affair, a point where you could draw back; that point once passed, there was no drawing back. Three weeks together might take Victor and this woman beyond that point. Bonds might be forged that were too strong to break. But instinct assured him that a surreptitious romance was out of keeping with Victor's character. Victor was too dedicated to tradition and his career. Himself, he had a different explanation for Myra's perplexity. There had been a play some years back called *The Seven Year Itch*; that was Myra's trouble. She had married very young, engaged in her first year as a débutante. She had had no "wild" period. And now, after five years of marriage, with two children, she was restless, subconsciously. She did not know it, but a side of her nature that had been only half expressed, or that had been rendered dormant by domesticity, had become insistent. Because she had not wanted to admit this to herself – she would have been astonished and indignant had he suggested such a thing – because she was vulnerable herself, without knowing it, she had focused her restlessness on Victor, convincing herself that he was up to mischief.

Dr. Clarke smiled. He was confident that he had recommended the right medicine. Three weeks by herself would work the trick. Something might happen down in Malta. It should do her all the good in the world, and it might well save her marriage. Would his father in pre-Freudian days have suggested such a cure? He continued his morning's work in a self-congratulatory state of mind.

4

A month later, on a warm May morning, a tall, rather slim dark-haired man in his middle thirties walked up to the reception desk of the Statler-Malta. "You've got my reservation, Francis Everett?"

"Certainly, Mr. Everett. Six days, I think."

"That's right."

He signed the register, giving his profession as "salesman", his address as Cape Town, South Africa. "Thank you, Mr. Everett. Philip, take Mr. Everett to Room 225. I trust that you'll be comfortable with us, Mr. Everett."

Everett stood on the balcony; his room faced south-east. It was a clear day; the Mediterranean was unruffled. The peak of clouds showed on the horizon. An aeroplane droned overhead. The white superstructure of a liner glowed in the middle distance. On a gentle hill a quarter of a mile away, a Palladian-style casino shone in the sunlight. The patio below was set with beach umbrellas; white-coated attendants were briskly busy with long cool drinks. A couple of children were splashing, three or four adults were floating in the pool. I'd better case the joint, he thought.

He took with him as a piece of camouflage the paperback that he had been reading on the plane. He did not want to sit and stare. He wanted to look like someone who was fully occupied. As a young man he had been advised by an experienced traveller: "On a long sea voyage, never strike up acquaintaces, in particular with females, during the first two days. You'll never get rid of them. I remember going to the West Indies, before the war. We sailed from London. It was in November. It was cold and wet and the sea was rough. There was an extremely handsome Englishman – of about thirty – who looked as though he were somebody. For the first four days he stayed in the bar playing bridge with three other men. He never went into the main saloon after dinner. Everyone felt curious about him. He was so much the most striking man on board.

"The other passengers did their best to be sociable with one another. But conditions were appalling. Everyone became weary of the sea and the ship and of one another. Then on the sixth day the weather cleared; the sun shone, the waves were ripples; the crew appeared in whites. Everyone was cheerful; everyone wanted to forget the first five days and the passengers with whom they had spent them. It was at that psychological moment that this man, about whom everyone had been wondering, emerged from his seclusion. In spite of his concentration on the cards, he had kept a close watch on his fellow passengers. He had noted which girls were unattended, which ones appeared most promising. He had addded up the score. He knew exactly where he was going to deliver his first

38

attack. And on that first day of warmth and unswaying decks, he could not have been more welcome."

Everett had never forgotten that advice. One didn't nowadays have the chance often of taking a long sea voyage, but the same principles applied to a week's visit in a beach hotel. Make no move for the first few hours, take a loitering recce.

Between the patio and the sea was a short, rocky beach. He had been warned that there was a lack of sand in Malta. But a raft was floating fifty yards from shore. A white flag indicating safety was flying from the steps. I'll try that first, he thought.

The water was refreshingly cool. He pulled himself up on to the raft and waited. But no one joined him. One or two paddlers were splashing near the edge of the water. None of them looked to be strong swimmers. It was close to twelve. Perhaps the younger set had already gone back to the pool. But by now the pool too was empty. The children had been taken to lunch. He sat on the edge. Among the forms recumbent on the long chairs were several admittedly attractive females, but they all had escorts. Better try the bar.

The bar had a terrace projecting over the patio. It was hot, but he found a seat under an umbrella. He ordered a Pimm's No. I. It was cool and fresh and strong. Even if nothing transpired from this visit, it would be pleasant to spend six days idly in the sun, drinking from a long, cool glass. He waved his hand to the waiter. "Yes," he said. "The same again." He lifted the replenished glass, toasting the crowded patio, "Six idle days, *skol* to you."

But the glass did not reach his lips. A woman whom he had failed to notice was finishing her swim. Slowly as she climbed up the ladder, her attractions were revealed to him. Her shoulders, her waist, her hips. The water was now up to her knees; another step and he would be able to see whether her legs were straight and slim. They were. With her hands on the rails, she turned and he saw the line of her figure, taut and trim. She's young, he thought. Definitely young.

She took off her cap and shook out her hair. It was sandy-coloured, of medium length. It had a wave. He drew a long slow breath. Then he looked at her left hand. A ring on the fourth finger. Damn.

He went into lunch early; from a table near the door, he watched the guests arrive. The parade depressed him. Whenever an attractive female appeared, a reasonable escort followed her. Whenever a female was alone, she was uninspirational. That was the trouble nowadays. A shortage of women. Forty years ago, though more male babies had been born, fewer had survived. Something to do with the size of the head. But now, owing to superior medical skill, there was a surplus not of women but of men. If a man wanted an attractive woman, he had to pull up his socks. She could put what price she chose upon herself. A buyer's market had become a seller's market.

It was getting late. Fewer were coming into the room now than were going out. Perhaps she was having a cold snack on the patio. He ought to have stayed in the bar, watching to make sure; perhaps he should hurry his lunch and have his coffee there. Yes, and find her sitting with a tall, handsome proprietary male. His lunch spoiled and to no purpose. Better, perhaps ... but he never reached the alternative. Here she was, coming through the door; and – his heart bounded – she was alone. A group of six were leaving; she stood aside to let them pass. She was barely three yards from him. She was even more attractive than he had thought. From a distance, he could not appreciate her colouring; but he liked the short straight nose and the full mouth. She gave the impression of being warm and friendly, an outgiving person.

His eyes followed her across the room. She moved easily, smoothly. I'll bet she dances well, he thought. An idea struck him; though she was alone now, she might be on her way to join a group. He watched anxiously. No, it was all right. She was alone. The head waiter was showing her to one of a series of single tables, lining a banquette. The table next to her was occupied by a woman. As she took her seat, she spoke to the other woman. They could scarcely be travelling together. If they were, they would have been facing or at right angles to each other. But from the way they were talking, they were clearly on friendly terms. The other woman was dark; she was wearing a low-cut blouse. She had full smooth shoulders, regular features, and white, very even teeth. She looked over thirty. She was probably a little plump. From the angle at which his table was set to the banquette, when the women were talking

40

together, the dark woman was facing him, while the other was in quarter profile; she would not know that he was watching her. That had its advantages. Before the meal was ended the dark woman would have become aware that he was watching her. That would make it easy for him to approach her afterwards. Through her he could approach the other.

The conversation between the two women appeared to be a lively one. The younger woman seemed to be doing most of the talking. The other would nod, would appear to encourage her with an occasional query or remark. She smiled quite often. She had a way of slipping the tip of her tongue between her lips. She had short, practical hands; the way she used her knife and fork made him feel that she did something with them. Perhaps she was a sculptor. There were two rings on her right hand but none upon her left. She did not exactly attract him, but he felt that she was someone whom he could get to like. He wondered how long the dark woman had been at the table before she had been joined. She was drinking beer and her glass was almost empty. Would she wait for her friend to finish? It was not likely. At dinner, probably, but not at lunch. I'll be up in the lounge waiting, he decided.

He took a seat facing the short flight of steps that led from the main lobby to the dining room. Soon the dark woman arrived, alone. She was as he had expected – slightly plump. She was also a little short for her weight. At one end of the lobby was a shop. She walked towards it. Now that her back was turned he noticed that she had heavy hips. He followed her into the shop. They had it to themselves. A pile of English newspapers was on the counter. "I see that papers get in early here," he said.

"Earlier than you'd guess. They are here by nine, a direct flight from London."

She spoke with a foreign accent. "I'd guess you come from Germany," he said.

"You'd be right in guessing that."

"I've just come from there."

"Indeed."

"From Munich. I'm a South African on a business trip. What part do you come from?"

"I was born in Dresden."

"East Germany."

"Exactly."

41

"That means you don't go back there often."

"It means I don't go back at all."

She was smiling. He knew that she was making fun of him but it was not an unfriendly smile. Her eyes were long-lashed. She must have noticed that he was staring at her during lunch. "I live in Frankfurt now," she said.

He told her that he had only just arrived. "That's why I didn't know the papers got in early. Have you been here long?"

"A week."

"Then you can give me some advice. I see there are some tours. Would you recommend them?"

"There's a tour of Valetta which you shouldn't miss. The city's unique. There's nothing like it. But that tour was yesterday. There won't be another one till Monday."

"What about the others?"

"There's one to the catacombs tomorrow. I'm going on it myself."

"Then I'll go too. In the meantime I'll go into Valetta on my own this afternoon."

"It'll be very hot."

"It'll make my swim afterwards the better." With a copy of *The Times* tucked under his arm, he bounded up the stairs. An auspicious start. So much discovered in five minutes. As likely as not, the other woman would be on the trip tomorrow. Even if she were not, he would, by the end of a four-hour tour, know the German woman well enough to invite the two of them to cocktails before dinner.

He lingered late at the swimming pool that evening. The two women had not been at the patio when he had come down after his return from a hot, exhausting trudge around the steep streets and cathedrals of Valetta. He presumed that they had already had their swim and gone up to change for dinner. That suited him very well. He wanted to find them already in the bar when he came down, so that he would pause at their table for a moment and make the younger woman aware of his existence. She probably had not noticed him so far. How could she have? She had been looking across from him all through lunch. Then having made his two or three remarks, he would move over to the bar. He must not appear pushing.

But those few remarks should justify his asking her to dance after dinner.

It worked out as he had planned. When he came downstairs, conscious that he looked as elegant as he could ever make himself in a white sharkskin dinner jacket, he saw the two of them together. He smiled at the German woman, bowed to the other one. "You are right about Valetta," he said. "It's well worth seeing. But it is hot."

"I hope it made you enjoy your swim."

"It certainly did that. And I've booked myself on that tour tomorrow. I'll see you then."

"Who's that?" asked the other woman, as he moved away.

"A South African salesman who was staring at me all through lunch. I've an idea that I've made a conquest."

"Congratulations."

The German woman shrugged.

"Not interested?"

"He's not my type."

"What is your type?"

"It's hard to say. But I always know it when I see it."

The woman looked across at the bar. Everett was on the far side. He had a firm, strong profile; his hair had a gloss; his dinner jacket fitted neatly. He seemed very personable. She liked his voice. Its slight accent gave it character. Most women would have bothered to give him a second look.

Everett was up in the bar soon after dinner. This time he wanted to be ahead of them, so that he could suggest that they sit at the same table. Since the band played in the bar he assumed that the room would be crowded early. Again things worked out as he had planned. By the time the two women came up from dinner, there was not a table vacant. "I wonder if you would like to join me for a little," he said. "I shan't be staying here long. I'm tired after my journey." He introduced himself and learned their names. "You're English then," he said to Myra when he heard her voice.

"I'm English."

"But you live in Frankfurt now?"

"What makes you think that?"

"Because your friend does."

43

"I met Fräulein Hauptmann for the first time five days ago."

"I see."

He asked the German to dance first. The floor was small and packed, but she moved with ease and lightness. "Tell me about Mrs. Trail," he said.

"Tell you what about Mrs. Trail?"

"Who she is, what she does, where she lives."

"She's a wife and mother; her husband's in the Treasury. That's about all I know."

"What's she doing here?"

"What we're all doing here, taking a holiday in the sun."

"I see."

Once again there was that teasing expression in her eyes. She was rather fun. For a moment he wondered whether he might not be wise to address his attentions to her instead of to her friend. But he only wondered it for a moment. He remembered the glimpse he had had of Myra Trail that morning as she climbed out of the pool.

While he danced with the German woman, another man claimed Myra. He watched her over his partner's shoulder. He had guessed from the way she moved that she danced well. He had guessed right, clearly.

At last his chance came. For the first minute he danced in silence. Then he laughed. He said, "I made a bet with myself this morning."

He paused, waiting for her to take up his opening.

"What was the bet about?"

"That you danced extremely well. I've won my bet," he added.

It was her turn to laugh. "When did you make this bet?"

"At the swimming pool."

"I didn't see you."

"I was on the patio with a Pimm's. I watched you climb out of the pool. You looked so supple."

"That's an odd compliment. If it is a compliment."

"It's meant to be."

"That patio's a long way from the swimming pool."

"It is, but near enough for me to tell that you moved easily; too far though for me to tell that you were very pretty."

"Oh."

"I couldn't tell that till later."

"When was later?"

"When you came in to lunch."

"I see."

The music stopped. "I think it's going to start again," he said. It did. Again they danced in silence. "Are you going with your friend on tomorrow's tour?" he asked.

"I am."

"Then we'll have a chance to talk without all this music."

"There won't be much chance to talk if we have the same guide that we did this morning. He talks himself all the time."

"That's too bad."

Again they danced in silence. She was grateful to him for not interrupting the dance with chatter. He danced very well.

This time when the music stopped, he took her back to her table but did not sit down. "I look forward to tomorrow," he said and bowed.

Fräulein Naomi Hauptmann kept a bottle of Cherry Heering in her room. She and Myra had fallen into the habit of taking a final glass together on her balcony. It was a quiet, cool, cosy conclusion to a long, hot, noisy day. They retired to the bottle soon after Everett left them. Each felt that they had things to say.

"I was mistaken," Naomi said. "It's not me he's after."

"That's what I was thinking."

They laughed together. "You're not annoyed?" asked Myra.

"Heavens, no. A man said to me once, 'If two men are to remain friends, it's essential that they should like different types of women. Otherwise there'll be jealousies and competition.' It's the same with women. The moment I saw you, I knew that we wouldn't be getting into fights over the same man."

"What kind of man do you fall for?"

"Not a very satisfactory type, I am afraid." It was practically the same answer that Anna had given her. In a way Naomi reminded her of Anna; perhaps it was the foreign accent. "Did he say anything in particular?" Naomi asked.

"In a kind of way."

She told Naomi what he had said. Naomi raised her eyebrows. "What do you make of him?" she asked.

45

"He dances well. He's quite attractive."

"To me he seems so."

"It's all rather obvious, of course, a travelling salesman, spending six days in a beach hotel, looking for a pickup."

"Isn't that why most women come to beach hotels? To be picked up."

"That's not why you came here."

"Not altogether."

They laughed at that. They managed to find the same things amusing; that was how their friendship had begun.

On Myra's second morning, she had been the witness of a ridiculous self-important performance by a Central American couple who were objecting to the cavalier fashion in which their elegant luggage was being handled. "Treat that case with respect," the man was shouting. "It's genuine crocodile. I bought it in Buenos Aires. It cost me as much as you earn in a month."

Myra as she listened had become aware that from the other side of the room, another woman had been watching the scene with equal enjoyment. Their eyes met and they had smiled. It was a conspiratorial smile. They had known that they found the same things ridiculous. The next day they had booked on the same excursion. From then on they had become a team.

There was a thoughtful expression on Naomi's face, a ruminative tone in her voice, as she went on.

"I've an idea that books and films and plays spoil our enjoyment of a great many of the best things in life. They make one expect more than life has to offer. Particularly in the case of love. We feel that it has to be unplanned, spontaneous. 'The stranger across a crowded room'; Romeo going to a party in love with Rosalind, then meeting Juliet and forgetting Rosalind. But usually such loves are catastrophic because they run counter to the practical ordering of life. There's much more happiness to be found when two people feel a need for the same thing at the same time and guess that they can get that thing from the other person. The marriages that were arranged by parents often turned out very happily. Fifty years ago marriage bureaux were considered highly unromantic; no man or woman would have dared confess to going there. Yet the directors of these bureaux say that the results are very satisfactory because the men and women who go to them definitely want to be married and to make their marriages a success. Don't you think it's the same with an affair? One talks of the *coup de foudre* – and I've nothing against the *coup de foudre* except that it's disruptive – but there's nothing wrong either in a woman thinking, 'I've got a thoroughly satisfactory marriage. I've a pleasant home, adorable children, a husband with whom I see eye to eye. I don't want to alter the fabric of my life, but I would like to enliven it. I am going to spend two weeks in a beach hotel. I hope I shall find someone there who will enliven it.' What's wrong with that?"

"This is very dangerous advice you are giving me."

"It's very sound advice. Come now, be honest with yourself. When you decided to come to Malta, didn't you have at the back of your mind a hope that you might meet some equivalent for Francis Everett?"

"If I did, it was so much at the back of my mind that I didn't admit it to myself."

"And now that you have found him, what do you propose to do?"

"What would you have me do?"

"Whatever would make you happier. You are, you know, a very dear, sweet person." She paused. "Anyhow, to me."

To her surprise Myra found that she was blushing.

"We'll let tomorrow decide then, shall we?"

Tomorrow; it went the way that Everett had hoped. It was a warm day, but a tempting wind was blowing, as it usually did in Malta. There was nothing to stop it after all. A soft ochre-brown haze lay over the low limestone walls. The tour drove out to a river bed where the bones of prehistoric animals had been discovered. They saw some catacombs and a burial site over ten thousand years old that had only been discovered less than fifty years ago by chance because it was a local law in Malta that, in order to conserve water, every house had to have a cistern under it; so that a man digging under what had been a temple came upon these galleries. They also were taken to some Roman temples. And all the time, as Naomi had prophesied, the guide talked on and on. As he talked interestingly, it was hard not to listen to him. Yet even so, Francis Everett managed to get said a great many of the things he had upon his mind.

47

He talked of that first sight of her at the swimming pool. "It was the most astonishing experience I have ever had. You revealed yourself, you revealed the beauty of yourself inch by inch. You lifted up your arms. They are very lovely arms; not bony but not fat. You pulled yourself up; you must have taken one step on the ladder. The line of the water fell away; I could see your shoulders, down to the level of your bra. They are what one dreams of shoulders being – soft firm flesh; the shoulder blades not showing, but making you aware that they were there. Another step upon the ladder and the line of the water was just below your waist – and how the waist curved in, as though the hand of a god had modelled it. Then one more step and the line of the water was below your thighs; you seemed to be sitting upon the water, and what firm, rounded curves! This is too much, I thought, as one phase of perfection was added to another. Something must go wrong soon. The lower thighs must be too plump, the knees knobbly, the calves too muscled. But no, another step upon the ladder – you had pulled yourself right up, only the ankles hidden, those slim, strong legs; and then finally the ankles. Perfection achieved inch by inch, a series of miracles leading to the final miracle – complete perfection, and I had only realised how complete it was by seeing it achieved inch by inch." He said it all laughingly, flippantly, not as though it were a serious declaration. She was grateful to him for that.

"All the great painters have realised," he went on, "that the line of a woman's back is the loveliest thing God ever made. Have you seen that picture of Titian's, in the Uffizi gallery in Florence, the one with the hip raised? You surely know that story about Sir Thomas More – the *Man for All Seasons* chap. There was a father who wanted More to marry one of his daughters. More was to choose which he preferred. So the father had the girls undress, and then brought More up to their bedroom. The two girls were lying side by side under a sheet. The father pulled back the sheet. 'Now make your choice,' he said. More looked at them for a couple of minutes. Then he said, 'May they turn over on their faces, please?' He again looked at them for a couple of minutes. Then he smacked one of them on the buttocks. 'I'll have that one,' he said. Did you know that story?"

"As a matter of fact, I did."

"I hope it's true; I've always felt kindly towards Sir Thomas More because of it. I thought of it yesterday when you climbed out of the pool and I'll tell you what else I thought. I thought what bad luck it was on women that they can never see their most compulsive feature. They could only see it with an elaborate arrangement of suspended mirrors; then they'd have to crick their necks out of joint. Think of all the hours they spend in front of their mirrors; how differently they'd feel about themselves if they could see themselves as the rest of the world sees them. Had you ever thought of that?"

"I hadn't, no."

"I suggest you do sometimes. It might cheer you up. It was wonderful seeing you climbing up the steps, but I'm not sure that it wasn't even more wonderful when you stood at the steps and shook out your hair. I hadn't realised then that you were blonde, or that your hair would have such a pretty wave in it. Then you turned around and I saw how young you were. I couldn't tell seeing you from the back."

His stream of talk was constantly interrupted by the rhetoric of the guide, by descents from the bus, by the examination of this and the other relic; but in retrospect when she thought over what he had said, she had the sense of having been exposed to a ceaseless flow of adulation.

She had been expecting that its flow would be continued later in the afternoon when they lay side by side on beach mattresses at the edge of the swimming pool. But to her surprise and on the whole to her relief it was not. Instead he talked about himself and about South Africa. He loved his country; he spoke of it not boastfully, but confidently, and without resentment that her domestic policies had led to so much antagonism from other nations. "We have problems, special problems of our own that other countries don't understand. What's right for us in our country might not be right for them in theirs. It's a pity," he said. "But there it is."

He was proud of being a South African. He had a farm, he said, near Cape Town. He had cattle and vineyards and an export business.

"You're married, I suppose?" she asked.

"There's something wrong, isn't there, about a man of thirty-five who's not?"

"I suppose so."

Yes, he was married. And he had three children, seven, three, and a small baby. "Carefully spaced," he said.

There was a boyishness about him that she had noticed in other South Africans and had found attractive. They were wholesome, with an air of the open countryside and an exuberance that contrasted refreshingly with the bored superciliousness affected by so many Londoners. He was clearly having the time of his life and he was not putting out any alibi about being misunderstood at home, of being a frustrated man, a prisoner on parole, craving the indulgence of an hour. He stood firm on his feet. He was honest and straightforward – he happened to be spending a week in Malta; he had met a woman who attracted him, and he wanted to go to bed with her: a point of view that Myra could respect.

"There's nothing phoney about him," she said afterwards to Naomi.

"So I may suppose that you're looking forward to dancing with him later on."

"He dances very well."

But to her surprise he was neither in the bar at cocktail time nor was he at his table in the dining room.

"I guess that he's sampling one of the local bistros," Naomi suggested. "He's probably on demi pension."

"That's it, I expect."

"He'll be joining us in the bar after dinner."

"I shouldn't be surprised."

But he was not in the bar when they went up. "Let's take a stroll," she said.

They strolled slowly up the hill to the casino. "Shall we go in?"

"Why not. The hotel's signed us in."

They had been to the casino several times. They enjoyed gambling and the rooms had elegance. They sat at the roulette board and the ball ran luckily for Myra. Within half an hour she had accumulated over twenty pounds. Usually at that point she would split her winnings, put half in her purse and gamble with the remainder till she had either lost or doubled it. But tonight she felt restless and on edge.

"Do you mind, I think I'm going while the going's good."

"It's as you wish."

She quickened her pace down the hill. "Just one last drink," she said.

The bar was dimly lit; she looked from one corner to another, but no, he was not there.

She ordered a cognac and drank it quickly. A fellow guest invited her to dance. She hesitated before she rose. He did not dance badly, but her feet felt heavy. When the music stopped, she shook her head. "I'm packing up; I've had a long day," she said.

She excused herself to Naomi. "I don't think I'll have a final drink upstairs. I feel all in."

But though she was indeed all in, she could neither sleep nor concentrate upon her book. "I'd better have a nightcap after all."

She sat back among her pillows, sipping it. Outside the moon spread its long sash of silver on the water. She looked at her bedside clock – only ten past twelve. They were still dancing in the bar.

The telephone beside her rang. "Hi, what are you doing there at this hour?"

"At this hour. It's after midnight."

"The evening's only started."

"For you maybe. I left an hour ago."

"Then unleaven. Come down here right away. I've had a funny evening. I've a lot to tell you."

She hesitated. She felt she should be annoyed with him, but she could not be. There was such vitality in his voice. "All right, give me ten minutes."

"Seven."

"Eight."

"O.K., settling for seven and a half."

It was three o'clock before she was back in her own room.

"Even so I'm puzzled."

It was next morning she had gone to Naomi's room to share her breakfast; "Why should he have gone out last evening?"

"What explanation did he give?"

"That he had met an old friend in the bar, someone he'd played football with; they toured the hot spots."

"And that's exactly what he did do, probably."

"But why, when he'd made all that fuss over me all day? It's not as though he had all that much time to see me."

"He seems to have had several hours of your company."

"Only through a stroke of luck. Nine times in ten, I wouldn't have gone down."

"Perhaps he was running a calculated risk, to see what kind of impression he had made on you."

"Do you think that's likely?"

"As a matter of fact I don't. Some men enjoy what they call 'an occasional evening with the boys,' particularly Englishmen."

"But he's not English; he's South African."

"It's not so very different. What isn't English in him is Dutch. And the Dutch in that way are like the Germans. My people and yours. Rowdy evenings with a beer mug. French and Italians aren't that way."

"Even so I'm puzzled."

Naomi shook her head. "You shouldn't be. Men are incalculable. They call women the mysterious sex; compared with them we're a simplified equation. In the meantime has he made any plans for us today?"

"There isn't any tour. So he's hired a car to drive around the island."

"Am I invited?"

"I'm sure he'd be delighted."

"I bet he would. You tell me at lunch the way it went. I'll be at the table, not in the bar; I'll leave that to him and you."

"Well, how did it go? Just the headlines."

Myra laughed. "There were no headlines."

"No?"

"No. We drove around. I'd seen most of it before. You know how it is – those villages that look all the same, the dun-coloured streets, the succession of drab exteriors, with their first-floor balconies and their heavy doors, the dust-covered oleanders."

"Yes, yes, I can guess all that. And you went to Mdina and saw the old Arab gate; and you saw the weavers and he bought you a bag."

"He didn't. He bought me a bolt of cloth."

"Which you'll never have made up and that'll cost you a packet at the Customs. Well, go on."

"There's nothing to go on to."

"You mean nothing happened?"

"I mean nothing happened."

"Didn't he say anything?"

"Nothing pertinent."

"After all those speeches he made yesterday."

"Exactly."

There was a pause. "There are two things I'm wondering," Myra said.

"Yes?"

"I'm wondering if he's one of those men who are all talk, who make speeches when people are around, but suddenly feel shy when they're alone with you. Mightn't he be that kind of man? Particularly as he's married and may not want to get involved."

"It's possible. What's the alternative?"

"That he's hatching a deep-laid plot. He knows that he made an impression yesterday; now he's letting the situation simmer. He's working up to an assault on the last night."

Naomi shook her head. "Not the last night, the last night but two."

"Why do you say that?"

"First nights are rarely a success. You must know that."

"How should I know that?"

"From your own experience."

"The first night of a honeymoon doesn't teach you much – in that way."

"No, of course it doesn't."

Naomi smiled, a soft, fond smile. "*Liebling*, I forget how innocent you are. It's one of the things that make you so attractive."

During their morning's drive Francis had kept the conversation casual, but that afternoon by the pool he returned to the mood of the previous morning.

"I can't believe," he said, "that fifty hours ago I didn't know that you existed. I was ending a two months' trip. Things had gone better and quicker than I had expected. I had a week to spare. Why not spend it in Malta, relax there, swim, see what

53

there is to see. Go home refreshed. I came here for a rest, for nothing else. And then I found you."

She made no answer. Was that true, she wondered, or had he thought, "I've got a week to spare. Where'd I be likeliest to find a quick romance? Malta? I'll try that." A bit of both, she guessed.

"Fifty hours ago," he was repeating, "I had no idea that you existed. Now I feel that I know you better than friends I've known all my life."

That now is true, she thought. One meets a person at a party. One talks; one's at one completely, and one's lifetime friends seem shadowy.

"This is a funny thing too," he said. "We live in different countries. I don't come to England often. When I do, it's for a specific purpose, to put over a business deal. I'd have no contacts with your people. We move in different worlds, and nothing's more pointless than trying to keep up with someone whom you've met on a ship or in a beach hotel. In all human probability we shall never see each other again. Yet these four days here will remain alight in my memory till the day I die. I'll be thinking of them every day. I'll relive them every day."

That touched her. What he said next rather more than touched her. "There's something else," he said. "You'll change over the years. Little by little, imperceptibly, you'll note the changes in your mirror; that will sag, and this will wrinkle, your hair will lose its gloss. But to me you will look exactly the same as you do know. The years will not affect the picture that I have of you. I shall be seeing you exactly as you are on this patio here this afternoon."

She sighed. Yes, that should mean something. Thirty years from now and a grandmother, she would be able to say to herself, "Six thousand miles away, on the other side of the equator, there's someone for whom I still exist as a young woman in her middle twenties, who sees me as no one else in the world can see me now."

She had a wish to make that memory as rich for him as possible, to make herself unforgettable. Why not, after all, why not?

Yet afterwards when they danced, he returned to the neutrality of friendly chatter. Was he, after all, one of those men

54

who only talked, who were garrulous in public and tongue-tied in private?

Next day there was a whole-day tour of Gozo, the sister island, on which Naomi joined them. In the course of it, he said, "Listen. I don't want to force myself upon you, but I've only three days left. Why don't you both have dinner with me tonight? I'll order à la carte. And as Myra's husband's in the Treasury, I'll see if I can't charge it against expenses."

Only three days left. Three days was the radius within which a practised wolf, so Naomi had assured her, would organise his campaign. But there was no sign that Francis Everett had any such scheme under way. He was acting as though he were exactly what he had said he was – a contented family man enjoying a relaxed vacation at the end of a strenuous business trip. Why in heaven's name should he be anything else but that? Why should she be indulging in these fantasies? From the moment that she had learned that Victor was frequenting the Brompton Road at three o'clock on a weekday afternoon she had been picturing the whole world in a mad amatory spin. Pull yourself together, she adjured herself. Because an attractive South African appears to enjoy your company, don't cast yourself as Cleopatra. Relax, have fun. Let him give you a good dinner, and if, because of Victor, he can charge it against expenses, the best of British luck to him. Fortified with good intentions, she went down to the bar, resolved to enjoy her dinner.

She had set herself an easy task. A bottle of champagne was cooling in a steaming bucket. He had not ordered extravagantly; no caviar, no pâté de foie gras; straightforward dishes – smoked salmon, a steak with béarnaise sauce, a chocolate soufflé. She was grateful to him for that, for not making too much of an occasion of it. She was grateful to him too for the way in which he included Naomi in his talk, addressing himself to her as much as to herself, making Naomi feel that she was really wanted. He was a nice man.

And afterwards as they danced, in a continuing mood of warmth and gratitude, she let herself relax in a way that she had not before, drawing herself close, closer into his arms; subjected to the music, subjected to the sway and rhythm of his movements, letting him impose them on her. She half closed her eyes. "I could have danced all night. I could have danced all night." She was conscious of an abandon that she had rarely felt upon a dance floor. She had not danced much since her one season as a debutante. Victor did not particularly care for dancing. It was five years since she had danced like this. "I could have danced all night. I could have danced all night." Her eyes were fully closed now. Ah, this was wonderful. He led her with unfamiliar steps that she followed easily. As she swung and swirled and swayed, she became conscious slowly of the pressure of a protuberance against her inner thigh. She was instantly alert, startled out of her dream. This was a brand-new experience. It couldn't be. Surely it couldn't be. Her instinct was to draw away, but she could not; she had to know. Was it or wasn't it? Instead she drew closer, moving her right leg between his; pressing it sideways. No, there was no doubt at all, the protuberance lengthened, broadened, hardened.

Her nerves were tingling. He wasn't after all one of those timid men who only talked. Or if he was, her nearness had subdued him. However cautionary his mind, his body had controlled it, had taken over, issuing its own imperious commands. An exultant pride suffused her. She had not suspected that her mere dancing could have this effect. She wanted to look up at him, but her cheek was tight against his shoulder. Was he feeling awkward, ashamed of being trapped into this avowal? When they got back to the table, would he pretend that it had never happened? Would he manage to convince himself that she had not noticed? She was not going to let him have that alibi. That thing was certain. In a sudden flash of mischief, of resolution, she tightened her hand's hold on his shoulder, glided her leg between his to its extremity, and forced herself grindingly against him.

He gasped. He ceased to dance. He stood, close clasped to her, his hips moving against hers.

"It would be wonderful to make love to you," he said.

"You should try sometime and see."

She forced into her voice an amused, teasing lilt.

"What's the number of your room?" he asked.

"It's 207."

He shaved and showered. He rubbed himself with Old

Spice toilet water. He looked at the clock. Quarter of an hour since they had said goodnight. That should be long enough. Should he dress again? Was it presumptive to go in pyjamas and a dressing gown? Suppose he met someone on the way. Lucky that she was in the same wing, on the same floor as he was. It seemed very formal to walk into her room fully clothed; and then all the palaver of undressing. If he did meet anyone in the passage he would walk down to the front desk with some inquiry about transportation. Yes, much better to present himself in a dressing gown. Another glance at the clock. Nearly twenty minutes now. Time to be on his way. Had he ever known such acute excitement? Had his earlier years any equivalent for the experience that awaited him? It was the kind of thing that only happened to characters in books.

He walked down the passage with an unhurried stride. 201, 203, 205. Here it was. He turned the handle, pressed, but the door did not give. He looked up at the number to make sure. 207. That was it, all right. Could she have forgotten to press the opening stud? He tapped; there was no answer. He tapped again, more loudly. Still no reply. He could not very well tap any louder. Could she have fallen asleep? Had he misheard the number? He tapped again. He rattled the door. Still no result. He'd have to go back to his room and telephone.

He called the front desk. "Could you please put me through to Mrs. Trail?"

He was not going to give the room. He had to be sure that he was ringing the right number. He waited; there was the ringing tone, then there came a click. "Darling," he called, "your door's locked. What's the matter?"

There was no reply. "Myra," he called. "Myra." Silence; an utter silence. He flushed hotly, angrily. She had taken up the receiver. She must have laid it down on the bedside table.

"The bitch," he thought. "The bloody bitch."

Naomi woke late next morning, late at least for her, at half past eight. She ordered a continental breakfast. Was Myra up yet? She was tempted to ring through but decided not. If things had turned out as she presumed they had, Myra would be in no mood for early calls. She lingered so long over her

57

own tray and the morning papers that it was after ten before she came down into the lobby. When she did, it was to find Francis Everett at the cashier's counter, in a dark city suit with a couple of suitcases beside him.

"What on earth are you about?" she asked.

"I'm checking out. I'm hopping the next plane to London."

"I thought that you were staying on till Saturday."

"That was my intention."

"I hope you haven't had bad news from home."

"I've had no news from home."

His eyes were stern. He certainly was good-looking. "You're German," he said. "You speak English perfectly. But you may not know all our slang. Do you know what a C.T. is?"

"Yes, I know what a C.T. is."

"Then you can tell your friend Myra Trail that that is exactly what she is. And you can tell her that I'm on my way to London. I'm going to Soho. I'll find a prostitute, give her the ten or twenty pounds she needs, and have an honest time with an honest whore. You tell her that. Stress the word honest," and he picked up his suitcases and was on his way to the porch before any of the porters could intervene.

Naomi whistled. That very certainly was that. She crossed to the house telephone. She called 207. There was the sound of a lifted receiver but no reply. "Myra, it's me here, Naomi," she called.

This time there was an answer. "Oh, thank heavens. I haven't dared speak into the machine all day, and people have kept on calling me."

"You needn't worry any more. He's gone."

"That's something anyhow."

"Should I come up to see you or will you come down?"

"I'll come right down. I'm tired of this room."

They sat together in the lobby. The bar was not open yet. Anyhow it was too early for alcohol. "What did he say?" asked Myra.

"He wasn't complimentary."

"I'm not surprised. I behaved disgracefully."

"What happened?"

"Nothing. I locked my door and took my receiver off the hook."

"He seemed to think you had encouraged him."

"I had. I meant it, too. It was the kind of thing you read about in books. Meeting an attractive stranger, without any impediments, without any complications. Someone that I'd never see again. No subsequent embarrassment. I never will have such another chance. I'd made up my mind halfway through the evening. The way he danced decided me. I knew that he'd be good in bed. I was going through with it. And then . . ."

"And then?"

"I don't know how it happened. I was sitting, waiting. I'd showered, anointed myself with oils, the works, you know. I'd arranged the lights, left the door unlatched; and then suddenly I found I couldn't. I belonged to Victor. I couldn't do this with another man. I didn't try to argue with myself. I got up. I latched the door and switched the centre light on. I lay there waiting. I watched the door handle. I heard him tap. A pause; then another tap, a louder one. 'Come on,' I told myself, 'don't be a ninny. If you don't open that door now, you'll be regretting it all your life.' Maybe I shall. Don't they say that it's the things you haven't done, not the things you have done that you regret? But it was no good. I couldn't move. He didn't rap again. I presumed that he'd gone back to his room. Then the telephone rang, as I'd guessed it would. I lifted the receiver. I put it on the table. I could hear his voice. It sent a storm along my nerves. I hated myself. I despised myself. But I couldn't lift the receiver. I couldn't go through with it. I belonged to Victor."

She paused. Naomi said nothing. She waited for Myra to go on – as she did hesitantly, searching for the exact words to express what she really meant, repeating herself, contradicting herself, restating this and that, in terms of what she had contradicted.

Naomi, thinking it over afterwards, revolved it into this confession. "You must remember," Myra said, "that I was engaged in my first season, when I was nineteen; I was married when I was twenty. As a schoolgirl I had had flirtations in the holidays – of course I had – but I had been very carefully watched. England wasn't like America in that way. In those days you didn't have teenagers rushing about in groups, petting in the back of cars; if not going quite the limit, almost going

59

it. In that finishing school in Switzerland, we were watched even more closely. The French are very strict; and this was French Switzerland. No one could have been more of a novice than I when I went in with all those others to the Queen Charlotte Ball which is where I met Victor. Everything stopped there and everything began there. I was more than a virgin when I married. I had never been touched by anyone but Victor. He was the initiator; I was entered by him. I was possessed by him. Between the knees and the navel I belong to him. How could I deliver myself to any other man?"

"To any other man. Yes, I see that. But . . ."

It was at the end of a long, long talk in that hotel lobby, waiting for the bar to open, that Naomi reached that "But".

"Tell me," she said. "We've told each other quite a lot, this way and that, and though I've guessed it, though you've implied it, you've not said so in so many words. But you are having troubles, aren't you, with your marriage."

It was then that Myra told Naomi about her problems, her own heart searchings. Naomi nodded as she listened, not interrupting, but interjecting an occasional comment, an occasional query. She let her hand drop over Myra's, stroking the long thin fingers with her short ones. "Yes," she said. "Yes, I see."

When Myra had at last reached the end Naomi stood up. "We've got to have a long talk about all of this. I've quite a lot to say. We all have to talk about ourselves when we're in trouble; if we don't, things inside us fester. The psychoanalysts have taught us that. I think that a young wife is far better off talking to a woman a few years older than herself than she is to a priest or a psychiatrist. It's lucky that we've got a whole week together."

That was how it began. That was how it went on. They followed, on the surface, the conventional tourist routine. They swam and sunbathed. They went on trips. They had, through letters of introduction, contacts with some residents; the Maltese are very hospitable. they were invited to a lunch at the fashionable Union Club and to a couple of cocktail parties. One party led to others.

Their time was fully occupied; when Myra wrote to Victor she could present herself as leading a varied and enlivening existence; but all that was on the surface. Below the surface she was conducting with Naomi a sequence of confessions that in retrospect she saw as a continuous dialogue.

Myra had an instinct to confide. She had kept her feelings bottled up too long. Naomi had a strong personality and a persuasive manner. Moreover she was a foreigner, who rarely came to England. She knew none of Myra's friends. Myra would not be embarrassed later on by having made admissions, a thing that could happen so easily in one's own setting. You let down your hair with your oldest friend and then, ever afterwards, felt awkward in her presence. That would not happen now. No secret was too intimate for her to betray to Naomi.

Naomi asked if she had noticed any change in Victor's manner. "Does he make love to you less often?"

"No, I don't think so, no."

"How often do you make love?"

"It's hard to say. Sometimes three or four times over a weekend, then not again for ten days or so."

"Nine or ten times a month?"

"Yes, I suppose so, yes."

"Did you keep a score of the number of times you made love on your honeymoon?"

"Good heavens, no."

"It wouldn't have been an unwise precaution. Presumably you made love all the time."

"I suppose so, yes."

"Did you hear that old saying about the married couple who during the first year of their marriage put a bead into a vase every time they made love? At the end of the year, they put the beads into a bag. At the start of the second year, they started again putting a bead into the vase. At the end of fifteen years they had not collected as many beads as they had during the first year."

Myra laughed. "That wouldn't be true in my case."

"Not altogether. But remember this, if your husband was making love to you thirty times a month during your honeymoon and now makes love to you less than ten times a month, he has a certain amount of unexpended energy."

"He wasn't going to an office during our honeymoon."

"Did he make love to you any less often during the first six weeks after you'd got back?"

"Not as far as I remember."

"That's what I mean. He's capable of making love more than he does. He has some surplus energy, for another woman."

Naomi's questions became increasingly intimate. "You like lovemaking, don't you?"

"Of course."

"There's no 'of course' to it. A lot of women don't. Do you enjoy it very much?"

"I think so, yes."

"Do you feel restless if you've not been made love to for several weeks?"

"I've never not been made love to for several weeks."

"Are you beginning to feel restless here?"

There was a mischievous look in Naomi's eyes as she said that, a titillating look. Myra's zest for these questions quickened. What on earth will she ask me next, she'd think. When the dialogue was discontinued as they swam, as they listened to the guide's flow of explanation, as they were separated at a cocktail party, she became impatient for its resumption; at the day's end she would go over it phase by phase. She was fascinated not only by the questions themselves, but by the way in which Naomi set them. A roguish glint would flicker in her eyes. The tip of her tongue would slip between her lips. Naomi had a mesmeric effect on her. "Have you noticed any change recently in his ways of making love?" she asked.

"What kind of difference?"

"A different position, a different trick, something he might have learned from another woman."

Myra shook her head.

"What position or what positions do you use?" asked Naomi.

"The usual ones."

"That's not an answer. There are according to the Kama Sutra some sixty different positions. Let us be more specific."

Myra became specific. At the end of her interrogation, Naomi shook her head.

"It really boils down to only three. It was a pity that you had your first child so soon."

"Why do you say that?'

"Because this is, I suspect, what happened. You were completely inexperienced when you married. You'd read the little

62

books, the manuals; but there's all the difference in the world between actual and theoretical experience. You were puzzled by it all at first. It didn't seem quite natural for you to be behaving in this way with a man; you didn't feel at ease with him, you didn't enjoy it very much."

"Oh, yes, I did. I was so proud of myself at not being a virgin any longer, at knowing all the things about which as a schoolgirl I had been inquisitive. No woman could boast her superior knowledge; I was tickled to death. Oh yes, I enjoyed myself all right."

"But the actual act itself, how enjoyable was that?"

"It hurt at first, but then I had been warned it would. It didn't hurt as much as I'd expected. It was uncomfortable, but that didn't last for long."

"What about the orgasm?"

"What about the orgasm?"

"How long was it before you got one?"

"I can't be sure. It's hard to tell, isn't it, with a woman. There's not the explosion that there is with a man. I enjoy it more sometimes than I do at others. I get excited when Victor does; there's a feeling of achievement then, but really I don't know. I wonder if we don't make too much fuss about the orgasm, feeling that there must be with women an exact equivalent of what there is with men. I've an idea that with a woman it's all more diffused."

She looked at Naomi questioningly; but Naomi let the implication pass.

"Why," Myra persisted, "do you think it was a pity that I had a child so soon?"

"Because it checked your amatory development."

"How do you mean?"

"A honeymoon's an education, an initiation; a woman's shy at first and awkward. She's uncertain of herself. Gradually she becomes accustomed to the whole ritual of love-making. She becomes audacious. You remember Juliet's 'Strange love grown bold' thinking 'true love acted simple modesty'. That's what happens during the first year of marriage. The love-making gets more and more elaborate till there isn't a thing you haven't done together. That's unlikely to happen if there's a baby right away. A playmate becomes an invalid; she cum-

63

bersome, she has to be treated gently. Love-making becomes limited. It isn't, how shall I put it, a hurly-burly any longer. You fall into a routine, and once you've fallen into that, it's difficult to shake out of it. When the wife has recovered after her baby, she picks up the routine that she had followed during her pregnancy."

"Does that matter provided the routine is pleasant?"

"In my opinion, yes, because it prevents a couple from learning all the varieties of love-making."

"You think that's important?"

Naomi answered her obliquely. "How much pornography have you read?"

"Not very much. *Fanny Hill*, of course."

"That's the greatest fun, but it's not very explicit. Have you seen any blue films?"

"No."

"You haven't read any of those books that go into exact detail?"

"Modern novels go quite a long way, don't they?"

"Perhaps, but they can't go all the way. There are semi-medical books that do. Most men have read them and they wonder what it's like in these elaborate ways. I don't say those ways are more satisfactory, but they are different and there's a kick about doing things that perhaps are frowned upon. If a man doesn't do them with his wife, he'll be tempted to do them with another woman. It holds good for the wife, too. If she suspects that another man can give her a new experience, she'll very likely give herself an opportunity of finding out."

Naomi was asking fewer questions now. She was talking as an instructress to a pupil.

"It is essential in marriage," she went on, "that each should satisfy the other's curiosity. You will hear a woman say, 'I couldn't let my husband do that to me,' or a husband say, 'I couldn't do that with my own wife.' But the wife who says that may be very sure that some other woman will, and the husband can be very sure that some other man will be less punctilious. The wife will be grateful to that other man."

Naomi developed her theory amusingly, lightly, with no undue solemnity. She kept Myra laughing half the time.

"If Victor is being unfaithful to you," she said, "it's not that he's not devoted to you, that he doesn't love you, it's not even that he may not be in love with you. If he's unfaithful, it's because some woman is giving him some trifling assuagement that you never have."

She paused. She looked at Myra quizzically. "Has it ever occurred to you to whip your husband?" Myra was so astonished that she could only gape. Naomi laughed. "I can see that it never has."

"It couldn't occur to anyone to think of that in connection with Victor."

"Why?"

"He's so conventional, so formal; Winchester and New College. So completely the Treasury official."

"That's the very type for whom that treatment might be effective."

"But one can't imagine anyone like Victor submitting himself to anything undignified."

"That's the very type of person who responds to it. You have heard of flagellation."

"Of course, yes. But . . ."

"But you thought it was only neurotics, decadents, who indulged in it. Men whose nerves were so jaded that they needed an extra kick. But that isn't the way it is. It's solid citizens who fall for it. Which race of men would you say were the most ponderous, the most formal, the most self-important, the most insistent upon protocol? The English, the Germans, and the Swedes; and they are the three races most addicted to it. They want to escape from their robes and chains of office. They want to be human. It means nothing to the light-hearted Mediterranean types – the French, the Spaniards, the Italians; nor to the South Americans – with their comic-opera revolutions. But the stodgy, hide-bound northerners! Think of how bored a judge must get sitting in a high seat, pretending to be shocked by the misdemeanours of some hippie. What a relief to him to drive straight from the law courts to a small flat in Maida Vale, to be ordered about by a trollop, to be told to take off his clothes, go down on his hands and knees, then to have her mount him as though he were a horse and flog him round the flat. Of all the past presidents of France, who is the one who is held now in most affectionate esteem, who has the most streets named after him? Félix Faure. And why? He was on his way to a high civic function. He was seated at his official desk; he was wearing a frock coat and a high starched collar. His gleaming silk hat was on the desk beside him. But in addition to all that, a naked girl was on her knees between his legs; his hands caressed her head. In a sudden spasm of pleasure, he had a heart attack and died. His fingers fastened in her hair; the girl could only be released at the cost of her shorn locks. Félix Faure is a national hero."

Myra could not help laughing. Naomi made it all sound so ridiculous, and yet at the same time, inviting.

"Men need to come down from their high horses. They want to become human beings, and what a relief it must be to them if it's with their own wives that they can slip out of that magisterial saddle instead of slinking away surreptitiously to a squalid flat.

"And think," Naomi was continuing, "of the kick a wife must get when she looks up at her husband, pontificating on a dais, remembering how he behaved only a few hours ago; thinking of the romps they would be indulging in in a few hours' time, saying to herself, 'If only these people here could see him as I know him.' Myself I'm precocious. I know that; and I'm a bitch. But when I was only sixteen I seduced the dean of my college. He thought he did the seducing, but that's where I had him fooled. He didn't attract me particularly, but oh, what a kick I got out of watching him strut across the campus, and of listening to his sanctimonious sermons. I did the most outrageous things to him, I made him do the most outrageous things to me, not because I enjoyed it, at the time, but because I could chuckle afterwards when he stood up there in the pulpit."

"You are opening a whole new world to me."

"That's what I'm trying to do *meine Liebling*. I'm trying to save your marriage for you. The more prominent a man, the more he needs to be relaxed. He'll always be grateful to the woman who does that for him, and if it's his wife who does it, that marriage is built on very solid rock."

At first it was Naomi who had cross-questioned Myra. Now the roles were reversed. It was Myra who asked the questions.

"This business with whips," she said. "I can't see what pleasure it can give a man. It must hurt a lot."

Naomi shook her head. "Not necessarily; not if it's done

gradually, gently at first, then harder. You don't feel pain when you're excited. A footballer doesn't realise that he's been hurt till the game is over. Haven't you heard of women biting and scratching their lovers? Hasn't Shakespeare said something about that; 'the pinch that hurts and is desired'? Besides it's reciprocal in this. A woman gets to like it; it excites her. And if a man knows that a woman is being excited through him, that's inflammatory. There are a good many angles to it."

She elaborated the theme. "Man is excited by a woman taking all that trouble over him, by her assuming the active not the passive role. As a legacy of Victorian prudery, there is in many men a built-in suspicion that women don't get much kick out of sex; it's so easy for a woman to pretend. She can put on an act. It is so much in her interest to. That's her *métier de femme* – to exploit his physical need for her; to make him pay for the indelicate favours that she accords him. But it is a different matter when she's in the dominant role, using him as an instrument for her pleasure, ordering him about, lashing him to the bed posts."

"Lashing him to the bed posts!"

"That's a later stage. All this is an acquired taste, remember. One thing leads to another. When a woman says, 'I'm going to gag you so that you can't scream.' that's reaching a high bracket."

Myra's eyes grew wider. She could begin to see the point to it. Yet it all was very foreign to her. She could not picture Victor in such a role.

"You've done this kind of thing yourself?" she asked.

"Of course. I'm German, don't forget."

"How do you start?"

"It's easy with a little guile. If the man has a taste for it you'll find out pretty soon. There's a mental shorthand. In the same way, I suppose, that masons recognise each other. The woman has to take the first step, naturally. She's the active one. Often, she has to put the idea into a man's mind. That's when it's exciting – when he hasn't realised that he is that way, or what is more likely, hasn't admitted it to himself."

"But how do you put it in his mind?"

"As a joke to start with. Find fault with him on some account. Suppose that he's unpunctual. Then you can say, 'Next time you are late I shall have to whip you.' Watch how he

67

reacts. If he seems to relish the idea, if he says, 'Oh, you wouldn't do that, would you?' you'll know he's nibbling. 'Oh, yes I will,' you'll say, 'and it won't be a laughing matter, I can promise you.' But though you say it isn't a laughing matter, you must keep it a laughing matter. Don't be solemn. That's the mistake so many people make. They invoke high heaven. They deliver portentous vows. They talk about the soul; as though love-making was only justified when you have God on your side, angels and archangels and all the company of heaven. Let it be frivolous and fun. That's the whole point of it. Then one day you will produce a whip, or a birch – there's a lot to be said for a birch. It stings rather than bruises; you show it to him and say: 'Do you see this? This is for you next time you're late. One stroke for every minute.' As likely as not he will be late on purpose."

"You take my breath away."

"That's what I'm trying to do, my silly sweet. You're an adorable kitten. I want you to have the very best of everything." She raised her hand. She laid it against Myra's cheek, letting it rest there in a half caress. "There's another thing too about it," she went on. "It is a very definite aphrodisiac. It brings the blood to that part of the anatomy. It genuinely is what doctors recommend."

Next morning Naomi returned from a shopping visit in Valetta with a gift-wrapped package. It was two and a half feet long, and in a narrow box. She handed it to Myra. "For you to take home as a secret weapon."

The box contained a leather riding crop. The leather was painted and embossed. At the end of the handle was a soft, thin leather tongue, three inches long. "You show that to your Victor and mark the expression on his face," she said.

Myra held the handle at its end and flicked the tongue. "This doesn't seem a very lethal toy," she said.

"It'll do. If handled right. I told you to start gently. We'll have a dress rehearsal; tonight, after a hot bath."

That night there was a gala dance in the neighbouring hotel, the Sheraton. Two days before, they had planned to go to it. "What about that dance?" asked Naomi.

Myra shook her head. "It's too much bother. There'll be nobody there I want to dance with. Let's have a brandy with our coffee and then go up."

Naomi made no comment. But the tip of her tongue slid between her lips.

It was only just ten o'clock when Naomi knocked on Myra's door. Myra was in her bed jacket, sitting by the balcony.

"I'll have your bath ready in five minutes. Then I'll call," said Naomi.

Myra listened to the water running; a thick sweet smell came from the bathroom. Her impatience, her restlessness were mounting. Naomi's head came round the door. "All set."

Naomi had taken off her robe. She was wearing only the bottom half of a bikini. Myra, seeing her in a bathing dress, had fancied that she would be over-plump; she wasn't and her breasts were firm.

Naomi held out her hand. "Come along. Off with that jacket."

The streaming bath water was bluish, covered with whitish foam. "Nuns used to put white powder in their baths so as not to be shocked by the sight of their own bodies. I'm giving you a blue bath, to spare your blushes."

The bath was low, with a wide square brim. "I once worked in a hospital," said Naomi. "Giving the patients baths was my favourite chore."

She knelt beside Myra and began to soap her back. Her fingers were strong and firm. They kneaded the back of her neck and the flesh round her shoulder blades. Myra felt a slow hypnotic peace descend on her. "Lean back. Yes, like that, against the bath." Naomi put a sponge underneath her head and began to soap her breasts, rotating the palm of her right hand over each in turn, till the nipples hardened. "I've been so wanting to do just this," she said.

The massage went on, went on. "Stand up," she said. Standing up now beside her Naomi drew the film of scented soap over her stomach, over her navel. "Turn around," she said. Her hands lingering over the swelling haunches. "That South African was right," she said. "It *is* the loveliest line. Lie down again."

She eased Myra back into the water. "Now your feet," she said. Once again she was on her knees herself. She lifted Myra's right foot and laid it on the edge of the bath. She washed it carefully, toe by toe; she bent her head. She took the little toe between her teeth. "I could easily be a foot fetishist," she said.

She stood up again. Bending over the bath, she lifted the left foot and set it on the edge. "No, leave the right foot there. It'll make it easier later."

Her hands were now moving slowly over Myra's shins; they were kneading her calves. They moved over her knees. When they approached her thighs, Myra could no longer see them through the opaque blue water. It was tantalising to feel them mounting, mounting, coming nearer, nearer. "In the hospital," Naomi said, "when I used to bathe a good-looking man, at this point I'd say, 'Would you like me to wash you here?' I'm going to wash you there."

Nearer and nearer the approaching fingers came, nearer, nearer, nearer, then thrillingly they were there, lingering, loitering, entering, caressing. "The little boy in the boat," she said. "He likes it, doesn't he?"

"If you go on like that you'll have to gag me or I'll scream," said Myra.

Naomi laughed.

"That's right. You haven't lost your sense of humour. Never be solemn about love-making. Now for that secret weapon."

Noami slipped a pillow under Myra's stomach. "Never forget the pillow. It's symbollic as well as practical. The raising of an altar." She passed her hand slowly over the long smooth curve. "So lovely, so soft, so exquisite." She picked up the whip. She ran the point of it slowly from the nape of the neck, down the spine, between the line of the haunches. She raised it and struck gently. "That's how you start," she said, "so softly that it's a caress." She struck again, this time a little harder; a third and fourth time, each time harder.

"That one has left a mark," she said, "but not a big one; I must kiss it well." She let her cheek linger against the soft, marked cushion. She struck again, again; and each time harder. "It isn't hurting, is it?"

"No, not really."

It tingled, it stung, it smarted; it wasn't exactly pleasant, but it pleased her. It was an utterly new sensation. She had lost count now of the strokes. They were getting harder all the time. There was a little pause. Then suddenly, there was one much harder. Myra gasped and shuddered. "Oh, *Liebling,*" Naomi cried, "that was too hard. But you looked so tempting. I couldn't resist and it is thrilling you a little, isn't it?" She dropped the whip. She slid her hand under the pillow between Myra's thighs. "Oh, yes, you *are* excited. You're damp. I can't resist."

Before Myra could appreciate what was happening, she was on her back, on the edge of the bed. The pillow was beneath her hips; Naomi was kneeling on the floor, with Myra's legs divided across her shoulders. She looked up at Myra, a pleading, imploring expression in her face. "Please, please, please." Then lowered her head.

It was a sensation for which Myra had no standard of comparison. Nothing like this had happened to her. She had read about it; she had felt curious about it. She had been repelled and attracted by the idea of it. She had thought of it as something that no one would ever do to anyone like her. But now, but now ... a soft, pointed tongue was stabbing at her, was caressing her; firm, strong fingers were exploring her. Everything that had happened during the last week had found a sudden shattering culmination in this dynamic moment. She writhed, she sobbed out loud. "You're killing me, you're killing me," she cried. There was no mistaking the complete, the shattering nature of the explosion that convulsed her.

Her head was on Naomi's shoulder. She was back now at the head of the bed, among the pillows. Naomi was whispering in her ear; now and again the tip of Naomi's tongue toyed with the crevices of her ear. Naomi's hand was slowly stroking her from breast to knees.

"It's what I've been praying to happen all these days ..." she murmured, "for your sake even more than for my own. ... I wanted you to have the best there was – and it was, wasn't it? ... It wasn't just vaguely diffused, it was localised, too, wasn't it?"

"It was localised. It was diffused, oh, it was everything."

Naomi took Myra's hand, guided it between her own thighs, enforced its pressure. Myra was conscious with her fingertips of Naomi's gathering response. "*Leibling*, please, won't you now, in return, you to me?"

Myra hesitated. She felt a spasm of repugnance. "Please,"

71

Naomi was repeating. "Please, please." Myra still hesitated. I suppose I must, she thought. It would be churlish to refuse. Besides, she was curious. If she didn't try this now, she might never have another chance.

She slid onto her knees beside the bed. The sense of repugnance still remained, a little; but the skin of Naomi's inner thighs was soft against her cheeks. There was also a sense of challenge: to give as much as she had received. Her hand slid under Naomi's hips. Naomi's hips lifted to meet her kiss; moved in a circle, undulated, plunged, retreated. The feeling of repugnance slid away. The warm, luxuriant dampness was a lush intoxicant. She clasped Naomi's hips, gripping them, steadying their rocking movement, enforcing her dominance, as though she was mastering an opposing force. Naomi's hands were pressed upon her head. Myra tightened her grip, letting her nails dig into the firm, soft flesh, the pinch that hurts but is desired, waiting impatiently, eager, for the muscular contraction, the broken signs that would prove her triumph.

"I thought, at first, I wasn't going to like it, but I did," she whispered.

Naomi laughed. "You'll like it even more tomorrow. The second night's always better than the first, and I've so much to show you. We've three more nights. You'll see. The last will be the best."

It was.

5

Myra's return flight landed her at the Gloucester Road Air Terminal in mid-afternoon. It was a bright early summer day, too warm for her to wear a coat. The trim gardens that lined the road out to Hampstead were alight with irises. The ochre-brown fields of Malta belonged to another universe. It was hard to believe that six hours ago she and Naomi had toasted each other in a valedictory Tom Collins.

"It's unlikely, *meine Liebling*, that we shall ever meet again. But I shall never forget you, never, never. I shall relive these few days, oh, how many times."

Which was exactly what that South African had hoped to

say to her. How astonished he would have been could he have foreseen that that identical speech was to be made to her by a woman.

"Will the world be the same again?" That had been her answer then, as she had sat on the terrace overlooking the patio. Now with the taxi climbing Fitzjohn's Avenue, so seemingly unchanged, she was on the verge of wondering whether it had ever happened. Might it not be an episode in a novel that she had read on a vacation, identifying herself with the heroine, as one does when one reads a novel, in a deck chair by the Mediterranean?

As she got out of her taxi, a voice shouted from the nursery. "Mummy, Mummy, welcome home." Jerry had been watching for her. A minute later Jerry was in her arms; and under her nostrils was that familiar wholesome smell of soap and powder.

Jerry insisted on her unpacking right away. She wanted to see what her mother had brought her back, but she also wanted to have her mother to herself. She had so much to tell her mother. It took her a full quarter of an hour to tell it all. The sentences fell over one another. She was still talking, as at last she allowed her mother to come to the nursery. As she trotted up the stairs, tugging at her mother's hand, her mother thought, No, it has never happened. It was all a dream.

Five minutes later she was recognising in a startling flash of illumination that very certainly it had. When they came into the nursery, Anna was tidying Jerry's bed, which had been ruffled by the afternoon siesta. Frankie was in his pen, and Lena was bouncing for him a large India-rubber ball. Seeing the two girls together, Myra recalled how she had wondered what they did together. She looked at Lena first. She knew now what it was to be a passive partner. That, very certainly, was Lena's role; and one day, no doubt, when the need for domesticity, for a family became assertive, she would be passively receptive of some man. Anna was a different proposition. She was not only older, she was settled in her ways. She was a woman who knew herself. Myra looked at her, thoughtfully, noticing her hands as they smoothed out the bed. They were not short-fingered as Naomi's had been. Anna's fingers were long and thin, but they were firm and sensitive. She passed them slowly in a final sweep over the counterpane. It would be exciting to have them pass in just that way over one's shoulders. What would it be like to make love with Anna? At that moment Anna, her job completed, stood up and turned. She was about to give her employer the conventional smile of welcome. But instead, as their eyes met, her expression changed. She stood transfixed with a look of surprise, of wonderment, of recognition, then of delighted warmth. She knows, Myra thought, she knows. They stared at one another, each knowing what was in the other's mind. No, Myra told herself. It isn't something that happened to someone else. I'm never going to be the same again.

Would she, she wondered, have looked different to Victor if she had succumbed to that South African?

Whether she would or would not, she was very certain that Victor looked different to her in the light of the last week. Under the handkerchiefs in her drawer was that little riding switch. Would she ever use it? She could not believe she would, and yet, and yet . . .

On his return that evening from his office, he looked so exactly as he had always done, so formal, so correct, in his dark blue pin-stripe suit, his stiff white collar, his Burgundy dark tie with its pearl pin. Was it possible that beneath that stern exterior was a rebel, avid for outrageous practices? Was it? Was it? At any rate, he was going to be shown that whip.

He was, later that very evening. She was still at her mirror when he came in from his dressing room; he took up a stool and set it by her. He passed his arm around her shoulders, fondling them. His face was reflected beside hers in the mirror. He smiled at her.

"All this trouble to make up a complexion that's going to be tousled within seven minutes."

They laughed together. He was in the right mood to be shown the secret weapon.

"I've brought another present too, one that I'm shy of showing you."

"That sounds intriguing."

"It's not actually a present, and it's not in fact from me. It was given to me, for you, if you see what I mean."

"I'm afraid I don't."

74

"Well, it's like this. There was a woman in the same hotel as me in Malta. She gave me a good deal of advice."

"What kind of advice?"

"That's what I'm coming to. She was a German."

"I see or at least, I don't."

"She told me that German men were very much like Englishmen, that the same treatment that suited the one would suit the other."

"There's something in that, maybe. But we're still a long way, aren't we, from that ambiguous present."

"I'm coming to that. Be patient. I have to explain how all this came about. What she said was this, that Englishmen, like Germans and Swedes as well, were very correct and disciplined; that at school they were subjected to extreme discipline; and that if they weren't subjected to strict discipline they felt lost. Would you agree with that?"

"I suppose I would. But then I don't think that most of us ever get an opportunity of being lost. We are still subjected to discipline. All our lives a man like myself for instance is just as punctilious about punctuality, about being at his office desk on time, as he was in the sixth book at Winchester."

"I know you are, but that's not quite what she meant. She was talking about the methods by which this discipline was enforced."

"I'm still not following you."

"It's like this, or rather this is how she said it was." She hesitated. She had to bring it out into the open now, to use the actual word. "She said that Englishmen were accustomed to being flogged at school, that that was how they became subject to discipline, and if that type of discipline was not continued, they felt lost without it."

"This is all very complicated. I don't see what you are leading up to. I thought we were talking about an unusual present."

"We were. We are."

"What's this present?"

"This."

She opened the drawer. She slid her hands beneath the pile of handkerchiefs. Her fingers closed around the handle of the whip. "Now," she thought, "Now," and pulled it out.

She noted in the mirror an expression of startled surprise

cross his face, startled but at the same time pleased. She noted it with amused relief. Perhaps Naomi was right.

"And what may be the purpose and point of this?" he asked.

"She said that since a whip was the symbol of an English-man's obedience during his ten formative years, he would as a man respond to the influence of this symbol."

"Like Pavlov's dogs?"

"I don't know about them. But this woman said that if a wife wanted to get the best out of her husband, she should introduce this symbol of discipline into her home."

"Now that *is* something." His eyes were twinkling and a smile was flickering on his lips.

He's catching on to this, she thought.

"Did she give you any idea of how a wife was to employ it?"

"Oh, yes, to use it as a threat to start with. She took the example of an unpunctual husband. She should say to him: 'Next time you're late, I'll have to use this on you.' "

"And if he goes on being late?"

"She uses it."

"Did she give any other examples of its use?"

"Oh, yes."

"Such as?"

"A husband who was negligent. It sounds rather ridiculous, I know, but Germans are so formal, aren't they?"

"Negligent in what?"

"The fulfilment of his marital obligations."

"Is that the way she put it?"

"Yes, that's the way she put it."

"And that was why she made you a present of this toy?"

"She called it a secret weapon."

"I once read that Russian women in the Czarist days took a whip with them on their honeymoon."

"But that was different; that was for their husbands to use on them."

"You don't think your German friend had that same idea?"

"No, no. That was not her point at all. Englishmen aren't like Russians. Englishmen are conditioned to the whip."

"I see."

He frowned thoughtfully. She noted that frown, expectantly. Naomi was right. The idea did appeal to him. She was con-scious of her heart beating quickly. He put his arm around her shoulders, caressingly. "Let's go to bed," he said.

76

They had been apart for twenty days, the longest time since their marriage. You would expect a young husband to be ardent after a three weeks' absence. He was. She had never known Victor so ardent since their first weeks of marriage. If there *was* another woman in his life, he couldn't have been seeing much of her, she thought; or maybe it was the idea of the whip that had excited him. She'd got to play on this.

On their honeymoon, she had felt that one of the pleasantest things about love-making was the quiet talking together afterwards. One of the slightly melancholy things about marriage, she had later come to think, was how very seldom one had that talking together afterwards. Victor was tired after a long day's work. He usually fell asleep within ten minutes. Another of the pleasant things about that talking together afterwards had been the knowledge that within half an hour or so he would be wanting to make love to her again. The first recognition of that mounting need had made her heart beat faster. Nowadays that hardly ever happened.

But this night was exceptional. Their talk together lingered on, for fifteen minutes, twenty, half an hour. A mischievous idea occurred to her. During her honeymoon, and on their post-marriage, honeymoon-style holidays, she had lain passive at his side, awaiting the first signal of his need for her; but during the last three nights she had been far from passive. She had learned the magic power that lay within a woman's fingertips, within her own fingertips. Why ignore that lesson? She turned towards him, on her side. She let her hand slide across his knees. Slowly she drew her fingers upwards, upwards, with the lightest, the most electric of all touches. She remembered how Naomi had asked her whether there was any change in Victor's love-making, some trick that he had learned from another woman. Myra was on safe ground here. She could not have learned this from another man. Her fingertips fluttered over him. Yes, it was working. It had worked. "Darling, oh darling," she sobbed, as he turned towards her.

Afterwards, a long time afterwards, he said, "I don't think, do you, that you would be justified in using that whip on me tonight."

She chuckled to herself. The idea had excited him.

6

Ten days later Myra was rung up in the morning by a man who said: "You do not know me; you have never heard of me. But I have to see you about something of great importance to you. My name is Montagu Frank. I would like to see you alone, when there is no likelihood of our being disturbed. I shall need half an hour at least to explain the situation to you." Myra arranged to see him at three o'clock.

Recalling it all afterwards she was to think: If anyone were to say to me, "Describe him," I don't know how I'd answer. I don't know if I'd recognise him in the street.

Montagu Frank was the most negative person in his appearance that she had encountered. He might have been thirty-five years old, he might have been fifty-five. He was of medium height. He wasn't heavy, though he had a slightly protuberant paunch. He had no distinguishing features, no moustache, no scar. He was neatly dressed, but without any air of fashion. He looked the kind of man who had been at a minor public school and had made no mark there. He was carrying a small black attaché case. He said, "It is very kind of you to grant me this interview." He had an educated accent to the extent that it had no provincial inflection. It gave the impression of having at some point had a genuine accent filtered out of it. He tapped on the attaché case. He said, "I think I can best explain the purpose of my visit with the contents of this case; or rather I can let this case explain it."

He opened the case. He took from it a small tape recorder. He put the machine on the table and turned the switch.

Two voices came from it, two female voices; one had a German and the other an English accent. The German voice was saying, "It wasn't just vaguely diffused, it was localised too, wasn't it?" The English voice answered, "It was localised. It was diffused, oh, it was everything."

Mr. Frank switched off the machine. "It is," he said, "difficult to recognise one's own voice when one first hears it on a tape recorder; but I presume you will have no difficulty in recognising the voice of the woman with the German accent."

"No difficulty whatsoever."

"No one who knew you would have any difficulty in recognising yours."

"I accept that."

"I possess a great many hundred feet of tape of conversations that took place in Malta between you and this woman. What I have brought here this morning is an abridged version containing the more . . . How shall I put it?" He hesitated. Was he going to say "juicy." It was the kind of adjective that a man like this would use. But no, after a pause he found a word that was sufficiently definitive, the word "significant." Yes, she thought, that gets his message over.

"No one hearing this recording," he went on, "would have the slightest doubt as to the relations that existed between you and this woman. What your husband's reaction would be, in his capacity as a husband, I cannot say. There are, I believe, a certain number of husbands who would welcome a situation such as this. It would add a dimension, a fascinating dimension to their marriage."

He certainly is a revolting creature, Myra thought.

"But however he might accept this record personally as a husband," Mr. Frank went on, "there can be no doubt how he would receive it professionally, as a man occupying a prominent position in government service. This record makes him a security risk."

He paused. He looked interrogatively at Myra. "I am not contradicting you," she said.

"The fact that the other woman was a German makes the position the more delicate."

He paused again, and again with that interrogative expression on his face.

I must keep my head, thought Myra. I mustn't be aggressive. I mustn't put his back up. At the same time I mustn't be too docile. "I quite agree with you," she said. "Those tapes could be of the greatest damage to my husband. What price are you putting on them?"

For the first time Mr. Frank permitted himself to smile. "It is a relief to deal with a practical woman of the world, who recognises the point of issue and comes straight to it."

"I'm glad you appreciate that; I will be quite straightforward with you. It would be absurd for me living in a house like this, surrounded with some quite valuable china, pictures, furniture, with my husband receiving a substantial salary, to pretend that I am poor. I am not. Nor is my husband the kind of man who lives above his income. He is prudent and he is cautious. We could, if a crisis arose, raise a considerable amount of money. If, that is to say, it was a crisis in which we could work together as a team. This is not such a case. On the mantelpiece is a rather charming Meissen figurine. I could sell that for a hundred pounds, but it is not mine to sell. I could not explain its absence to my husband. I am sure that you will see my point. What I suggest is that you should name your price and that I should consider if I can meet it."

Whatever I do she told herself, I must not make any deal on the instalment plan. She had read enough novels dealing with blackmail to be assured on that point. Better to throw herself on Victor's mercy than lead a life of continual deceit, always wondering where she could raise the hundred or so pounds that would keep the transaction fluid. It must be a lump sum down, then the tapes handed over.

Once again he smiled. "That point had occurred to me. I was not planning to ask you for any money. I was going to ask you to perform a service for me."

Ah, here it comes. This was how spies got enrolled and enough novels had warned her on that point. Was this Mr. Frank a Soviet spy? He looked the very kind of man who would be – impersonal, negative, hard to identify, a citizen of no man's land.

"What kind of service would you want of me?" she asked, though she felt that it was an unnecessary question. Through Victor, if she were adroit, she would surely have access to a considerable amount of information that would be of paramount value to a foreign power. If that was what he wanted – and she was very sure it was – she had her answer ready. "No, no, no."

But no, that was not the service he required.

"I had better," he said, "lay my cards upon the table. I am one of the representatives of a small international group whose main activity is the transference of drugs, heroin, hashish, and opium between one country and another. It is a very profitable business. A package of heroin that can be slipped into a handbag is worth several thousand pounds. But it is a very risky business. We have to choose our agents with the greatest care.

As you will have realised by now, it is through blackmail that we recruit them."

"But that's impossible."

She was taken off her guard so completely that she could not maintain her pose of detached, amiable co-operation. To become a drug courier . . . with all the risks that were attached; sooner or later she would be caught, inevitably. She would not know a second's peace of mind. No, no no, it was impossible.

He raised his hand. "Please let me explain. I said it was a risky business. It is; that is why we have to employ exceptional precautions, precautions that are extremely costly. You will be aware that it did not cost us nothing to obtain these tapes. But the profits in this business are so great that we can afford to underwrite expenses such as those. And because those profits are so high, we can afford to diminish the risks of discovery, to reduce them to a point where they are non-existent. I will explain to you how we work, or rather by explaining how the police work, I can show you how we outwit them. Police work of this kind comes under the heading of defensive security. The police watch for anything that is unusual. They throw out a net. They check movements across frontiers – roads, trains, ships, airports. They check means of communication. They watch cables. In wartime they impose censorship; they tap telephones. Their effectiveness depends on how tightly the meshes of the net are drawn. You will hear policemen say, 'The small fish may get through, but we catch the big ones.'

"Now let us see how this affects us. If we had the same courier or couriers working for us all the time, we should awake suspicion. A woman like yourself can make one journey to Malta and no questions are asked. But suppose that you made four or five trips a year, that you went to Tangier, Beirut, Alexandria, Crete. They would want an explanation. For most of the time since the second war, residents of Great Britain have had a restricted travel allowance. How, they wonder, does she get the currency for this series of trips? They will make inquiries. If it is a question of her health, well, that's all right. Again she may have a professional reason, she may be a painter or a writer, or she may have a French or Italian lover who can finance her trips. That again is fine. The police are not concerned with private morals. But if there is no obvious reason for her making these excursions, they will search for one; and they will go through her luggage with a magnifying glass. We have found, in consequence, that there is only one way of defeating the police and that is by using the same courier only once. That should be very comforting for you. We will give you one assignment and that is all."

He paused. His expression was that of a salesman, who has put over an irresistible proposition. "You mean," she said, "that I will carry out one mission and then you will give me those tapes?"

"Exactly; after that one mission, neither you nor those tapes are of the slightest value to us."

"You could blackmail me, I suppose."

"Only in a minor way. We agreed on that a few minutes ago. I don't say that we don't use blackmail when it can be profitable – that's particularly true in the case of men. But in your case, my dear lady, one trip with an envelope of heroin in your handbag will amply repay our trouble."

"The profits in your business must be considerable."

"They are, indeed they are."

She thought of the trouble and the cost that must have been involved in the acquisition of these tapes.

"By the way," she asked, "how did you get these tapes?"

He shrugged. "One of the first rules in this kind of game is never to betray the sources of one's information. More people than you would imagine are in our pay. Bellhops, chambermaids. It isn't difficult to hide a receiver."

Yes, she thought; but who tipped off the chambermaid? It was a line of thought she did not want to pursue. There was only one incident in the whole transaction that disgusted her, one picture that she could not face: Naomi saying to some underling, "Tonight in her room and on the following nights." She prayed that it was not in that way that it had happened. It was something that she did not want to visualise.

Mentally she shook herself. It was time to be matter-of-fact and practical. How, she asked, was she to set about this mission?

"It will be very simple," he assured her. "We have a number of agencies along the southern Mediterranean. Beirut is the best. Hashish is grown there, along the valley between Damascus and the coast. But it may not be easy for you to get there. Tangier might be simpler, or Tunis. It is a question of your finding the place that will be most convenient for you."

"It wouldn't be convenient for me to go to any of those places. The doctor recommended me to take that trip to Malta. That was an exceptional case."

"Precisely; and that's why we don't want you to repeat it. This next trip of yours must be entirely above board. It must be a family trip taken with your husband; with your children as well, preferably."

"My husband and the children?"

"Indeed, why not? You are, I imagine, going to take a family holiday this year."

"I don't know about the children. But my husband and I had thought of taking a cruise in July."

"A Mediterranean cruise?"

"We had thought of going to the Norwegian fjords."

Mr. Frank shook his head. "Scandinavia, no. We have depots there. We deliver goods, but we don't collect goods. The Mediterranean through its links with the Orient is our source of supply. Surely you could persuade him to go to the Mediterranean instead."

"I suppose I could."

"It shouldn't be difficult. Every Englishman feels the need for sunshine. Almost anywhere along the southern shore will do."

As he presented it, nothing could be simpler than the project which he had in mind. "I will keep in touch with you. I will telephone you every other Tuesday, starting on Tuesday week. As soon as you have worked out your trip you will let me know. Then I will arrange a place where it will be easy for you to collect the packet. It will be a certain tobacconist, let us say in Tunis. We will fix a time, roughly. You will have a code. You will say. 'I want some mild cigarettes, because I have a weak throat.' You will be given rather a large packet and that is all that there will be to it."

"It sounds very simple as you set it out."

"And believe you me, that's exactly how it will prove to be. I have been in this business for ten years. Nothing has gone wrong yet."

Myra watched him from the window. He paused on the

pavement, looked from right to left, then crossed the street. He did not hurry. There was nothing particular about his walk. He did not limp or drag his feet. He was wearing a dark grey felt hat; it was not particularly new. He turned to the right, towards Church Row. On his way to the tube station probably. A car went by and then a truck. A youngish woman pushing a baby carriage was coming up the street towards him. She did not look at him. He was not the kind of person at whom anyone would look. He was completely ordinary.

He reached the end of the street and turned right again. Another minute and he was out of sight. The street looked just the same. Everything looked just the same. On the table was the novel she had been reading. She picked it up, sat down in the chair, and started reading where she had left off. Her eyes travelled down the page but her mind did not take in the meaning of the words. Everything looked the same. But everything was not the same. Nothing could be the same again.

She closed the book, rose, went into the kitchen. She habitually made her preparations for dinner directly after lunch. She had planned a casserole. It was simmering quietly. There was nothing that needed doing for at least an hour, when she would stir it and add a little wine. She had laid the table. She had looked forward to a quiet hour with a book before she went into the nursery for tea. That would be at half past four. It was now five to. She went back to the sitting room. She turned on the TV – a cricket match. She changed over to ITV. A cowboy film she had already seen. She switched the machine off. She stood in the centre of the room; she needed company. She wanted to talk to someone on the telephone. If only her mother did not live so far away. Long-distance calls were for occasional use and then after seven. Who else was there? Someone she could ring up, to talk to, as she had when she was a débutante. But then it had been different. All that ringing up after a dance and comparing notes. You had as a débutante so much in common with so many others. You had not, as a young married woman. Who was there she could call? She ran over a list of names: Barbara, Jocelyn, Edith, Kitty. Kitty. Why not Kitty? It was through Kitty that all this had started. She had an excuse for calling Kitty. It was time for a cutlet-for-cutlet project. Kitty? She dialled the number. But no answer. Kitty. Why hadn't she asked Victor right out on that first evening? None of this would have happened if she had said, "Kitty saw you in the Brompton Road today. What on earth were you doing there?" Why had she been pettily anxious to "have something on him"? If only at Severods' that Friday that guest had not arrived at the very moment when Kitty was going to say, "When I saw you from that bus on Wednesday." None of this need have happened. Chance had loaded the dice. It could all so easily not have happened. If only she had spoken at the very start. Now she was in too deep. Or wasn't she? Was not there still a chance of getting out? Might she in two months' time find herself thinking, If only I had confessed when that miserable weed first called. I had my last chance then. Now it is too late.

Pacing the room, she rehearsed the phrases which she could use if she had to break the news to Victor. She wouldn't be diplomatic. She couldn't lead up to it. She would break right in. "I'm in trouble," she would say. "I'm in serious trouble. I've been very stupid. You remember my telling you about the German woman whom I met in Malta? Yes, the one who gave me the whip. She made a pass at me. Out of curiosity, for the hell of it, I let her; now I'm being blackmailed." No apologies; no explanation. The facts. That was the way to do it. If she was to do it. Was she though? Was she?

As usual, soon after six, she heard the click of Victor's latch-key in the door. Then the tap of his umbrella in the stand. His feet fell lightly on the stairway. The handle turned. There he was in the doorway, urbane and trim. With his tie fitting exactly in the centre of his collar, his shoes shining as though they had been freshly polished, the evening paper in his hand, the cuffs of his shirt projecting a precise two centimetres beyond his sleeves. Under his thin moustache flickered a half smile of well-being, of self-satisfaction, almost but not quite of smugness. "How's your day been?" he said, and in his tone of voice was the assumption that her day – since it was his day too, since she was a part of him – must necessarily have been as good as his. Her hackles rose. How the hell could she tell him how her day had gone? It's all your fault, she thought. If you weren't the kind of man you are none of this would have ever happened. Why aren't you the kind of man to whom I can confess a thing like this? Why should you have the kind

85

of job that a scandal like this would damage? It wouldn't hurt an actor, a lawyer, a professor. Because you are a security risk, I'm vulnerable. That's the only reason. It's all your fault. No, there was no way of telling him. She had to go through with it.

Once again he had brought back a record, this time a long-playing one. It lasted almost to the end of their martinis. As the last notes vibrated along her nerves she took her first step along the road that was to lead her heaven knew where.

"I've been thinking about our summer holiday," she said.

"You've only been back a fortnight."

"That was my rest cure. I'm talking about *our* holiday."

"But you don't want to go right away, do you?"

"I'm not thinking about myself. I'm thinking about you. You need to get away, regularly."

"I don't say I don't."

"You work very hard. You must be getting tired. We'd planned to go after the Lord's test match. There isn't any reason why we shouldn't."

"I wouldn't say there was."

"Then let's stick to our programme. The first week in July."

"That's fine by me."

"Only I'm not so certain about Scandinavia."

"No?"

"You can't rely on the climate there, any more than you can here."

"That's true."

"I'd prefer the Mediterranean."

"Even though you've already been there?"

"That's why. It's made me greedy. The sun, the sand. What about a packaged tour?"

"I've nothing against that."

"I've never seen the Arab world. Tunis, Beirut; aren't there tours which take in six or eight different places?"

"I'll have my secretary get to work on it tomorrow."

"You're very amenable."

"Why shouldn't I be?"

Indeed why shouldn't he? But a great many men wouldn't be. They made their plans and didn't want them changed, by anyone except themselves. I'm lucky. I shouldn't be peevish. It's all of it my fault.

But was it? He was charming during dinner. He complimented her on the dish she had prepared; he toasted her as he raised his glass of wine. *"Skol,"* he said, looking into her eyes again. "How lucky we are," he said, "to live in a world that has no servants. How I'd hate to have a maid popping in and out, or worse still, standing behind your chair. We don't have to hurry. We can dawdle or we can break off when we want. I feel that I'm a Victorian roué taking a chorus girl to supper in a private room; and you look so pretty. As if you were a chorus girl."

He was gallant, witty, affectionate; no, no, she wouldn't have him any different.

But later, after they had done the dishes, the rankling mood returned. It was half past nine. "Anything good on the box?" he asked.

"Not very much; only an old movie."

"Then I'll pack up after the news. If I start watching a film, I'm certain to fall asleep; and that spoils my real sleep later."

"You sound as though you were fifty."

"I feel it after a full day's work."

And a long lunch in the Brompton Road maybe. She glared at him, suspiciously. Was he really tired out by work? How could she tell? What did she know about him, really know?

He picked up the newspaper. A man was supposed to read his paper in the tube, then tell his wife what was in it during dinner. He wasn't supposed to bury himself in it after dinner.

The TV news ran its course. Student riots here, race riots there; conferences to save the franc; conferences to stop the Vietnam war; finally the cricket scores. He stood, his hand upon the switch. "Shall I leave it on for you?"

She shook her head. "I might fall asleep over it myself."

He did not say goodnight. A quiver shot along her nerves. Did that mean that he was planning to see her later? He had been especially gallant across the dinner table. Since her return from Malta, she had marked in her diary the nights when they made love. The last time was six months ago. Her heart was beating quickly as she went into her room. She had taken a bath before dinner; but now she stripped and sponged herself. She let a drop of scent fall into her palm. She smoothed it over her neck, behind her ears, across her breasts. She slipped on a nightdress that exposed her shoulders. She looked at herself in the glass; she thought, "Naomi would like the way I look. I guess a husband should."

She pushed open her bedroom door. The bed was empty. No sound came from Victor's dressing room. Her eyes flashed. He couldn't, no he couldn't have. She opened his door gently. Yes, he had. There he was, curled up, breathing steadily, asleep. A savage indignation surged within her. You've had it, chum, she thought. If you're ever going to have it, now's the time. A red and holy wrath consumed her. She went back to her bedroom. From beneath her handkerchiefs she extracted Naomi's secret weapon. She brandished it, gloatingly, flicking the leather thong. She hesitated, she went back to the bathroom. She slipped off her nightgown. She picked up the phial of Auberg. She let it drop into her palm; this time she spread her palm and fingers downwards from her navel, over her thighs, between her thighs. She put on a low-cut chiffon dressing jacket, a flimsy thing that barely reached her knees. She went back to Victor's dressing room. He was still asleep. I could murder him, she thought; how dare anyone do this to me?

She stretched her hand out to his shoulder and then she checked. Suppose it didn't work. Suppose that Naomi'd been wrong, that she herself had mistaken what had seemed to her a suddenly wakened interest on Victor's part. Suppose, suppose ... Everything might go wrong. Yet the surging wrath was stronger than her tears. If everything went wrong, then she would abdicate, break down, confess her folly, ask forgiveness, apologise and explain. Pray God, though, it wouldn't have to be that way.

She put her hand upon his shoulder, shook him. "Wake up," she said.

He sat up, blinked. "What the hell is this?" he asked.

"You'll know in good time. Do you see what this is?"

She held the whip before his eyes. "I warned you, didn't I? This is my secret weapon. Now's the time for it. Do you know what a C.T. is? Yes, of course you do. You've used it against women. But a man can be one, every bit as much. All that talk about taking out a chorus girl to supper, getting me worked up, then going off to sleep. Come along. Get ready for your medicine."

She said it fiercely, but she said it laughingly. "Keep it light," that's what Naomi had said. But her nerves were trembling, with fear and with excitement. Would he give way? If he did, it would be the most thrilling adventure of her life. But if he refused, if he sat up and told her not to be an ass ... She almost hoped he would. What a relief to break down completely, to get all this off her chest, indulge in the luxury of confession; be a weak and silly woman that had to be looked after.

He raised himself upon his elbows. The room was in semi-darkness, lit by the light from her own room that shone through the open door. She could not read the expression on his face.

"Come on," she ordered, "take off those pyjamas."

He hesitated. Was he going to? This was her most dramatic moment. The whole course of her marriage depended upon what happened in the next thirty seconds. Their entire relationship would be changed. He lifted his right hand; his fingers went to the top button of his jacket. He's going to, she thought, he's going to. Slowly he undid the button. Her heart exulted. Now she knew what to do. Her role was clear. "Come on," she said, "hurry up. Off with that jacket. Now the trousers. Lie down on your face. Put a pillow underneath your stomach. Yes, that's the way."

She stood above him. It was the first time that she had seen him quite like this: naked, with his hips lifted. She caught her breath. He was certainly a handsome creature. Not a ripple of surplus fat. Please stay that way, she thought. She lifted the whip and just as Naomi had done drew its tip slowly from the nape of the neck, down his spine, between the division of his buttocks. Then she struck, gently, just as Naomi had done. She chuckled. "Don't think it's going to be all like this. It's got to be a long, long lesson. Not the way it was for you at school. Six of the best and quickly over with. This is going to last quite a time."

She struck again, a good deal harder. "That one made a mark," she said. "And so will this one."

The third stroke was definitely hard. "The next's going to be even harder." It was delivered with almost her full strength. "That should leave a weal," she said. "You won't dare to take a Turkish bath for several days." She paused between each stroke; watching each one's effect. She was enjoying this, enjoying the sense of power that it gave her: of power over Victor; that she should be subjecting this punctilious civil servant to this treatment. The blows were getting stronger now. They must be hurting him. That, too, gave her a kick. He deserved this. It was his fault that she was in this mess. "At school you used to make it a point of honour not to squirm when you were being beaten. You'll squirm tonight before I've finished with you. In fact I shan't stop until you do. So now you know."

The next stroke was as hard as she could give, but he did not stir. She noted the mark that it had made. The next stroke would land in exactly the same place; so would the one after, and the one after that. He couldn't stand many more of those. Two, three, four, each in the same place. But still he didn't move. This was ridiculous. She had been challenged. She struck with every ounce of strength that she possessed. She was almost out of breath. She raised the whip again. Please let him move, she prayed. At tennis, she had been taught, "Hit through the ball, hit beyond the ball," She'd hit now not at Victor but the pillow under him. The blow was so fierce that it jarred her wrist, but yes, yes, it had made him squirm.

She sighed. "I said I would and I have, haven't I?" She flung the whip on the floor. She laid her hand on his hips, stroking them gently. They were so warm, they must be tingling. What next, she thought. There had to be a continuation, there had to be a climax. She remembered how Naomi had turned her over, had drawn her to the edge of the bed. Was there no equivalent for that?

An idea struck her; a flash of inspiration. "There's one thing more," she said. "You must beg my forgiveness."

She sat on the edge of the bed. "Come on your knees in front of me," she ordered. He'll do anything I order now, she thought. She sat on the very edge of the bed and spread her legs. She took him by the shoulders, and drew him to her. Their eyes met, but in the half light she could not read the expression in his. His head was a little above the level of her knees. She put her hands on his head and pressed it down. She remembered what Naomi had said, of certain things that a man was shy of doing with his own wife. She would give him his chance now. Gently, but firmly, she pressed down his head. His cheeks were rough against the soft flesh of her inner thighs.

She drew him closer and closer. She was conscious of his breath warm against her. Was he going to take advantage of this chance, now in the heady aftermath of that long encounter? Was it true that a whip acted as an aphrodisiac? Please let him, she prayed. Oh please, please make him want to. He couldn't conceivably not guess. She closed her eyes. She was tense with anticipation. Did she fancy it or wasn't he of his own volition drawing closer; it wasn't only her pressure on his head. Please, please, please, she prayed. And then even as she prayed, she felt first the sharp bristles of his moustache, then thrillingly, shatteringly, the soft touch of his tongue. "Yes," she cried. "Yes, oh yes, oh yes."

Never had she been more excited. He might not be as adroit as Naomi. Perhaps only a woman knew what a woman really liked; but that he, her correct husband, should be indulging her in this caress, that was the secret of the thrill. It was not so much what was being done to you, but who was doing it that counted. Her hands tightened in his hair, a series of short cries shook her; spasm followed spasm. Was he excited too? Was this a new experience for him? She remembered with Naomi her own first repugnance, a repugnance that had changed into delight. Was Victor feeling that? She stretched out her foot, raised it between his legs, turning it over, so that the soft flesh of her sole caressed him. Yes, he was aroused all right. The tangible proof of his excitement swelled, lengthened, hardened. It was more than she could stand. She lifted her legs, rested them on his shoulders, holding his head in a vice between her thighs, then pulling at his hair, dragging his head away, lifting it to hers as she fell backwards on the bed. Never had she suspected that life had such delights for giving.

On the following evening Victor returned with a series of travel folders. "My secretary has been very active. I shall show you what she has worked out."

There seemed every kind of tour, at every price, from a Greek Islands tour by ship, to a package seventeen-cities-in-twenty-one-days circus from Lisbon, through the Straits of Gibraltar, along both flanks of the inland sea, finishing in Istanbul. The prices varied, but in no case did they seem exorbitant.

"Have you any preferences?" she asked.

"I want to please you. I'd suggest a twenty-three-day tour. That takes me away for only three weeks from my office."

"Would you like to leave the folders with me and let me study them?"

"That's precisely what I'd hoped you'd say."

But she had no intention of studying them. They were for Mr. Montagu Frank to study, not for her. He was due to telephone her in two days' time.

He was, as she had known he would be, punctiliously prompt.

"I've a number of folders here. I'd be happy if you'd make your choice."

"May I call round at ten tomorrow?"

"Certainly."

He was extremely business-like, as she had known he would be. He quickly sifted out the tours that were most promising.

"These rushed tours are no good for our kind of project," he explained. "You're too busy. Every hour is occupied. You can't get away to the little bar or boutique where you collect your parcel. Now look at this one. Arrive Tangier eight a.m. Tour of the Casbah; visit the caves of Hercules. Lunch at Robinson's Beach. Afternoon see the weavers. Cocktails at the Rif. What time have you to yourself? Rule that out altogether. Now this one is more like it. Three days in Beirut. An afternoon at Baalbek; the Old Vic Company staging *As You Like It*. But the whole of the next morning free. You can easily say to your husband, 'I want to spend the morning in the bazaars.' He'll be delighted to get away from you for a little. Let's put that folder on one side. We can go back to it."

In an astonishingly short time he had made his choice. "It boils down to these three. I suppose you should discuss it first with your old man. Give him the impression that he's making the decision; as far as I'm concerned, it doesn't matter which you choose. I'll telephone you on Friday. You can tell me then which you have chosen, and I'll be round within a week with the operation orders. Is that oke-doke?"

Heavens, but he's an awful man, she thought.

That evening she showed Victor the folders. "It's one of these three," she said. He did not go over them very carefully.

But he took notes of the dates, the prices, and the itineraries. "I'd like to confer with Martin Severod."

"Why on earth with him?"

"He had an idea that he and Kitty might like to join us."

"Do you think it's a good idea?"

"It might be. I lunched with him today. I told him that we were going on a tour. He said that he and Kitty had had the same idea. The advantage of our going with another couple is, as he pointed out, that we could try more wines. That's one of the great inducements for him of going abroad, to taste the wines of another country; and if you are four instead of two you can sample twice as many wines."

Wine, wine, wine; so that was what this tour was going to be about. Anyhow she'd have somebody to drink martinis with.

"There's another thing too," said Victor. "You and I don't always want to be doing the same things. I shouldn't feel guilty leaving you alone if I wanted to see museums. You and Kitty could go on shopping sprees."

And how am I going to pick up packages of heroin if I've got Kitty on my heels, Myra thought.

"You like the idea of their coming with us, don't you?" Victor asked.

"Of course. Kitty's one of my oldest friends. We're always complaining that we don't see nearly enough of one another."

"That's what I thought. And I was sure that you'd be glad at my asking them to the Odde Volumes' Ladies' Night."

"That's on Tuesday, isn't it?"

"That's right."

The Odde Volumes was one of London's oldest dining clubs. It had been started in the 1870's by an affluent book-seller who had grown tired of paying for his friends' lunches, so decided to amalgamate them into a club where each member would have to meet his own expenses. Each member had a special cognomen, by which he had to be addressed. He was known as Brother Viking or Brother Peculator, and he wore around his neck an order that symbolised this cognomen. There was a very elaborate ritual based on Masonry. After each dinner one of the brethren read a learned paper. Once a year there was a Ladies' Night. Victor had been a member now for several years. He was known as Brother Trencherman. He was president and was addressed by the other brethren as Your Oddship. Ladies' Night would be for him a considerable occasion. He would be on his feet a great deal of the time, controlling the proceedings, interjecting comments. Every brother in turn introduced his guests by name. On masculine nights it was the tradition to be insulting towards one's guests. Facetiousness was the keynote of the occasion. In the rules, for instance, Rule XVI read "There shall be no rule XVI."

It was the first time that Kitty Severod had been to an Odde Volumes dinner. She was fascinated. "I can't believe it's true," she said. "Martin's been once or twice. I thought he was pulling my leg: isn't it odd how some really sophisticated men remain schoolboys at heart all their lives."

"Isn't that what's so appealing for us as women? We see these men standing up there with their medallions around their necks and their wands, and then we think of what they're going to be like in three hours' time when they are alone with us."

At that moment the company was on its feet. Victor was holding a gavel in his hand. He struck the table. "Brother, Master of Ceremonies," he anounced. "Bring to me the body of the Keeper of the Archives." The Master of Ceremonies carried a tall silver-tipped ebony wand. He walked between the tables. He laid his hand upon the shoulder of another member. He led him up to the high table as though he were leading an arrested prisoner before the magistrate. The Keeper of the Archives carried a small embroidered cushion on which reposed a large wooden key. He placed the cushion in front of Victor. Victor picked up the key; he held it raised high. "Brethren, I hold the key. The eight hundred and seventh dinner of the Sette of Odde Volumes may begin. *Incipit feliciter coena.*"

Kitty was seated immediately across the table. Victor, as befitted his position, had brought eight guests. She looked at Myra reflectively, as though she were setting herself a question. "Do you really get a kick out of that?" she asked.

"Get a kick out of what?"

"Thinking how different Victor is going to be when he's alone with you, in three hours' time."

"Don't you, with Martin?"

94

"Of course. I didn't know that you did. You are more sophisticated than I guessed. I don't think we see enough of one another."

Myra smiled. Would she have thought that before her trip to Malta? She looked back a year. How had she felt about all this at the last Odde Volumes dinner? Had it not all seemed rather childish to her – the cognomens, the badges of office, and the wands? Now she saw Victor differently. As a complement to the wand of office there was under her handkerchiefs the secret weapon. The one adjusted the balance of the other.

More than once during the dinner, she noticed that Kitty was watching her with a self-questioning look. Kitty was three years older than herself; though they had been at that finishing school in Switzerland where there had been no question of seniority, they had never met quite as equals. They had never let down their hair with one another. Kitty had always seen her in terms of the Clos des Abeilles – as someone considerably junior. Am I a new person to Kitty too, she thought. As they left the hall, Kitty slipped her arm through hers and pressed it against her side. "We're going to have fun together on that trip."

"I felt so proud of you." That was the first thing she said when she got home. And it was true, she had felt proud, in quite a new way, that this remarkable man should be her husband. In these last ten days he had become a new person to her: someone mysterious, someone to be explored, someone so unlike the public figure that the world respected. She was so well contented that he was that figure, but so relieved that he was this other one: this new-found one.

"It was the best Ladies' Night you've ever had," she said.

He smiled. "I think it went all right."

"You must have taken a great deal of trouble over it, insuring that none of the turns went on too long."

"It needed some rehearsing."

"And you never worried me about it."

That was one of the things about him. He never brought his problems home. "The cat that walked alone."

"I wanted it to be a surprise for you."

"It was a very pleasant one."

"The Severods enjoyed it, didn't they?"

"They certainly did."

"They should be fun on this trip."

She nodded. But the thought that Kitty would be with her in Beirut sent a cautionary shiver along her nerves. She had received very precise instructions from Mr. Frank. The tour allowed for three nights and four days in Beirut. The first day had billed a preliminary tour of the city. On the second day there was an excursion to Baalbek. "You get back at half past five. That might be the best time, when your husband's resting. But probably the next morning will be best. It's marked as 'free' on your programme."

"But I can't fix an exact hour in advance. I can't be sure when my husband will be resting."

"Of course you can't. There are a number of alternatives. We are a rich organisation. Someone will be on duty all the time that you are in Beirut. You cannot miss the shop. It is among a cluster of small boutiques between the St. George and the Normandie. You will enter, you will look around a little. You will pick up a packet of Camels. Then you will say to the assistant, 'I want to try a Turkish cigarette. Do you have one?' It is as easy as that."

It had sounded easy enough when Mr. Frank had given his instructions. But she had not then known that Kitty would be with them. She remembered how Kitty had looked at her at dinner, how Kitty had pressed her arm, how she had said, "We're going to have fun together on that trip." She had underlined the word "together." Kitty had something on her mind. She was curious to know what that something was. But how was she to find out, if she was going to be fussed trying to get away from Kitty to that small shop along the waterfront? Oh damn this secret mission. If only Victor was a different person, someone in whom she could have confided. But did she want him to be a different person? No, she didn't. He was perfect the way he was. It was things, not he, she wanted different. Damn, oh damn, oh damn.

It was well after eleven. But she did not feel sleepy. Nor did he, she supposed. He would want to talk things over. "Have you got a half bottle of champagne on ice?" she asked.

"That is precisely what I have."

In their first year of marriage, they would usually after an evening such as this have sat tonight on the sofa. A mood of intimacy would have been created. Very soon they would have found themselves in each other's arms. "Why don't we take these glasses in with us?" he would say.

They had changed that pattern now. They would sit in chairs facing one another. In a house where you had children and *au pair girls,* you ran the risk of being interrupted. But the atmosphere was little different. It was not so often now that at the end of an evening they sat talking it all over across a half bottle of champagne, but when they did, almost invariably the same cosy sense of intimacy crept over them. Before the bottle was half finished, they knew they would be making love in half an hour's time. Beyond doubt, Myra knew it now. She was tempted to hurry her wine, but she refrained, almost dragging the last sips out, heightening the anticipation. She tilted the glass back. The last drop gone. She stood up. "That's that," she said.

She had loitered over her wine. She loitered now over her undressing. She put on the Empire-style nightdress that she knew he liked. She pushed the door of her room open. He should be in bed by now.

He wasn't though, and to her surprise there was no sound from his dressing room. The door was ajar. She looked in. To her astonished incredulity he was in bed, curled up, his back turned to her. He couldn't, it was unbelievable, he couldn't. . . . She stared, she listened. A slow smile crossed her lips. So that was it then, was it? He wasn't asleep; she knew from his breathing that he wasn't. He was pretending to be asleep, so as to invite the secret weapon. If that was what he wanted . . . She went back into her room, lifted her nightgown over her head, took the secret weapon from the drawer. She shook it gleefully. If this was what he wanted, he had found the right person to give it to him.

Later, quite a little later, they lay side by side. Her head was on his chest.

"Tell me," she said, "do you think all those beatings in public schools give Englishmen a taste for this?"

"They say it gave Swinburne one."

"How often did you get caned yourself?"

97

"Not very often; four, five times. I got into the sixth book pretty early."

"Did it give you any pleasure?"

"Good heavens, no."

"Not even afterwards? Wasn't there a kind of glow?"

"I don't remember it. Before we were going to be caned, we used to sit on the hot-water pipes; it hurts less then. Did you know, by the way, that Nelson when he had his arm amputated complained of the coldness of the knife? After that he insisted on having hot water in the sick bay."

"It was a good feeling, wasn't it, when the actual pain subsided?"

"It was a good thing when the whole thing was over. One felt something of a hero too, you know, like troops coming out of action."

"I suppose now and again you had to cane a boy yourself?"

"I was a prefect for three years."

"Did you get any kick out of it?"

"I can't say I did. As far as I recall, it rather jarred my wrist; perhaps at first it gave me a sense of superiority, of having the right to beat somebody, but after that wore off, and it wore off very soon, no, I don't believe I got any kick out of it."

"But then . . ." She paused. After that first time she had longed to talk to him, to find out what he had felt, how he had felt it. She had felt shy then; the illusion of punishment had to be maintained. It was different now; but even though he had invited the visit of the secret weapon, there were some things she could not ask. There were, though, quite a few things she could.

"Of course you couldn't choose whom you caned. It had to be somebody who had broken a rule of some kind."

"Naturally."

"You couldn't look down the hall, see a good-looking boy who attracted you and think, I'll give him a good thrashing."

"Naturally I couldn't."

"And of course they were wearing trousers."

"Of course."

"Mightn't it have made a difference if they hadn't? If, for instance, it had been a good-looking young boy whom you found attractive."

98

"That's a very hypothetical situation. I can only say that as far as I was concerned, it didn't happen."

"Then would you say that in spite of what the psychiatrists are saying there is no sex element to all these canings?"

"Ah, no, I wouldn't quite say that; there are some celibate masters, who are homosexuals without knowing it, who get a kick that way. But for the boys themselves – well" – he paused – "it's something I've sometimes asked myself. My first school was a new one; it started in the very year I went there, when I was nine. At the start there were only six of us. There were forty when I left; now there are a hundred and fifty. We were very ignorant, very innocent; there were no older boys to teach us anything. We knew nothing of the facts of life. We knew how babies were born, but not how they were conceived. Not at least in any detail. But we were oddly enough very interested in whipping. We used to whip each other."

"You did what?"

"Yes, whip ourselves, in the dormitories at night."

"What with?"

"Knitted bootlaces or with hairbrushes."

"Which side of the hairbrush?"

"The prickly side. At home when I had a hot bath at night, I used to beat myself and I'd arrange my father's shaving mirror so that I could see the reflection. It was exciting to see the blood come."

"The blood?"

"It's very near the surface after a hot bath."

"But blood, didn't it hurt a lot?"

"Not in the least; it barely stung. I told you that we used to sit on the hot water pipes before we got a caning."

"When you beat yourself in the dormitories were you naked?"

"Yes."

"That must have made a difference then?"

"I suppose so, yes."

"It must have been more exciting, seeing the effect, the marks, how the muscles would contract."

"I guess so."

"And you think that all that, when you were only twelve, did have something to do with sex?"

"I've wondered that." He hesitated. "There was a kind of
99

prurient curiosity about it all. We were so innocent at that particular school. I'm wondering if it wasn't a natural development, a normal prelude. I've noticed that old-fashioned school stories used to pander to that prurience. A friend of mine was doing an article on Edwardian school stories. He showed me some of Desmond Coke's. They came out in *The Captain* in 1909 or so. They had very luscious descriptions of boys being beaten. And the publishers reissued after the second war a school story called *Teddy Lester's Chums* that came out in 1960 – chock full of it. I'm sure it had a sexual undertone – a premature interest in what doctors call erogenous zones. We used to talk about canings in the furtive way that at public schools we discussed normal cases. Look at this now as an example. As I told you we knew nothing about the machinery of fatherhood. One day when we were in the changing room, about three or four of us, and we were talking about beatings, one of us lifted his shirt and called our attention to himself. He was in a most rampant state. He said, 'Isn't it funny that I get like this whenever I talk about beatings?' "

Myra chuckled. "It seems to be having that effect on you right now."

Myra slept late next morning. She fixed her breakfast before she took her bath. She was still sipping her coffee when Lena came into the kitchen.

"I'm afraid I have bad news," she said. "I shall have to leave."

"Why?"

"My sister is getting married to a German. She is going to live in Hamburg. That means that my mother will be all alone."

"Are you going to live with your mother?"

"Oh no, that wouldn't work at all. There's nothing wrong with her. She's not an invalid. She's not fifty yet. She's not infirm. But she's a widow. She's lonely. She does need a daughter that she can talk to on the telephone, whom she can run-round to at a moment's notice, who'll be five minutes away if she's not feeling well."

"I can see that."

"She wants to have someone she can do things for."

"I can see that too. You will be missed though. You don't need telling that."

"I'm sorry to go. I've been very happy here. You've been most kind to me. I love the children."

"What about Anna? Is she going too?"

"She said she would."

It was what Myra had expected. She did not feel that it was any use trying to persuade Anna to stay on, but she made the attempt. She waited till they were alone together.

"I don't suppose it is any good my asking you to stay on with us?"

Anna shook her head. "I'm afraid it isn't."

"I understand."

"I believe you do."

Once again there flashed between them a look of understanding. Almost a conspiratorial look. They could talk in shorthand. "If things change for you, if you were alone, if ever you should want to come back . . ."

"I'll write, don't worry." There was a wistful expression in her face. "I'd like to think I had a harbour here."

"Yes, think of it that way." There was no hurry about their leaving. They would stay on till after Myra's return from her tour of the Middle East. In the meantime Anna was going to try to find another Swedish couple.

"Do you think they'll be such a team as those were?" Victor wondered.

7

The plane was late getting into Beirut. There had been a delay in Cairo. Every seat was occupied, three seats on each side of the aisle. Kitty was next to Myra. As the plane circled over the airport, she whispered into Myra's ear, "They say it's the wickedest city in the world. This has taken on from where Tangier stopped. It looks so little from here. Think of all that's concealed beneath that stretch of rooftops."

They had been due to arrive soon after lunch, but it was five o'clock before they landed.

"Time for a quick look round anyhow," said Kitty.

There were some two hundred passengers about. they had been split up among the various hotels; the four of them had been booked into an old Turkish building on the waterfront. It was a very long way from the best or the smartest hotel but it had a cachet. It looked Oriental. It had a large central hall with small rooms opening off it. Rugs hung upon the walls. There were large leather cushions on the floor. There was no air conditioning, but fans were circling from the ceiling. Below the ceiling ran a first-floor gallery off which a series of small doors opened. The porters were dressed in Moorish uniform, with short-cut red jackets, skull-caps, and baggy trousers. A courier from the tour had met them at the airport. He had seen their luggage through customs, their passports through immigration; he now arranged their accommodation at the desk. The suitcases of the group were stacked together while they sat and waited. It was all very restful. They had every bit as much privacy as if they had travelled independently. And they had saved so much on the fare that they could afford to order à la carte.

"The St. George is *the* hotel," said Kitty. "Let's go there as soon as we're unpacked."

Myra had read of the St. George. It had appeared in so many wartime reminiscences, in so many espionage novels. It had a wide terrace, on the waterfront. Sand stretched below it. A mighty range of mountains flanked it. It was still hot and humid. But the St. George's terrace caught the breeze. It was crowded and polyglot and many-coloured. There were dark-skinned, dark-haired men; there were very pale girls with shining black hair lying low upon their shoulders; there were those who looked like film stars. There were Muslims in long white robes, their head scarves held in place by gold and black fillets. There was an air of wealth and elegance.

"Now this is the place where we must come tomorrow, by ourselves, when we can dodge the boys. We must make friends with the head barman. He can tell us what it is we need to know."

What was it that she needed to know, Myra wondered. Kitty certainly had something on her mind.

They dined on the terrace under the stars. This was the kind of place that in books and films had typified for Myra the glamour and glory of the East. Well, here she was at last. And all she could do was worry about a boutique along the waterfront where she would collect a parcel, and how she was to find the time to get it. That was her main problem: how to get away from Kitty?

Directly after the last course, before the coffee, Kitty was on her feet. "Myra and I are going to case the joint." But she was not in search of the powder room. "I've got to locate that barman."

There was no difficulty about that. He had the magisterial, apostolic look of a man who has listened to confessions and offered solicitude and guidance for a quarter of a century. He was tall, handsome, clean-shaven, olive-skinned, with hair smooth and shining. A sharkskin suit fitted closely over his ample shoulders. He was the complete, the perfect Levantine. "I bet he's called Pierre. Every smart Mediterranean barman is called Pierre. Let's go."

They perched themselves on stools in front of him. "Two Cherry Heerings, please."

She raised her glass to him. "So many people have told me about you. I must introduce myself. I'm Kitty Severod; this is Myra Trail. We're only here three days. We want to make the most of them. You're the man who can tell us how."

He bowed politely. "I am flattered to have been recommended by your friends." His voice was unctuous. His accent was neither American nor English.

"We won't bother you now. You are very busy."

"I am, alas, always busy, but never too busy to be able to succour a charming lady."

"When are you least busy?"

"Just after the evening begins, and just before it ends."

"We'll remember that. Back to those men of ours, Myra. By the way," she said as they slipped off their stools, "have you ever been inside a brothel?"

"Heavens no, have you?"

"Not really. Not a proper one. That's what I'm looking for. If I can't find one here, where can I?"

So that was what Kitty had on her mind.

Their hotel was only a quarter of a mile from the St. George. They strolled back along the waterfront. The noise of pop dance tunes welled up from a dozen doors. Uniformed porters importuned custom. Small boys held out their hands for money. Horse-drawn open cabs clattered down the middle of the street. Myra noticed the restaurant Saad's that she had been given as direction post. She counted the shops past it. Yes, there it was. Valentina; but it was closed now. Of course it was. But she knew where it was. She would slip in there to-morrow.

Or at least she hoped she would. Next day there was an excursion to Baalbek. They started soon after breakfast. They took a while collecting the tourists from the other hotels. It was after ten before they started. They lunched at Stoura, at a charming little restaurant beside a stream, where they were served Lebanese dishes and arrack, the white liquid onto which water was poured and which turned cloudy; it had a flavour of licorice, but went well with the small savoury-type dishes that were served with it, radishes, white cheese, anchovies, olives. You sipped arrack slowly; you did not like the taste of it. But it induced a sensation of well-being.

The lunch was too copious. That was the trouble about package-tour meals, so Victor had assured her, but it was quite good and the wines that went with it, though by Victor's Odde Volumes standards they might be negligible, were adequate to her. Musicians played to them as they ate. The river supplied a satisfactory undertone.

Kitty sat beside her. The moment they were alone, Kitty reverted to her topic. "When I asked you if you'd ever been in a brothel," she said, "I didn't mean a bistro where there are tarts whom men take home but a *maison*– where men buy women on the spot. I've always felt curious about that. There's a place outside Casablanca called the Sphinx; they've changed the name of the town, I forget what they call it now. It had a great sphinx in lights over it. I made Martin take me there. Could I have been more disappointed? It was a brothel, right enough. There were girls and there were men; the men could take the girls upstairs, but they couldn't take upstairs the wife or the girl that they had brought with them."

"What would have been the point of that?"

"The whole point: to see what goes on. Haven't you ever felt inquisitive about that? To know what married couples are like when they are alone. Don't you want to know what other people are like together, what other people do together? Don't you? I do. Shall I tell what I'd choose if a genie came wreathing out of a vase and asked me to name a wish?"

"What would you choose?"

"To be invisible. The Ring of Gyges. A lot of people might ask for that so that they could steal. I wouldn't. I'd like to see what other couples do together. Do you remember your saying at the Odde Volumes dinner how it gave you a kick to see Victor standing up with that medal around his neck, looking so solemn and self-important, and to be able to reflect on what he was going to be like in three hours' time? You remember saying that."

"Of course I do."

"It gave me quite a jolt your saying it. I thought, Little Myra has grown up. She's much more sophisticated than I thought. She's become my kind of woman. I felt inquisitive about you and Victor. Three hours later I found myself wishing I could be invisible in your bedroom."

Myra chuckled. You might have been surprised if you had been, she thought. Or would she? Had Kitty a secret weapon too?

"Even so," Myra said, "I don't see what you're going to get out of going to a brothel."

"Don't you? Why, the looking on of course. Seeing what the girls do together. Seeing . . . oh damn, here are those men back again."

The conversation was broken off, but it was resumed the moment they were alone together. At the day's end it seemed to Myra that she had listened to an uninterrupted monologue.

"Doesn't it give you a thrill to see things being done?"

"I never have."

"Then believe me you've missed something. Haven't you ever arranged a mirror so that you could see yourself and Victor in it? You haven't? Oh, but it's quite a thing."

Myra remembered how Victor had arranged his father's shaving mirror so that he could watch the blood run down his legs. There might be a kick to that.

"In some brothels they have glass roofs fitted to the beds. And some beds have glass sides so that you can see yourselves endlessly repeated. That would be wonderful."

"Are there such places now?"

"That's what I must find out. There used to be. An uncle of mine told me about one he went to in the war, in Asmara, the old Italian colony. There was a place they called "The Glass House.' Of course eventually the British authorities closed it down. So much has been closed down. Have you ever seen a blue film?"

"I haven't, no."

"I have, in Bangkok: it wasn't really very good. That same uncle told me about a place there used to be in Nice. The room in which they showed the films was lined with mirrors. He used to watch the reflections in the mirrors. He said it was more exciting that way, although you couldn't see the action so completely. It was more real. You seemed to be spying on something."

"Your uncle seems to have been quite a person."

"He certainly was. He told me a lot. I fancy he got a special kick out of it: a kind of incest."

"Is he still alive?"

"Alas no."

"I'd have liked to meet him."

"He'd have liked you too, too much perhaps; it might have made me jealous. The things he told me. I sometimes feel I was born twenty years too late. The thirties were the time. Still there must be something left. If it isn't here, where is it?"

They got back from Baalbek in the early evening. It was the time when Myra had planned to call on Valentina. But there was no getting away from Kitty.

"Now's the time for our conference with Pierre. Let's take a quick shower, not put on anything special; the men are sure to want to read their papers. Then we'll come back and get dressed up."

They were planning to go to the casino. They would be dining very late. "Hurry up," she urged. "Not longer than twenty minutes."

As Pierre had promised them, there was no one in the bar. The bathers had gone to their rooms, the diners were not ready yet. "So now we've got you to ourselves," said Kitty. Pierre inclined his head. "Tell us, Pierre – your name is Pierre, isn't it?"

"That is what many people call me. There was a famous Pierre here during the war."

"Were you here then?"

"Madame, we are talking about 1942."

"Weren't you in Beirut though then?"

He inclined his head. He did not commit himself. "I did not start to work here until '56."

"Beirut must have been very different in '42."

"From what my friends have told me, yes."

"There was a lot of fun going on here then."

"It was a leave centre. You know what troops are like on a two weeks' leave. They had nothing to spend their pay on in the desert."

"There were houses where they could find girls, weren't there?"

"Of course."

"What has happened to them now?"

"Alas, what has happened to all such places now."

"There's not one left, you mean?"

"Not to my knowledge."

"But surely, surely . . ."

"If I knew, madame, I would surely tell you. It is a matter of fact a question that I am rather often asked."

"And I'll bet," Kitty said afterwards, "that he knows the answer. Only he's not telling somebody he scarcely knows. We ought to have had a proper, or rather an improper, letter of introduction. There must be places. Look around you."

They had taken their cocktails onto the terrace. The sun had gone down. It was beginning to crowd up again. "Think of all the money that is represented here. What proportion of the world's black market does not send its one-tenth of a per cent here? This is where money changes hands. There must be every kind of accommodation for the men – and women too who bring in that kind of money. Somebody must know the answer. What about the hairdressers? They often know. I think I'll have my hair done tomorrow."

It was what Myra had planned herself. It would give her an opportunity to escape from Kitty. Now she would get her opportunity, but not of having her hair done.

"I want to buy some brocades. I'll join you afterwards for a cocktail and learn your news."

At last she was alone in Valentina's. It was a very ordinary shop, catering to the casual tourist. There were cigarettes, there were chocolates, there were scents and liqueurs. It was perhaps a little cheaper than the large shops, but Myra questioned that. It was made to seem cheaper, that was all. Probably it was more expensive. There were three or four customers in the shop. There was only one saleswoman. She was a nondescript Lebanese, cumbersomely middle-aged. She might have been attractive once. Myra idled her way along the shelves. She picked up one or two objects and replaced them. She asked the saleswoman if she had any Kodak films. "Of course, over there." But she did not go to the shelf where the films were stocked. Instead she crossed to the shelf where there were various packets of cigarettes. She knew that the saleswoman was watching her. She picked up a packet of Camels. She held it up so that she could see it. Then she returned to the counter. "I want to try a Turkish cigarette. Do you have one?"

The saleswoman looked at her very straight, then nodded. "I have exactly what you need," she said. She opened a drawer and took from it a long oblong package that was prettily gift-wrapped. In the top corner was a label marked "Valentina. Chocolate liqueurs." "You should find these satisfactory. That will be ten shillings."

Myra took up the package. It was rather heavy. Was Victor going to say, "What the hell's that damned thing you've bought? You know that on these package tours one has to keep under that twenty-kilo limit?" Would he suggest that she break open the package and distribute its contents among other parcels? What did the contents look like? She had never seen opium or heroin or whatever the hell it was. You didn't realise the complications till you were faced with them. What do I do with it now?

She remembered a play called *Ten-Minute Alibi* in which a man had worked out the perfect alibi for a murder, but then one little unexpected miscalculation upset the entire schedule. Was weight going to be the problem now? Could she slip it into her handbag? She judged the size. She judged its weight. Scarcely. What about that brocade? Did she really need it? She had thought she did. It was going to have been her one extravagance: silver-shot Damascene brocade. But if weight was to be the problem, and on a package tour you simply could not go beyond your allowance ... It wasn't like a standardized commercial BEA flight where you paid excess.

Back in her hotel, she weighed the package between her

hands. Why hadn't she brought the scales? Three pounds, four pounds, who could say? How could she tell what Victor was planning to buy? They had weighed their suitcases very carefully, forty pounds to each; that left four pounds extra for each. She couldn't with these Valentina chocolates carry brocade as well. What was Victor buying? He'd be expecting her to bring back something special. Valentina chocolates? She herself never ate chocolates. She watched her figure. Whom had she bought them for? In what unexpected complications she had found herself.

She sat in the window annexe, the package between her knees. What would happen to it? What would the gangster world do for it and do with it? What lives might not be corrupted by it? Could she be blamed for that? Were those lives not already ruined? If she did not bring this package through the Customs, someone else would. And was it fair to argue that because she was bringing this package, some innocent fifteen-year-old girl at present absorbing an English Lit course at Roedean might find herself destined for destruction? Could you go back that far? Earth "ailed from its prime foundations". If you were to look for first causes, ultimate results, where did you land yourself? Yet if you were to say, "If I didn't do this, somebody else would," what a contemptible alibi was that. Could you ever do more than face each immediate problem by its effect on you, and on those dear to you? Was she not forced to prevent that tape being allowed to ruin her life with Victor and with her children, with Victor's career, with all that Victor's career meant not only to himself and to her, but to the country? Victor was someone who had to be protected. It was useless to ask herself what damage this elegantly boxed package would spread and in what lives, any more than the bomber over enemy territory could afford to think, That bomb may have killed a potential Einstein, Pasteur, Mozart.

She put the box at the bottom of her suitcase. Victor and Martin had gone to a museum. Kitty would not be due at the St. George for another hour. It was no use buying brocades that would make her overweight. Better read a Maigret. There was a certain impersonality about those records of detected crime that harmonised with her mood. Simenon withheld judgment. He recorded what happened, when and where and how. Things happened in such a way, inevitably, step by step. That's how it had been with her; that's how it was continuing to be with her. And what else was there for her to do about it?

She shrugged, and read about Maigret, and Madame Maigret and Janvier, and all those cold beers and sandwiches, until it was time to go down to the St. George.

"Now tell me what you've bought. I see you haven't brought it with you. I can't wait to see it."

Myra was evasive. "I've not made up my mind. I'll go back later. You tell me what you've found out."

Kitty laughed. "I got as little there as I got out of Pierre. I played it the wrong way. I'll plan my campaign more carefully next time."

"Why not stage it in Soho? There's nothing that can't be found in London."

"By foreigners, I know. But not by Londoners. Englishmen are quite different out of their own country. Every American will tell you that. You can't imagine a husband who's spent his whole day in Whitehall going to a striptease in the evening."

"A lot do, don't they?"

"Not Londoners. Or if they do, they're taking out-of-town customers from Birmingham. You don't get men like Martin and Victor going there, but here it's different. English let their hair down when the white cliffs of Dover fade. If we'd gone, the four of us, to one of those places that my uncle used to describe, and had put on an exhibition . . ." She paused and an eager light flickered in her eyes.

"What do you think would have happened?" Myra asked.

"That's what I'd like to find out. Anything might have happened. Did you ever read that novel *La Garçonne* that caused so much scandal in 1921?"

"I thought it rather good."

"So did I. Do you remember that scene where they all went to a bordello, men and women?"

"I certainly do."

"You know what a *partouze* is?"

"Yes."

"I don't say that that would have happened, but something

110

would. I want to know what that something is, and that something would have led to something else."

Myra closed her eyes. She tried to picture a *partouze*. It seemed bizarre. But the idea excited her.

"Look, here they come," said Kitty. It was a hot, sultry morning but the two Englishmen looked very spruce and cool in their well-pressed summer-weight light trousers, their sandals, their short-sleeved sports shirts with foulard four-in-hands knotted at the throat. Each was wearing a light Panama hat with a club ribbon around it.

"Look at them now," said Kitty. "Don't they look formal and correct? Don't your fingers itch to muss them up? Mine do."

The tour itinerary marked the afternoon as free. "I'm for a siesta," Victor said.

Kitty caught Myra's eye. An eyelid flickered.

Victor and Myra had a twin bedded room. On one side of the wall was a wide cupboard, with a long glass mirror. From the pillows you could not see your reflection, but if you sat on the bed halfway down, you could. An idea came to her. I'll get him in the mood, she thought. He was lying on his back outside the sheets, his hands crossed under his head. He had on only a light silk dressing gown, nothing under it. She lay beside him. "Tell me," she asked, "did you ever beat a woman?"

"Once."

"How come?"

"She drank too much. She got rather silly when she was tipsy. I said, 'The next time you get drunk in public, I'll thrash you when we get home.' She did, so I did."

"How did you do it?"

"I put her across my knee."

"What did you beat her with?"

"My hand."

"Then she can't have been wearing any clothes."

"She wasn't."

"What about you?"

"I had my trousers on – the first time."

"So it happened often."

"Once a week or so."

"It was more fun with your clothes off, for you I mean."

"Of course."

111

"So it was fun?"

"I was angry with her for being tipsy. She embarrassed me in public. I wanted to hurt her. Yet at the same time, yes, I did enjoy it."

"Not like those schoolboys you caned for being late for chapel."

"Oh, no, quite different."

"What about her? How did she take it?"

"It's quaint but I've an idea she rather liked it."

"What made you think that?'

"I think she got drunk on purpose."

And that, thought Myra, was where you got the idea of pretending to be asleep.

"She sounds an interesting female. You must tell me more about her."

She looked down the bed. She slid aside his dressing gown. As she had expected. "That's a very ambitious profile you've got there," she said. She moved away from him and off the bed. She went on her knees. In the mirror she could see her head reflected, looking down at the centre of his body. He could not tell from the pillows what she was seeing. She stretched out her arms, the one across his stomach, one across his knees; she pulled him towards her till he was on the very edge of the bed. She lowered her head above the surgent column. She watched her tongue flicker along its length, saw her lips close over it; her fingers were about its base. How firm and yet how soft. Kitty had been right. It was exciting. She recalled the film advertisements of children sucking lollipops, how they slid them in and out, nibbling at them. She knew exactly what to do, as a child could derive the maximum enjoyment from its sweetmeat, tantalising itself in its delayed fulfilment. Why had she never done this before? Was it new to him? It couldn't be. He'd been with tarts. But it must be different for him, with her. How long would he be able to hold out? They had made love last night. He had had quite a bit to drink at lunch. It depended probably on her. He wouldn't have the same control over himself as he had when he was making love himself. With her left hand she stroked his stomach, running her fingertips over it. He was beginning to stir and tremble, to heave his haunches. He was breathing fast. Should she hurry? Yes, better hurry if she could. His hands were in her hair. He was trying to lift her

112

head, to raise her to his level on the pillows so that he could take control. But she would not let him. She was resolved to follow her experiment to the close. She might never have such a chance of watching it again. She quickened the pace, the tempo of her voracious lips. She was conscious of a throbbing tautness; now, now. It must be now. If it were she who was being made love to, she would close her eyes. Not this time though. She could watch from the first explosion to the final spasm, conscious, acutely conscious of the last shuddering sigh.

She knelt, her chin rested on his stomach, brooding peacefully. Then she lifted her head, drew away from him, stood up, moved to the head of the bed, looked down on him. Their eyes met. In his there was an expression of adoring gratitude. She put the palm of her hand upon his forehead. The skin was damp. She lay down beside him. He put his arm around her shoulders, holding her close. He said nothing: there was no need for words. They were utterly at one.

The aircraft tilted on its side. The No Smoking sign flashed on. "Fasten your seat belts please." She jerked her chair into an upright position. Below her she could see the Thames, and the proud bastions of Windsor Castle. This was the moment she had dreaded, the passage through Customs. They said that Customs officers could always spot the passenger who was concealing something. Years of training had taught them to detect a way of walking, an over-confidence, or a furtiveness. Something that seemed unnatural or exaggerated. She had put the Valentina package in her airline night bag. She would display that right away; no attempt at concealment. It was so very obvious. It took up nearly all the room there was. Victor had grumbled at first. Then he had made a joke of it. He had over-played his joke, or at least to her he had. When they reached Istanbul, he had adjured Kitty to keep his wife away from sweetshops. "If she buys chocolates in Lebanon, she'll go mad over Turkish Delight. I went mad over it as a schoolboy. Didn't you, Kitty?"

As the bulk of his own purchases had increased, he had grown impatient with her chocolates. "Let's open the box and eat them now," he said.

"But it's a present."

"Who for?"

113

"That's my secret."

"Why don't you take off the wrapping, buy some chocolates in London, then fix that Lebanese wrapping on it?"

"Because . . ."

She was exasperated by his persistence, but she could see his point. Why should she have bought chocolates in the Lebanon; with all the trinkets that there were to buy there, why choose chocolates? And if she had been going to buy a present, why hadn't she thought first for whom it was intended? Thank heavens she had had the sense not to say "The *au pair* girls." If she had, and she so easily could have done, he would have carried his joke into the nursery. He would have been certain to say, "Now let me see by what manner of sweets I have had my travelling plans upset."

As it was he would insist on knowing who the sweets had gone to. That would mean her having to buy some chocolates in London and send them to somebody whom Victor scarcely knew. "Ah, what a tangled web we weave . . ."

There was inevitably always some factor you had not foreseen. This had become hers. The final test now lay ahead. What would crop up at the last moment? Something would, something always did. What would it be?

She looked at her watch. Ten past three. Within an hour it would all be over. By the time the hour hand had passed the four, she would be on her way to the airport bus. An hour, what a little time that was. She looked back an hour. At ten minutes past two she was finishing her lunch, sipping a duty-free cognac; that only seemed a minute or two ago. She had barely finished her cognac when the "Fasten your seat belts" sign had flashed in front of her. How swiftly she had lived through that hour. In an hour's time she would be looking back to this moment thinking, What was I making all that fuss about? How quickly that hour went.

Would it though? Might she not have been taken into a small back room for cross-examination, a cross-examination that would be the curtain to Victor's whole career? The very thing she had striven to avoid when she undertook this mad assignment. She closed her eyes. Why did I ever do it? Why, oh why, oh why? If I get through this next hour safely, never again, never, never.

She was standing inside the Customs shed, waiting for the number of her flight to be announced. Her airline bag was on the floor beside her. If Victor makes one more joke about those chocolates I'll scream, she thought. There was the strident but garbled voice of the announcer. "Flight —" she couldn't catch the number. What was their number, when it came to that? Victor nudged her. "Come on now, this is us." They moved into the big hall. She saw the accumulated, variegated, many-coloured collection of suitcases with which she had grown familiar during the last three weeks on this and the other pavement, in that and the other hotel lobby. Victor was onto their two suitcases quickly. He was in a bustling mood. "Got your keys?" he asked her. "Fine."

He had his and her case open. "Yes," he was telling the inspector, "we've got several things. I've bought some Damascene brocade; we've got between us a bottle of whisky and four hundred cigarettes. My wife, will you believe it, bought chocolates in Beirut. Chocolates from the Lebanon, I ask you. You've got that in your airline satchel, haven't you? Show it to the inspector. Then I got some silk shirts in Istanbul. Here's a list of what I bought and spent. What else did you get, Myra? Oh of course, that leather writing case from Tunis. Have you your list? Here it is, Inspector. I'll settle the duty on it all. A wife's dividend on a holiday; I don't suppose it'll be a lot."

He had gone over to the desk with his cheque-book. In three minutes he was back. "Only seven pounds, three and threepence. Not much really. Now we're through. With any luck we'll be in Hampstead by six o'clock."

We're through. Had he any conception of what that meant, to her, of what it was that she was through? It had been so simple. Why had she been worried? How effortlessly he had taken control of everything. They were through. It was over. The nightmare was at an end. Never again, she vowed, never, never again. Yet even as she vowed it, she was forced to think, But how could I have helped it? Where did I go wrong? One thing led to the next. If I had it all to do again, what would I not do that I did, what would I do that I omitted? She couldn't see where she had been at fault.

The coach swung to the right, eastwards towards London. Two hours and she'd be home. There'd be the children and the *au pair* girls to welcome her. She had her revolting pack-

115

age. In a day or two the telephone would ring and she'd hand the package over, receiving that tape in return. The chapter would be closed. Never to be reopened. She sighed. She had had a bad time and it was over now. Yet even so, as there was to everything, there was a credit balance. Did she regret those three days' dalliance in Malta? Wasn't her marriage on a sounder, deeper base because of them? Hadn't she learned something about herself that might be useful later? Hadn't she been brought much closer to her husband? They had been settling into a rut, she and Victor. They had been shaken out of that rut now. Her husband had become a different person to her; she must have become a different person to him. Had she had an affair with that South African – as so well she might – new doors would have been opened to her. He would have been probably a dashing and imaginative lover. And when those three days were over, she would have thought, If one man can teach me so much, what might not another do? She would have been encouraged to experiment. She knew herself, or rather, she was beginning to know herself. Her curiosity would have led her to accept each new opportunity. Her relations with Victor would inevitably have become increasingly tepid, a routine exchange that would have left Victor vulnerable to any fresh temptation, as he already had proved himself to be ... if those suspicions about the Brompton Road were justified. And from what she had learned of Victor during these two months, he could not be blamed if he had gone elsewhere for what he could not get at home.

All that was over now. There mustn't be anything, but anything at all, he couldn't get at home; nor must there be anything she couldn't get from any man that she could not get at home from her own husband. That was what marriage was, what marriage should be, the sharing of everything, yes, everything between two people. We've only started, she thought. She recalled that long siesta talk in Beirut about the woman who had got drunk on purpose. She looked sideways at Victor. He was so composed, so controlled, so much the conventional, turned-out-to-pattern Englishman. It was hard to imagine those pale cheeks flushing suddenly, those eyes ablaze. She envied that girl who was able to break down that composure. It would be fun to see that look of anger, to be suddenly seized upon, thrown across his knees, your skirt tossed over your head, to feel his hand upon you, one, two, three; then to be flung backwards and treated like a slave girl, no preliminaries, a sudden fierce entry and possession. I wonder how I can annoy him enough to have that done to me. I'll find a way – there must be a way; I'll search. I'll find it. She drew into her lungs a long slow breath of taut, fearsome anticipation. They'd only started. That girl in the Brompton Road wouldn't stand a chance.

As the taxi drew up in Holly Place, she could see on the second floor two small heads leaning out of an open window waving their hands.

Anna or Lena must have been watching specially. That's dear of them, she thought. She was going to miss them, miss them a great deal. The presents she had brought back for them were minute: a hand of Fatima for Lena, a string of beads for Anna; but they would take up very little room. They were the kinds of things that might lie upon a dressing table for a lifetime. The two children were eager for their presents. They, too, were modest ones. Turkish dolls that would look pretty for thirty hours, that would be discarded before the week was out. "They look as though they've been good, have they?" Myra asked.

"They've been very good."

"And we're going to have two such pretty new nurses when they leave," said Jerry.

"You are?"

It was the first Myra had heard of it. Correspondence had been impossible during their tour, with its constant changes of address.

Anna nodded. "I've found two young students whom I'm sure you'll like. They've graduated from the London School of Economics. They wanted to stay on another year."

"When will they be ready to come?"

"As soon as you want them."

"That means as soon as you want to go."

"I suppose it does."

"And when will that be?"

"As soon as you've got settled back. The week after next, if that's convenient."

"It'll have to be, won't it?"

117

She said it wistfully. Yes, she would miss them. Particularly Anna.

Two mornings later, as she had expected it to do, the telephone rang soon after ten. That flat, unaccented voice did not need to identify itself. "Did everything go all right?" it asked.

"Yes, everything went all right."

"When may I come round?"

"As soon as you like."

"The sooner the better, don't you think?"

"I quite agree."

"I'd like to be able to have a little uninterrupted talk with you."

"I don't see why you should."

"I'll be able to explain why I do."

The tone of his voice did not alter, but it seemed to her that it contained a threat.

"How long would you need?" she asked.

"An hour."

"What could you need an hour for?"

"I'll be able to explain that when I see you."

Again she detected a note of menace. What on earth could he need an hour for! "All right," she said. "What about this afternoon?"

"This afternoon would be most convenient."

"At three o'clock." Then she could have tea in the nursery, with her mind and conscience clear, every cloud dispersed. At least that was how it should be. That was how she prayed it would be. But why had he needed a whole hour? What could he have to say to her that would take an hour?

He arrived punctually at three. He was carrying a small plastic briefcase that looked as though it were made of leather. She had half forgotten what he looked like. If she had met him in the street, would she have recognised him?

He put the briefcase on the table, beside the package labelled Valentina's chocolates. He picked up the package.

"Is this it?"

She nodded.

He undid the gift wrapping, lifted the cardboard lid; Myra could not see what it contained. She was curious to know what

118

it looked like, but she could only have seen by standing up. She did not want to do that. He licked the tip of his forefinger, put it inside the package, licked it again, then nodded. "Fine, fine. Isn't it strange to think that so small a parcel is worth half a million dollars?" He rewrapped the package, opened his briefcase, put the package in it, and took out a smaller one.

"Is that my tape?" she asked.

He shook his head.

"But you promised that you would give me the tape if I brought you back that package."

"I didn't quite say that."

Rage and alarm struck at her simultaneously. This was what she had dreaded, the surrender to a long course of blackmail, where the fee was raised each time. She would become a slave, never knowing an instant's peace of mind, her whole life poisoned. No, she vowed. No, I will not stand for this. I'll go to Victor. I'll confess. I know him better now. He'll be furious but he'll understand. We'll go to the police. You can always trust the police where blackmail is concerned. He thinks he's got me because I've taken that first step. He hasn't though. I'm no longer the inexperienced woman he frightened that first time. I'm not afraid of Victor any longer.

"No," she said. "No, I'm not standing for it. I've done this once, but not again. You told me that you never sent the same courier twice, and I believed you. It seemed logical. That's why I went. Now you're going back on your word. You've lied to me."

"Please, Mrs. Trail, please." He raised his hand. "I did not lie to you. But I did not tell you the whole truth."

"You told me . . ."

He interrupted. "I did not tell you what I believe you are trying to say I told you. I told you that you had to recover that tape by earning it. I said that in order to get it you had to collect a certain package. And that was perfectly true. You had to get that packet and you have got it."

"You said . . ."

"Please do not interrupt. I did not lie to you but where I was not quite honest was in letting you believe that the collection of that package was all you had to do. It is not all you have to do. There is one further forfeit that you have to pay."

"You told me that I should only do one mission."

119

"And that is perfectly true. I am not going to ask you to go on another mission. But there is, as I said, one further duty before I give you your tape."

"And what is that?"

"To recruit another courier."

"What?"

"Exactly what I said. Recruit another courier."

She stared at him. "Explain."

"It's very simple. The operation that you carried out was a two-barrelled or perhaps I should say a three-barrelled operation. First of all you were yourself recruited."

"I was recruited?"

"Of course you were. In Malta. How else do you think we got that tape? Then because we had that tape, you went to the Lebanon and brought back that package. That is the second barrel. You have been through Customs once. We never ask anyone to go through Customs twice. That is a rule we never break. But the circle has to be completed. The third barrel has to be charged and fired. You have got to acquire a piece of tape containing a confession that will make an unsuspecting person accept the role of courier. That is why I needed to spend an hour with you this afternoon. I have to explain how the machinery works."

He tapped the parcel that he had placed upon the table. "It is quite simple. You can learn it easily."

First of all you were recruited. So Naomi had been in the same position as she was now. She had wondered how that tape had come into this wretched man's possession. She had felt aggrieved and cheated. She had been exploited. She had wondered if she would ever know the truth. Now that she did, her resentment left her. Poor Naomi; it must have been a bad time for her. She was dear and sweet and kind. Had she had any sense of guilt? How had she felt? Had she shrugged her shoulders? *Sauve qui peut.* She was a citizen of Dresden. Had the war contained a more pointlessly Philistine act of violence than the saturation bombing of that lovely city? Could anyone who as a small girl had had her home and family exposed to that feel any moral compunction about the temporary inconvenience, embarrassment – for it had been temporary – of a national of the country who had been responsible for that outrage? Poor Naomi, she thought. Poor, poor Naomi.

Yet why poor Naomi? Had it been for her such a penitential project? All the same . . . in her case.

"I can't do that," she said.

"I don't see why not. Is it any worse than what you've done already? I'd have said it was much easier. You smuggled this package through Customs. In doing that you ran a considerable risk. You've come through safely. There's no risk now. Listen." He began to speak not wooingly but practically. "What you have to do," he said, "is to inveigle someone into behaving or talking in such a way that a record of it will make him or her ready to collect an illicit article to prevent the publication of that tape. It is as easy as all that, you see."

"But I can't do that."

"Why not? What you have already done is far more serious than anything you have to do. May I now explain to you how to manipulate this machine so that you can obtain the tape that we require?"

"Please, no, please."

"You have taken the first step; the second will be much easier."

"But how could I meet the person who would provide that tape?"

"That is exactly what the lady who enrolled you said to me. I answered, 'It doesn't matter whom you enrol.' It may be a man, it may be a woman. It could be a schoolboy. It has to be someone who, confronted with a certain proof of a certain aspect of his or her behaviour, will do anything to prevent its being publicised. You have to find someone vulnerable. Artists, actors, authors, they're no good: they don't mind what is said about them. Someone like yourself does. That's why you were such a good choice. But a man would be just as good. Very likely it would be easier for you, with a man. A man's more vulnerable – if he's in public life. And there's this, too, that you must remember: the tape has to identify the man or woman. You have to get the name on, the position occupied, if possible the address. I didn't play over the whole of your tape to you, but our courier had been very careful. Everything was down."

"But the person from whom I get this confession will know it came through me. I'll never be able to look him in the face again."

"Choose someone in whose face you don't want to look again."

"It'll make things very awkward."

"Not if you're tactful. I can recall a case when one of our couriers taped a series of scenes with a very high-born lady. He confessed to her. He said, 'You'll never forgive me. I've done a fearful thing. I had a tape machine concealed in my flat when you came to see me. It was because I loved you that I did it. I know this won't last forever. How could it? Comparing our positions. I wanted to remind myself that it had really happened. You understand that, can't you? Well, a terrible thing has happened. My flat's been burgled and the tapes were stolen.'

"Believe it or not, he got away with it. She believed him and she kept on with him. But that's unusual. It's best to choose a stranger, someone you won't see again, as your friend did with you. And there's this to be remembered, it doesn't have to be sex. A fiddle over income tax would be just as good, a numbered bank account in Switzerland, a piece of bribery perhaps. It's up to you. Now let me show you how this toy works."

It was an intricate piece of machinery, but it was not difficult to install or operate. Naomi should have found it very simple. So will I when my time comes, Myra thought. For there was not much doubt that she would have to go through with this. She had got in too deep. She had taken the first step; why not the second? She was already beginning to rehearse the list of acquaintances who might be suitable. Kitty – what about Kitty? Or one of Kitty's friends.

"I suppose," she said, "that you see quite a little of what is called the seamy side of life."

He smirked. "I have friends who do."

"Then can you give me the address of a good London brothel?"

He raised his eyebrows. He pursed his lips. He looked as though he were preparing to whistle, then changed his mind. "You're going in for this in a big way, I see."

"It might be a handy thing to know."

"Of course, of course ... But ... it isn't easy. London's been cleaned up. What are you interested in especially? I can put you on to see blue films."

122

"That's an idea."

"Or anyone who's keen on rubber."

"Rubber?"

"Those tight-fitting rubber clothes, you know."

"I don't, but still . . ."

"Don't you? It's very much the mode. I can put you on to that."

"What I was really wondering about were places like Polly Adler wrote about."

He shook his head. "That's gone. Even in Paris now. Too many people needed to be bribed. It's all done privately. Girls on their own, or girls in couples, in their own flats. You see their advertisements in Shepherd Market, hung up outside tobacconists. I can tell you what I can do, though. I can give you the name of someone who might help. He's a barman in a mixed club in Soho." He took out a memorandum book, wrote an address, tore out the sheet. "Ask for Grantie. Say Frank sent you. Good luck. I'll ring up every first Tuesday of the month."

Once again she watched him from the window. No one turned to look at him as he walked down the street with his plastic case that contained half a million dollars' worth of illegal merchandise. What a world I'm moving in, she thought.

She looked at the clock. Five minutes to four. Kitty might be in. If she were, it wasn't a time when she would mind being disturbed. But Kitty was out. Her daily help answered. "Please ask Mrs. Severod to call back any time before dinner." She went into the nursery. It was extraordinary that she should be conducting two such different lives; this one so sane, so ordinary, so normal.

The two new Swedish girls were to pay their first visit on the following day. Jerry was enrapturedly excited.

"But you will miss Anna and Lena, won't you?" Myra asked.

"Oh yes, of course, but we know them."

The new thing, always the new thing.

"I expect that you'll miss them more than they'll miss you."

"I'll certainly miss them, and I'll miss England too," said Lena. "I've made good friends here." She wanted to spend the Tuesday night away. Friends in Sussex had asked her to pay them a goodbye visit. "They want to show me how good English cooking can be in an English country house."

"Of course, of course."

Tuesday was one of Victor's Odde Volumes evenings. This time the dinner was to be held at Oxford and Victor would be spending the night away. "Would you like to go too?" she asked Anna. "I can easily sleep in the nursery. I'll be alone."

Anna shook her head. "They're Lena's friends more than mine. They'd prefer to have her to themselves. I'll enjoy a quiet evening, writing goodbye letters."

Kitty rang back shortly before seven. Victor had been home half an hour. They were listening to records, he over a whisky and soda, she over her habitual dry martini. She guessed that it might be Kitty. "I'll take it in the bedroom," she said, put down her cigarette in the ashtray, and hurried through. "Kitty? Yes, I thought it might be you. I can't talk to you about it now. But you know that information we tried to get in the St. George from Pierre? I've found out where you can get it from a barman called Grantie in Soho. When can you lunch with me? On Tuesday? Fine. At the Jardin at one-fifteen."

She was back within a minute to find that the cigarette at which she had only taken a couple of puffs had been stamped out in the ashtray. She looked at it, surprised.

"If there's one thing I loathe it's the leaving of lighted cigarettes in ashtrays," Victor snapped. "They give off the most nauseous stench."

He was almost angry. She had never seen him angry like this before. Was that how he had looked at that girl friend who got drunk at parties? It might be worth remembering.

"But how did you find out all this?" Kitty asked.

"Never reveal your sources of information. But we might as well look around."

"Of course, of course."

"You have seen blue films, haven't you?"

"One or two."

"Did you get a kick out of them?"

"To begin with, yes. But they're so repetitive. It's only the beginnings that are any fun."

124

"How so?"

"It's the introduction, the seeing how they start. There's a chauffeur, say, driving a couple of girls along a country lane. The car breaks down. They all get out to try and put it right. Then suddenly you find that it's only a bluff, so that he can get them out of the car and in a hedge. The real kick is over before it's been running for two minutes. The men always look pretty ghastly too."

"What about the girls?"

"They're not so bad. Quite attractive, most of them. But then that isn't surprising, is it? If they weren't attractive, they wouldn't have got started in that kind of game. It's the exact opposite with men. If they were attractive, they wouldn't ever get caught up in it."

"I suppose they wouldn't." Myra paused. "All this stuff about rubber. What do you make of that?"

"It doesn't attract me. Does it you?"

"I can't see how it could."

"Anyhow we'd better see what Grantie has to show us."

The Bamboo Club was halfway down Greek Street. It had a bright sign outside announcing "Members Only".

"I don't suppose that means anything," said Kitty.

The club was on the first floor. The front door was not locked. It consisted of a single L-shaped room at one end of which was a bar. It was rather dark. A radio was playing. The walls were decorated with travel posters. In the L of the room were a number of tables. It did not look as though any solid food was served at them. A section of the L had been converted into booths. Two of the tables were occupied; there were three people at the bar; ten in all of mixed sexes and mixed colour. They seemed reasonably tidy. It was not a tough spot. Myra and Kitty walked up to the bar. The barman looked as though he were half Indian.

"You ladies members? I not see you here before."

"No, we're not members."

"You want become members? Five shillings each a week."

"We've come to see Grantie."

"That's who you is seeing."

"We've got a card from Frank."

Myra handed across the slip of paper.

Grantie put on his spectacles and examined it. "That sure

125

is Frankie's handwriting. Now what can Grantie do for two nice friends of Frankie?"

"What we had to ask you was a little private."

"It was. Well, there's a quiet table over there. What'll you have to drink? I'll make you honorary members for one day, as friends of Frankie. What did you say you'd have? Two Cherry Heerings. That'll be ten shillings each and the tip's included. You take them to that table. I'll join you in a minute."

The table was relatively out of earshot, provided that one did not raise one's voice.

"This is not the atmosphere in which your uncle was brought up," was Myra's comment.

"I'll say it isn't."

They looked about them. So this was vice in the world's swinging city. Grantie joined them. "The point about us here," he said, "it's where things begin. No funny business on the premises. We keep the law. We're a proper club: registered. We can serve drinks eight hours a day. We serve them from noon till eight. Members can get a drink in the afternoon when the pubs and restaurants are closed. Very useful for some people. Now how can I help you?"

Myra and Kitty looked at one another. It's up to her, isn't it, Myra thought. But Kitty remained silent. Oh well then, since I brought her here. "We're concerned about our husbands," Myra said. "We want to show them something new. We feel that they're getting in a rut. Now what would you suggest?"

"Most anything. You pay the price. You tell me what you want; I find it."

He looked from the one to the other, interrogatively. Myra and Kitty exchanged a glance. Each knew exactly what was in the other's mind. They rose to their feet.

"I can't thank you enough," Myra said. "I now know where we are. You know who we are; we know who you are. If we call and say 'Kitty and Myra,' you'll take care of us. What we want is something that will make our husbands think the world is a somewhat different place."

Grantie broke into a loud guffaw. "I get you now. I see exactly what you want. You let me know. I fix it."

Myra and Kitty blinked as they came out into the bright clean air. "What about a coffee?" Myra asked.

"That's precisely what I feel like."

The Coventry Street Corner House was only a five minutes' walk away. They both ordered chocolate sundaes as well as coffee. "Why don't we come to this kind of place more often?" Kitty said.

"Why don't we? They say that the Cheese and Grill is fabulous."

They sat in silence. Then Myra spoke. "That's not what we're looking for."

"Most certainly it isn't."

"We're between two groups. Though we're twenty-four and over, we belong to the pre-Pill generation. It's all different now. Our fathers, or maybe our grandfathers, had their special problems. They were worried about V.D. It made sex a problem for them. Pencillin settled that. Young men today aren't worried there, though perhaps they should be, and the girl's problem is cured by contraception. They don't need to worry any more about getting babies – that lies within their control, unless they're Catholics, and are young Catholics bothering? In a way it's easy for a young man today. He finds a girl in his own class. It's only people like ourselves who want something special who find that it isn't there for them."

Myra paused, then chuckled. "Hamburg. That's what we should try. Take our men to Hamburg."

8

Myra had taken advantage of Victor's absence to enjoy the kind of supper that was only possible in her own house, when she was alone. Two ample dry martinis on the rocks accompanied an open-faced smoked-salmon sandwich; then she scrambled herself some eggs, and washed them down with a large white coffee. It was a warm night. She was wearing a light, quilted housecoat over her pyjamas. She had curled herself into the corner of the sofa. That afternoon at the tube-station bookstall she had found a Maigret that she had not read. She was looking forward to a quiet, restorative evening. How lucky to have a husband who dined out at least one night a week.

There was a tap on the door. "Yes." Anna was standing in the doorway.

"I've come to say good-bye," she said. She was wearing a pair of black beach trousers and a tight-fitting yellow sweater, long-sleeved with a rolled neck. She closed the door behind her. She stood looking down at Myra. Myra stood up. They were six feet apart. There was a smile on Anna's lips, a soft look of invitation in her eyes. It was for Myra a moment of complete revelation. She had no doubt of what was happening, no self-questioning. Slowly, without a word said, they stepped towards each other, into each other's arms.

It was a long, deliberate kiss. Anna's hands under the quilted jacket moved slowly over Myra's back; then they drew apart. There was no fumbling with the other's clothes. Each knew what was in the other's mind. They met as equals. Each undressed herself, without impatient haste. They had all the night before them. A minute and they were in each other's arms again, among the cushions. "It'll be better on the floor," said Anna.

It was the only thing they said for a long, long while. The floor was covered with a deep warm rug that had been hand-woven in Morocco; it was soft beneath them, giving them the resistant support they needed. It was a fever, a phantasy of changing positions; of lingering, wandering caresses; of breasts sweeping against breasts, of penetrative tongues and fingers. At one moment with feet beside the other's head, their legs were crossed like two pairs of scissors; with their hands clasped, they pulled on one another, rotating themselves against each other. Another moment and they had swung into reverse, their knees drawn close under their chins. Lying on their right sides. Myra's left foot pressed against Anna's shoulder blade; Anna, her left leg drawn under Myra's, pressed her foot under Myra's arm; her left hand, from beneath her leg, was clasped around the small of Myra's back. Myra's own left hand was curved between Anna's thighs. Their breasts were held apart by a confusion of knees and elbows, but each was completely, intimately exposed to the other's darting tongue.

Myra, her hands now joined, drew Anna closer and closer to her, subduing her to the same mounting rhythm to which she was herself subdued. She had not believed two people could be so completely equals, no question of seduction or of being seduced: two people meeting in, being joined by, an equal need for one another. Then once more they were face to face, drinking each other's kisses, their breasts stroking one another's, till at last the sequence of broken sighs sank to a quiet breathing.

They lay in silence. Then Anna spoke. "Tell me about her."

"Tell you about whom?"

"The woman that you met in Malta."

"She was German."

"It's always best with a foreigner, the first time."

"You don't seem to have practised that yourself."

"You mean with Lena?"

"Yes."

"Perhaps Swedes are different. Yes, I think we are. We're very tolerant about that kind of thing."

"You knew as soon as I came back."

Anna laughed. "How did you know I knew?"

"From the way you looked at me. It was a shock."

"Not an unpleasant one."

"I didn't say it was. But it was a shock. I wondered if I was so obvious to everyone."

"Oh no, only to someone like myself."

"What about Lena?"

"I didn't discuss it with her, but I shouldn't think so. It's not in her blood, as it is in mine; as I believe it is in yours."

"So you think that, do you?"

. Anna nodded. "I used to wonder about you. I felt that you'd really like women in this way but that you'd never been, do you know the phrase we use, 'brought out'?"

"I know that phrase."

"I was very tempted. But I couldn't be sure. I didn't dare to risk it."

"Did you think that I'd have sacked you?"

Anna shook her head. "If I'd guessed wrong, it would have been very awkward – between us two I mean. And then there'd have been Lena. Her feelings would have been hurt if we had had to leave, because of you and me. And even so, suppose I'd not guessed wrong, suppose that I had been able to play that German woman's role with you. It wouldn't have been easy, not with Lena here. You'd have resented her. She'd have been puzzled. I'd have had to lie to her. She'd probably have

129

found out. It would have been a mess. But I was tempted. Particularly after you came back from Malta, and I knew."

"Did you want to then, all that much?"

"*Alskling*, you're such an innocent. That's one of the things that makes you very special."

She raised herself on her elbows. She looked down at Myra. She lowered her head and brushed her lips softly over hers, moving them away, along her cheek, taking the lobe of her ear between her teeth, biting at it softly, sliding the tip of her tongue into the shell-like crevices; at the same time her hand slid downwards over Myra's body, her fingertips began their slow, tantalising, lingering caress.

It was the moment in love-making that Myra loved the most, when after an interval in love play, passion became resurgent. For a moment she regretted the difference between this moment and those others, when with Victor she had become conscious suddenly of his renewed, his palpably renewed interest in her. In a sense there was something here incomplete. Mentally she shrugged. In everything there was always something missing. And there was so much extra here. I need both, she thought. Once again, she turned into Anna's arms.

Later, once again, the sighs had sunk to an even breathing. Once again Anna was whispering softly to her, "I knew that you'd be wonderful. I had no idea that you would be *so* wonderful. If I had known, I don't think that I'd have been able to resist you all this time. Do you know what I first thought when I learned that Lena would have to go? I thought, This gives me my chance with Myra."

"It was luck Lena having this night away."

"Do you really think that it was luck? I fixed it. I knew that your husband was going to be at Oxford. So I suggested to those friends of Lena's that they ask her for that night. That would leave us alone together. It's going to be a night we'll never be forgetting, never. I've so often thought, have you? No, I guess you haven't; you're younger than I am, and a woman who likes men isn't promiscuous in the way that a woman who likes women is. I've so often thought, it may not be after the first night, it may be after the third or second —"

"Maugham makes one of his characters in The Razor's Edge say that the second night is the one that counts."

"I wouldn't contradict the maestro, but I have thought often at the very start of an affair, If only it could stop here. We've had the best that we can ever give each other. We've touched the heights. It can only be a repetition after this. And to repeat is to diminish. But one can't stop there, because of the other person, because of oneself, because you live in the same village, the same town, you have to go on seeing one another, and because you do, you have to go on making love to one another. That's why we're so lucky in this, you and I. We'll have this one long night, to say all we'll never have an opportunity to say again, to reveal each final secret, to leave no caress unused, no curiosity unsatisfied. That is what fate has given us. It is something that fate does not give so often."

The night was only a third spent when she said that. As she had prophesied, so it was. They talked and they made love and then they talked. As the night advanced, the air grew cool. Myra shut the window. She brought in a coverlet from the bedroom. In the intervals of love-making, they would lie on their backs, cushions under their necks, their hands crossed under their heads.

"Who brought you out?" Myra asked.

Anna laughed. "I guess I brought myself out. I seemed to know from the beginning the kind of person that I was."

"But surely the first time, wasn't it with an older woman?"

"Yes, of course, but there wasn't any seduction on her part. It was one of those holiday camps. I was a Junior Guide. She was a Guide leader. She was four years older, but the moment I saw her, at the very first reception, I knew. Our eyes met. I thought, this is it. When I came out from supper, she was waiting outside the tent. We didn't say a word. We went for a walk into the woods. And that was that."

"But when you yourself, when you've brought girls out, that's different, isn't it?"

"Of course, as it was with you and that German woman. If she'd made a pass at you your first evening, you'd have had a fit. It took me a long time to get the idea into Lena's head. But as I said, she isn't really my type at all. Sooner or later she'll see the man who's right for her. Then she'll go to him."

"Will you be very sad?"

Anna shrugged. "It's happened before. It's what I've known
131

from the start would happen with her. I'm on my guard. Live in the moment." Again they turned to one another.

It was Myra who first resumed their talk. "You say that Lena will find some man. Isn't there a chance that you yourself might find a man?"

Anna shook her head. "Not a man that I'd give up a woman for."

"You told me that the kind of man you liked isn't the kind of man who'd make a good father for your children."

"That's so."

"What kind of man would he be?"

"What kind of man would you expect him to be?"

"Well –" Myra hesitated, and Anna caught her up.

"I think I can tell you the kind of man that you'd expect. Because I'm masculine, he'd be feminine. That he'd be a fairy, in fact, who'd be vaguely bisexual. And that isn't paternal timber. Is that what you had in mind?"

"More or less."

"You couldn't be more wrong. The kind I like is excessively masculine, over-masculine. He's brought up under rigid discipline. He's spartan. Usually he's a northern type; a Prussian or a Finn, a Swede, someone who's on a ship for long periods of time, who rather despises women. Because he is virile, powerfully masculine, he doesn't suppress the sex side of his nature. He expresses it with men, as soldiers in the Foreign Legion or prisoners sent to Devil's Island do. At the same time it is really *faute de mieux*. He has acquired these tastes because no others were available. But that doesn't mean he doesn't find women attractive in their way and in their place; the trouble is that he only likes doing with women the things that he has got into the habit of doing with young men."

"And that is the kind of man to whom you find yourself attracted?"

"That's so."

"How did you find this out about yourself?"

"The first man who attracted me was like that."

"What kind of a man was he?"

"He was a German. He'd been in submarines in the war."

"Was that why you said I'd been lucky to meet a German woman?"

132

"If one has a kink, it's easier with a foreigner. One has no class distinctions. One's not afraid of being looked down upon. Something strange is justified by foreignness. I once heard a Frenchman say that English men and women, living on an island, had breathed the same air so long that they had become like brothers and sisters to each other. All strangeness gone."

And it needed a German woman, Myra thought, to introduce that note for her, so that Victor and she became alive for one another. "But wasn't it," she asked, "a shock for you at first? You couldn't have known he was like that."

"A surprise, but not a shock. I was surprised with myself for being attracted. I thought I knew myself so well. You mayn't believe it but I was a virgin."

"Are you still?"

"Heavens no. I had to try the other things, as an experiment. I didn't like it much."

"But with this other man, how did he explain?"

"He didn't explain. He started to do things I'd not expected."

"And did you like those things?"

"Not at first. But most tastes can be acquired. And the fact that he was different in that way made me feel that it was all right for me. I didn't want to be like everybody else. Being different in those ways gives me a sense of superiority. What may be good enough for the rest of the world isn't good enough for me."

"You're putting ideas into my head," said Myra.

Anna laughed. Once again her fingertips were moving gently, persuasively between Myra's thighs. "Not only into your head, I notice."

Once again the long colloquy was interrupted.

"Have you met many men like that?"

"Five."

"All foreigners?"

"Except one. One of them was a Moslem, an Iraqi. I liked him the best."

"What about the English?"

"I'd rather expected to find one here. I haven't."

They laughed together. Myra found it strange to feel herself so utterly in tune with this foreign girl with whom up till

133

now she had been on such formal terms, and whom she would never, in all human probability, ever see again. "With these other men," she asked, "did you know what they were like before?"

"Before what?"

"Before it started. With the German you said it was a surprise. The second time, did you guess beforehand?"

"There's a freemasonry about these things. If you have a kink yourself, you recognise it in other people. You'll find that out. One doesn't make a mistake very often."

"I've got a lot to learn."

"You'll learn it."

Again they laughed. It was fun that they could laugh together; that's what Naomi had said. Don't be solemn and serious and invoke high heaven. Treat it as light-hearted entertainment.

"Do you know what a *partouze* is?" Myra asked.

"Of course."

"Have you ever tried one?"

"Not a strict *partouze*; a *partie à trois* I have."

"Is that very different?"

"I think so, yes. A *partouze* is four people at least; and that's an orgy. There can't be any intimacy. With a *partie à trois* there is. It's an added intimacy."

"Tell me. Do you mean a man and two women, or one woman and two men?"

"In my case it would be two women and one man. It would be only with homosexual men that you'd get one woman and two men; there'd be the kick there of seeing someone you're attracted to doing things and having things done to him."

"So you yourself get a kick out of seeing things done to a girl that you're in love with?"

"Provided it's by the kind of man that I've described, then it would be something that we could share, she and I; it would be an added bond between us. But if it was a man who liked normal things, it wouldn't be something we could share. Besides, I would feel jealous, I might lose her. She might prefer the things she did with him. I'll probably lose her anyhow eventually. I don't want to anticipate that day."

"I think I see it, but it is a whole new world to me."

"That's how it was once with me. It's involved psychologic-

134

ally. Love comes into it. The need to give, to provide someone with a pleasure that you can't give yourself. That leads to gratitude. Then there's the devious attraction of, I won't say actually corrupting someone, though that perhaps is the word, but of initiating someone into practices that without you they'd never have known. There's a very definite attraction about that. She's more yours afterwards. Especially so with that Iraqi, his being a Moslem and dark-skinned."

"And you introduced him to girls you were in love with?"

"Girls I was having an affair with."

"How many?"

"Three."

"Have you done that with Lena?"

"No," she paused. "Not yet," she added, and they laughed together. I'll remember every minute of this night, as long as I remember anything, Myra thought.

9

Once again, on a Tuesday morning at ten o'clock the telephone bell rang. Myra's heart sank. She had been expecting this, she had been dreading this. For days on end she would forget that such a person as Montagu Frank existed. Her life was moving happily and smoothly. The nursery was well run; the two new Swedish girls were easy to get on with. They could not have been more different from their predecessors. They each went out with men on separate dates, different men too, as far as she could judge. The children did not seem to miss Anna and Lena in the least. Her marriage was as vivid and vital as it had been tame and routine before. It was hard for her to remember that this shadow was threatening to drift across the sun. For days she would forget. Then suddenly she would remember, I'm on borrowed time.

She took the call in her bedroom. "Yes," she said.

"Have you any news for me?"

There it was again, the flat, neutral voice with an accent she could not place.

"No," she said. "I'm sorry. I haven't yet."

"Isn't it nearly time you had?"

"It isn't as easy as you think."

"I don't think it's easy at all. If it were, my friends and I wouldn't have gone to all this trouble to enrol you."

"How long did it take to enrol me?"

"Rather less time than you might suppose. And I don't think that your predecessor was any more attractive or more competent than you. But perhaps she was more in a hurry than you are. She wanted to be rid of the whole business. Why not follow her example? You'll be so much happier when you have got this out of your system, so much more at peace."

"Suppose I don't do anything. Suppose I simply say to hell with you. You've got your package, you must be content with that."

"In that case the tapes would go to certain interested persons, and that would be the end of your husband's Treasury career."

"Would that do you any good?"

"Not immediately. We should have to regard this particular operation as a loss; but you would provide us with a very usual piece of ammunition. Suppose some other lady was to prove difficult, as you are now. It would be easy to say to her, 'You may not yourself remember a very promising young civil servant in the Treasury, but your husband is certain to have heard of him. Victor Trail. Ask your husband what happened to that promising young official and he will say, "Now it's very curious that you should have asked me that. It's something I've always wondered. He resigned and went abroad. I don't know where; none of us knows why. It's quite a mystery." ' Then I shall be able to tell that lady, 'I can solve that mystery for your husband. Mr. Trail's wife, who was in exactly the same position that you are, found herself dependent on our good services. But she was very foolish, as I am sure, my dear lady, you are not going to be. She would not do what was required of her, so we had no alternative to sending some very injudicious tapes to the people on whose good graces her husband's career depended.' "

He paused. She said nothing. He went on. "So you see if you are foolish, but I am sure that you won't be, we can make some use out of you, even so. But you aren't going to be foolish, are you?"

He'd do it, she thought. He isn't bluffing. He might even be
136

rather glad to have someone to quote as an example. There was a silence, then he spoke again.

"I wonder if you are setting about this in the right way. Grantie told me that you visited the Bamboo Club, but that isn't the place to meet the people who can be of use to you. I gather that you realised that yourself. Anyhow you've not been back. The people that you'd meet there have no social or business status. They couldn't do anything that could damage them, or, if they did, it would be so outside the law that you wouldn't want to be involved in that; you'd be picked up in the Thames with your throat cut. No, no, you want to concentrate on the Establishment. They're the vulnerable ones. They stand to lose a lot. Thirty years ago you could have operated in a country house, but country houses belong to a closed world today. You may have the entrée to it, but I doubt it. Better to stick to what used to be called Café Society, to the luxury hotels where the big spenders go, the men with expense accounts. You don't have to go outside England. What's that place in Kent where James Bond went? The one that's near the golf courses. Go when the big tournaments are on, and before you know where you are, you'll have seen the last of this dingy character. Good luck!"

She stared at the receiver she had replaced. The Royal Sandwich: it was not a bad idea. The children needed some sea air. She wouldn't mind a little change herself. Victor could come down for weekends. The Swedish girls could take alternate weeks off. What was there against it? Nothing that she could see. The family was in funds.

The Amateur Mixed Doubles were due to start early in September. Both the Bath Club and the Guards had held their meetings earlier. It would be a very social time. The sea water might be too cold for Myra and for Victor, but not for the children. Anyhow there was a heated swimming pool. There was no reason why it should not be a relaxing holiday.

Myra, the children, and the Swedish girl called Olga arrived in the early afternoon. She had booked a first-floor suite for them. From its terrace she could look over the Channel. She could see the stretch of the links with the white Coast Guards bungalows, and the fairway of the sixteenth green. She could see the port of Ramsgate in the distance. She wished that she

137

had taken up golf at school. There's plenty of time, she thought, but wondered if there was.

The front terrace of the hotel faced the eighteenth green. It was crowded by the time she got there, soon after six o'clock.

The first round of the Amateur Mixed Doubles was being played. She had never followed golf closely, though Victor had. She did not know who was who in the golf world. The buzz of talk around her conveyed very little. She was content to look about her, to absorb the atmosphere of the hotel, its elegance and wealth. Tomorrow she would try to find out who was who. She could relax tonight.

Suddenly, however, she became aware of a heightened interest around her. There was a murmur of "Ah, here they come." Then a queried, "Who's got the honour?" As the match had not ended on the seventeenth, was someone dormy, and if so, who? Or was the game still tied?

From the murmur around her she gathered that this was the key match of the day; two possible winners had drawn each other in the first round. She saw a tall, youngish man, slim and graceful, stand upon the tee. There was a hush of silence. The crack of the club upon the ball, then a murmur as it was seen that the ball had streamed straight down the middle of the fairway. "That won't cause Heather any worry," someone said.

The opponent took his place upon the tee. He was a short, squat man. He was bald and seemed middle-aged. His swing was short, but he appeared to put his full weight into his stroke. His ball too went straight down the middle of the fairway, finishing a few yards behind the first. The two players and their caddies left the tee. The first player had walked to join a rather short, slim, youngish woman, who was wearing green slacks and a yellow, long-sleeved sweater. She had on a cap with a long peak, which gave her a nautical air. They were a handsome couple.

"Who are they?" Myra asked.

The man to whom she had spoken looked surprised. "Heather Bennett and Gerald Armitage. They won last year, you know. I heard someone say they were one up."

Someone who overheard them turned his head. "They were one down on the fifteenth green. They won the last two holes."

I suppose, Myra thought, I should have heard of them. They're probably quite famous.

They had now reached their ball. They stood aside while their opponents played. It was a par four hole, but a wind was blowing, the green was over a hundred and fifty yards away. Most women would have preferred to play short. The green was guarded by an awkward bunker. The woman hesitated. She consulted with her partner and her caddy. She took out a wood from the bag. She was out to reach the green. She was one down and could afford to run a risk. She needed to win this hole. There was silence as she took her stance, silence as she swung her club. The ball rose into the air, white against the blue. It rose and flew, and then just as it was losing height and strength, it seemed to gather power and resist the pull of gravity. It fell to the left of the bunker and rolled to the edge of the green. There was a burst of clapping.

Heather Bennett walked to her ball. She did not hesitate. She took an iron. Clearly she was going to play short for safety. She had her back to Myra. She was a graceful creature, slim legs, firm, rounded hips, well-covered shoulders. She had an easy swing. She did not appear to be hitting at all hard; there was no sense of effort. The ball rose clear against the sky, straight, straight towards the green, clearly to fall short of it, but well to the right, with a run up to the pin. There was a much smaller burst of clapping. "They'll have to work for their four," Myra heard someone say.

Armitage deliberated behind his ball. He then walked up to the green, looked back from it towards his ball, then returned to it. He took what seemed to be a seven iron from his bag. He wasn't going to run it up then. He was going to pitch. There was a dead silence once again. He swung, the club cut into the turf, lifting a large divot, the ball rose high. It landed only a few inches from the hole, but it had a heavy back spin on it. It bit the green and checked, trickling to the very rim of the cup. This time there was a real burst of clapping. That was the match all right unless his opponent sank a putt right across the green. He didn't.

Armitage and his partner handed their clubs over to the caddies and walked towards the hotel terrace. He was certainly good-looking, in the classic Attic way, with a high forehead, a straight nose, and a firm chin. She was a good match for him, dark where he was blond, pale-skinned, with what Myra had heard described as an appealing pushed-in face. Her figure was firm and trim: the breasts pressing against the sweater. Myra looked again at Armitage. He had the look of a Greek god, yet he had an air of nonchalance, of being at ease with himself, self-confident but not aggressively. She watched him, fascinated.

As she watched, he turned his head towards her, became aware of her watching him, then checked, surprised, a look of recognition on his face. He seems to know me, Myra thought. I'm certain I don't know him. I wouldn't forget anyone like that.

He stared at her, hesitated, seemed on the point of coming over to her, then thought better of it and went away.

I must remind him of somebody. Lucky somebody, thought Myra.

But that was not the case. Within two minutes he was back. "Mrs. Victor Trail. I was sure it was you, but I couldn't be certain. I asked the reception desk. They told me, yes, that you were here alone with your two children and a Swedish nanny. I don't think we've ever met. But I know your husband. As you're alone, I wonder if you would have a drink with Mrs. Bennett and myself. We're thirsty after that round. I've got a suite. Let's go to it. I don't want to be caught up with golf fans in the bar."

He had not mentioned his own name. He had assumed that she would know who he was.

"I can't think how you recognised me," she said. "I know we've never met."

"I've a good memory for faces, where pretty women are concerned. I've seen your photograph in the papers, and you were pointed out to me at a party 'across a crowded room'. Victor Trail's a lucky chap, I thought."

"Do you know Victor well?"

"Not very. We've met at wine tastings."

"What a lot of time Victor does spend at wine tastings."

"And at Lord's. I've seen him there quite often."

All the same she was astonished at being recognised. She was flattered.

His suite was on the second floor, with the same view as
140

hers, but one room smaller. "I bet you pay the earth for it," he said.

"Don't you for yours?"

"I don't pay for anything. Hotels think I have publicity value."

"Do they set up your bar as well?" The cocktail cabinet was well stocked with bottles, with glasses and an ice bucket.

"They don't, but my employers do. I work for a wine firm. As long as I win tournaments they trust me to sell their booze. How long they'll go on doing it is another matter."

"As long as you go on winning tournaments, of course." This interpolation came from Heather Bennett. She was stretched out in a long chair with a long, cool drink beside her.

"From the way I was playing today, I shan't be doing that much longer."

"I didn't see anything wrong with your play today."

"I saw your last two shots," said Myra. "They couldn't have been better."

"There was nothing wrong with that final one, but there were a number in the middle that were ..." He paused. He raised his glass. "It's very nice to be meeting you, Mrs. Trail. I've wanted to for quite a while. They told me at the desk that you were booked in for two weeks, so that should give us several opportunities."

"When is your next match?"

"Tomorrow afternoon, at three."

"Then I'll gallery the match."

He shrugged. "Let's hope we take them as far as the eighteenth green."

"Now, Gerald, you mustn't talk like that."

"I mustn't, I know, but something's telling me that this is the last time I'll ever be your partner in this tournament."

"You'll be my partner as long as you can get around that course on crutches."

He laughed. "That wouldn't do you any good." He turned to Myra. "Mrs. Bennett is in her way as much an amateur professional as I am, though I'm sure that you don't need telling this. She's games mistress at that great school for young ladies, Annandale. It is as important for Annandale that she should win tournaments as it is for my employers that

141

I should. The trouble is that while Mrs. Bennett is twenty-seven, I am thirty-eight."

"Thirty-eight's nothing. You don't look any different."

"But I feel different. After thirty-five one year takes as much toll as three did. Something gives. It's hard to say what it is, but one becomes conscious of it."

He spoke lightly, humorously. It did not seem to worry him very much. He had probably a number of irons in the fire. And Mrs. Bennett teased him in an easy, affectionate way. They seemed very much at ease with one another.

That evening, after dinner, she called Victor.

"I met a friend of yours today. Gerald Armitage."

"Of course you would. He always plays in that tournament – and I suppose Mrs. Bennett was there as well."

"She was."

"Staying in the same hotel?"

"I gather so."

"She would be."

"Tell me about her; tell me about them."

"There's not much to tell. You know about his golf. He was a blue at Oxford. He played in the Walker Cup team. She's a schoolmistress. She's not in the same class that he is but she's very good. They've been playing in this tournament for five years. They've won it the last twice."

"Is there anything between them?"

"Everything, I'd imagine, wouldn't you?"

"Why don't they get married?"

"That's rather tragic. She married when she was very young, a perfectly appalling man, a bully of the worst kind – at least that's the story and probably it's true. She could have got a divorce from him under any reasonable conditions, but he, unfortunately, is a Catholic and he swears that he will fight to the last inch any action that she may bring. She doesn't stand a chance."

"I see."

There was a pause. "It'll be amusing to have a party, the four of us, this weekend."

"It certainly will."

"Darling, I'm missing you," he said.

"I, you."

There was a pause. Then he said something that made her

142

heart beat faster. "It's funny. It wasn't like this a year ago. But now I feel incomplete without you."

Next morning, soon after ten o'clock, Myra took the children to the swimming pool. "Take an hour off," she said to Olga.

"You can spare me?"

"I've got to learn how I can spare you. *Au pair* girls aren't going to last forever."

Mrs. Bennett was at the pool. She waved at Myra, then came across to join her.

"I'm surprised to see you here," said Myra. "I thought bathing was supposed to put your eye out."

Mrs. Bennett shook her head. "There are so many myths about that kind of thing. I've heard cricketers say, you probably have too, that they've never seen the ball so large as on the mornings when they've had to hold their eyelids up with matchsticks."

"So you're prepared to swim."

"But not to take dry martinis before lunch."

They laughed together. Myra had scarcely noticed her the day before. Gerald Armitage had done all the talking. Now she was seeing Heather Bennett as a person in her own rights. She wasn't "just a schoolmarm". Myra looked at her more closely. She was a definitely attractive object, yet at the same time she had an unawakened look. What had her husband been like?

"I'm coming out to see your match this afternoon."

"Thank you. Wish us well. We'll need it." Mrs. Bennett paused. "How well do you know Gerald?"

"Not at all. Last evening was the first time I'd met him. I'm astonished that he should have known who I was."

"Do you know much about him?"

"Nothing. I don't read the sports page."

"You don't know what his problem is?"

"As a matter of fact, I rang my husband up last night to ask."

"And what did he say it was?"

"You."

They stared at each other. Then they burst out laughing. It seemed extraordinary to Myra that they, two complete strangers, should be talking together in this way, laughing in

143

this way. I do like her, Myra thought. I feel in tune with her.

"You couldn't be more wrong," said Heather Bennett. "I'm not his problem. It's his mother."

"Oh?"

"Yes. Oh, she's a sweet dear person, but she's got him in her clutches. She's the sun he circles around. He's the spoiled child who was always nice to look at, who was always petted at children's parties, who won all the prizes at his schools, who brought them home to mother, his tasselled caps, his ribboned coats, all home to mother. You think that kind of boy is effeminate; oh no, not at all. Could anything be more virile, more masculine than Gerald Armitage? Yet all the emotional side of his nature is concentrated on his mother. And because of that he has never made a real mark for himself."

"But surely his golf, his agency for this wine firm . . ."

"Oh no, no, no, those are just appendages. They aren't a career. He's got a brother, Ernest. Have you heard of him?"

"I haven't, no."

"You're lucky. He's so worthy, and so dreary. He's in insurance. He's doing well. He's going to do better. He's got a highly suitable wife with money; they've got two children. He went to Westminster. The boys will go to Rugby. One step up all the time. He won't get knighted but he'll get an O.B.E. for public services, whatever that may mean. He's three years older than Gerald. He's desperately jealous of him, because Gerald's popular and good-looking, because he's in the public eye, because he's his mother's favourite; he's jealous of him, but he disapproves of him. He's always reading Gerald lectures. He insists that everyone should have a real career, should contribute to the prosperity of the state; you know the kind of thing. He dismisses Gerald as a playboy. He prophesies the most dire future for him. He says that within a few years he'll have stopped winning tournaments; within a year or two after that he'll have ceased to be of any publicity value to his wine firm. Then he'll be in a mess and Ernest gloats over the prospect. He believes that when that day comes Gerald, who's sat so lightly in the saddle for so long, will have to come with cap in hand and ask him for a job, for any job. How Ernest is going to enjoy that moment. What a lecture he will read poor Gerald. 'I told you so,' he'll say. And explain how impossible it is to find a job for an untrained man of forty. He may even

144

quote Kipling at him. That poem 'Back to the Army Again' – 'The man of four and twenty who 'asn't learned of a trade, Beside reserve agin 'im 'ad better never been made.' But I don't mind betting that Ernest will have a job waiting for him; he's got it all planned out. It won't be a bad job either, but it will be one that will humiliate Gerald. It will be one that will remind Gerald at every moment of the day that his brother is his superior, that he owes his very existence to that brother. That'll be the turn of the screw and with a vengeance."

Her eyes shone and her face was flushed. She looked almost beautiful. Certainly most appealing. Poor thing, thought Myra, she must really love him. She wanted to cherish and console her.

"And the worst thing about it all," Heather was going on, "is that Ernest is dead right. Gerald is a playboy. He's on a dead-end road. In ten years' time he will be finished. And the wine firm will want a younger man in the public eye to advertise their wines."

"Hasn't he saved any money?"

"I doubt it. And he hasn't been paid all that much. He doesn't get actual money, but the equivalent of money; travel expenses, first-class tickets on the plane, suites in hotels, a well-stocked cocktail cabinet. But that isn't the same as money in a bank."

"His mother will leave him something, I suppose."

"Something. All she has, presumably. But I don't suppose it's much. Part of what she has is a pension probably, and the income that takes care of an elderly widow doesn't go very far with a man of forty who has been used to living it up for twenty years. Not after death-duties have cut the capital. It's not a pretty prospect, and the trouble is that Gerald is beginning to realise that Ernest is dead right. You heard how he was talking last night."

"I didn't get all the implications of what he was saying. I was meeting him for the first time, remember."

"How did he strike you?"

"He's very good-looking and attractive."

"I didn't mean that. How did all that talk about being off his game strike you?"

"I'm not an athlete, but I'd have thought that one should always start a game believing one was going to win."

145

"Exactly. One should be nervous when one stands on the first tee. If one isn't taut, one takes one's play casually. You've got to be on edge before you start; then you can relax into a deep, calm concentration. But one thing you have to be and that's self-confident. You've got to believe that you are going to win, that you can win, that you're better than the other man. I had an uncomfortable feeling about Gerald yesterday. I felt that he'd like to lose."

"Oh, surely not."

"Oh, surely yes."

"How did he play yesterday?"

"Not really badly; he wasn't himself for a while. He had a bad patch at the turn, but he pulled himself together."

"Then why are you worrying?"

"Because I think he was almost sorry that he did pull back, then he let the competitive instinct take control. He'd as soon have lost."

"I can't think why you should say that."

"Because he knows he's on a road that has no turning. He's past the point of no return. He knows what's waiting for him. He wants to get there as soon as possible, to know the worst, to get it over quickly. He foresees how bad it will be." She paused. "I can see his point. But I'm not going to encourage him. Nothing's lost until the battle's over."

"He's lucky to have you."

"And he's going to go on having me for quite a little. You heard what he said about my having to get another partner for this tournament. He said it was as important for me in the eyes of my school directors to go on winning as it was for him. But that's sheer nonsense. It was important for me at the start when I was being taken on, to be someone capable of winning a tournament such as this. That gave me a status. But to be a games mistress you don't need to be in the public eye. You only have to prove that you are good enough to teach because you yourself once played in a high bracket. My position is quite different from Gerald's. But even if we lose this afternoon – and we may well do so – I'm not going to let him resign next year. He's going to enter with me again, and I'm going to shame him into putting up a first-class show. He's got me on his hands for quite a time."

Once again her eyes were flashing and her cheeks were
146

flushed. Once again there swept over Myra a protective need to comfort her. They were sitting on the edge of the pool, dangling their toes in the water. Heather's hand lay on the side. Myra put her hand over it, pressing it, in sympathy. "Don't worry," she said. "It'll be all right. If we want anything strongly enough, we always get it."

It was a warm, almost a hot afternoon, but a breeze was blowing from the sea. It was an ideal day for golf, but it was also a day on which you needed to play good golf. The slightest hook or pull would be taken by the breeze. Heather had advised Myra to wait at the fourth green. It was a one-shot hole. "You'll see us coming up the third fairway to the green; you can watch us putting out. You'll have a good view of our shots from the fourth tee. Then if you like, you can trail along with us."

Myra had borrowed a pair of field glasses. The third fairway was protected by a line of sand dunes. It was a doglegged hole that provided a high test both of skill and judgment. It was not difficult to carry the dunes, but if you took the cautious line, you could not hope to reach the green with your second. From the left of the fairway the green lay open for a two- or a three-iron shot; the easier the approach for the second, the riskier the shot from the tee. "It's an exciting hole to watch," Heather had told Myra. "You see the balls come over, and you wonder which is whose. Then the players arrive and you know."

The Armitage-Bennett match was due to start at half past three. They should be driving off from the third tee by four. Myra was at her vantage point on the hillock that backed the fourth green at the quarter to. She wanted to get the atmosphere of the day and match. She settled herself comfortably in a hollow of sand and grass. She savoured the warmth of the sun and the coolness of the breeze. The sea was calm, with a few white horses in the middle distance. Across the bay were the cliffs and spires and bungalows of Ramsgate. What a lovely country England was on one of these rare fine days; and how the English took advantage of these days with their sailing boats and picnic baskets. She watched what must be the foursome immediately ahead of Heather's take their course up the fairway. How light their tread was on the springy turf; how picturesque they looked in their bright pullovers and trousers; how they were relishing this lambent weather. Yet the English took the rough with the smooth; they would be trudging up the fairway with equal zest in four months' time on a rain-swept December morning, with waterproof coats and trousers and wide, bright golf umbrellas.

The foursome ahead had now reached the green. Another minute and there would be two white balls on the greensward. Ah, here was the first, she lost it against the sky, but caught it against the ochre brown of the dunes; for a moment she could not tell where it would land. Then she saw it, white against the green, a long way over to the left. Whoever had had the honour at that tee looked likely to retain it at the fourth. There was a brief pause. Then the second ball came over. It was a good deal further to the right. Who had taken the easier line at the third hole? The man usually played the first hole. Gerald would have played that shot from the tee. Had he the honour? Had he lost the last hole, and was playing now for safety, making certain of his five, letting his opponent make a slip? She waited anxiously. Ah, there was Heather, in those same dark green trousers and that canary yellow pullover. Which way was she going, to the right or to the left? There seemed a moment of confusion, of consultation. One caddy had been sent ahead to mark the stroke. There couldn't be any doubt. No, of course; there couldn't be any doubt. Yes, it was Heather turning to the left. Gerald had had the honour. He had taken the dangerous line and the hole stood open.

Myra watched the other couple. From where the ball lay, the woman could not hope to reach the green; she would have to play short and to the left, for safety, opening the hole. There should be no doubt about their five, and there was always the chance of a putt dropping. She played her shot. It was the most that she could do; it was the best that she could do. The five was certain, unless they three-putted.

Heather took up her stance. She had taken out a wood. How slim, how graceful, what an exquisite creature. It was only now in this modern age when women took their place in the arena that you could realise quite how exquisite they were, how smoothly the muscles flowed around and controlled the limbs. Myra held her breath. Had she ever seen anything lovlier than the harmony, the rhythm with which that club swung to and through the ball? Myra was so entranced that she did not follow the flight of the ball. She was held by the picture of Heather, with her club swung behind her back, poised, on balance, like a piece of sculpture.

She shook herself. She looked away. Yes, there it was, landed just short of the green. Trickling towards the hole. There should be no doubt of the four. There wasn't. How much are they up, Myra thought.

Heather had to play from the tee at the next shot. It was a one-shot hole, but a full shot, and the breeze was blowing across the course. It was not an easy shot, and the green was on a plateau. If the ball fell short, it was liable to roll down the hill.

Heather took her stance. Please, please, Myra prayed. Heather swung. There was the click of the wood against the ball. The ball rose, soared, seemed to gather strength, then lose it. Would it reach the green, would it? . . . Oh, it had, but only the extreme edge; it hesitated. It lacked the strength to climb those last two inches; it wavered, then slid back into the bunker. Myra sighed. Oh, she thought, oh, oh, oh.

Heather's opponent took her stance. She was a brisk, forthright woman. She teed up her ball, shifted her feet, steadied herself, swung. It was an admirable shot, four inches further than Heather's, which gave it the strength to mount the ridge and climb to the edge of the close-mown surface. It should be a three.

Gerald took a wedge out of his bag. He took a firm grip for his feet, then swung. A rain of sand was strewn about him, but the ball lifted through the fog. It landed ten feet from the pin, and ran another couple of feet further on. A possible three still; it had to be a three though. Gerald's opponent rolled his ball within three inches of the hole. Gerald struck it away. "O.K.," he said. Heather walked up behind her ball. She went down onto one knee. She walked over to the hole, knelt down again, took a line on her ball, returned to it, hesitated; stood up and walked away; then returned to her putt, stabbed at it, and missed it.

Heather looked at Gerald. Myra could not see the expression on her face; her back was turned to her. But she could see the way Gerald smiled. It was warm, friendly and encouraging. He stepped across to her, put his arm around her shoulder,

149

pressing it. Heather raised her head. Myra could guess now at her expression. They're a team, she thought. They really like each other.

Heather and Gerald separated, Gerald going to the tee, Heather to the fairway, waiting for Gerald's drive. Myra walked across to her. "Bad luck," she said.

Heather shook her head. "Bad play," she said.

"What's the score?"

"One up. We're one up. It's going to be all right. Gerald's on the top of his game. Quite different from yesterday. He's going to pull me through, even if it's by the scruff of my neck. I know him when he's like this."

"The best of luck, then."

Myra turned away, but Heather checked her, her hand upon her elbow. "Don't go away. Stay with me."

"Won't I put you off?"

Heather shook her head. "You'll be a help. I'll like your being there."

"I promise I won't talk."

"Please do. I like your voice."

They looked backwards to the tee. They saw Gerald's opponent swing. It was a very reasonable shot, not a very long one, but straight down the centre. Gerald took his place. He played with the minimum of effort, no trial swing. He teed up his ball, settled his feet, then swung. Heather gave a little gasp. "I told you, didn't I?" He had outdriven his opponent by thirty yards, in terms of carry, and the ball had a slight hook on it that gave it an extra run. Heather waved at him, then walked after the ball.

How good she looks, Myra thought. The sweater and the tight-fitting pants modelled every muscle of her figure; the swing of the club accentuated the harmony and perfection of that figure. You felt that every bone, every muscle, every nerve had been arranged in just that way so that the club should be swung smoothly. The one had been created for the other — this exquisite creature and the beautiful, ancient game of golf. Heather's approach flew straight towards the green, high and straight, landed on the edge and running on towards the hole. She does not need to be carried, Myra thought. No pulling by the scruff of the neck today. Another two minutes and the lost hole had been recovered. Two up.

For Myra it was an enchanted afternoon. She had never been particularly athletic. She had watched a little cricket; she had played a little of what in Edwardian days had been called "Vicarage" tennis. Skiing was the one branch of sport she deeply cared for, and that was different; it was a kind of picnic. It was uncompetitive. She had never known the excitement of pitting her skill and strength against those of an opponent. Now she did. She identified herself with Heather and Gerald, playing their shots with them, anxiously watching their opponents, dejected when an enemy's putt went down, elated when one of Heather or Gerald's approach shots cleared a bunker. It was a form of excitement she had never known, and she was enjoying the exhilaration, after the long months spent on city pavements, of feeling the turf springy beneath her feet, with the sun warm upon her face, but with the sea breeze cooling it.

She walked beside Heather all the time, except when it was Heather's turn to drive. Then she would wait in the fairway where she could expect the drive to land. Half the time Gerald would be beside them, and as they progressed from green to green, she felt mounting inside her not only the challenge of the match but a sense of kinship with the pair. She had identified herself with them, feeling that it was her ball that was rising against the sky, her putt that was rolling towards the hole.

In his way Gerald was as magnetically attractive as his partner, but on Myra he did not have the same effect, because the sight of a handsome, well-built man was familiar to her through films and through television. She had not before had an opportunity of watching, except at swimming pools, an extremely attractive woman occupied in sport. But even so they matched each other very well. And they were obviously in tune with one another, with Heather so absorbed in Gerald. It was cruel that he should be the kind of man he was. She had always been told that there was no worse bet for a woman, matrimonially, than a mother's boy. She looked at him. A sudden thought had struck her. The man who was desperately dependent on his mother might have some secret that he would do anything to prevent his mother knowing. Had Gerald such a secret? Might not the effect of his dependence on his mother be a devious amatory taste? Might this be the

151

quarry that she was seeking? She closed her eyes. What a loathsome person I have become, she thought: making new friends, then plotting to destroy them. She shrugged. She had been through all that before. Useless to go on crying about spilled milk. She was in this thing; the sooner she was out of it the better. If Gerald Armitage held the key that would unlock her prison, she must use it.

She turned to look at Heather. She was so graceful, so willowy, so gentle, so pretty with her unlined cheeks; it was cruel luck that she should have got messed up with a man like Gerald. The fact that she was in a mess, different though it was from her own, gave Myra an additional sense of kinship with her. That same protective urge was on her. She wanted to put an arm about her shoulders, to draw her close, to whisper consolation into her ear. Heather should be spared this kind of thing.

The afternoon wore on. Heather and Gerald's hold upon the game grew firmer. They were three up at the turn. Then they lost a hole. They had to work hard to square the eleventh, but there was no question of their cracking. They were soon three up again. At the fourteenth they were dormy. The fifteenth they lost, but when Heather at the short sixteenth landed her tee shot on the green, after their opponents had landed in the bunker, there was no longer any doubt. Their male opponent laughed. "That should be it," he said, "but I have in my time sunk an explosion from a bunker." He walked to the bunker, swinging his heavy wedge. But this was not one of the times when he was to perform a miracle. His shot hit the ball, instead of the sand behind it, and it soared high and far over the green.

Myra's voice was on the point of trembling. "Congratulaions, oh, I am so glad. The whole thing was wonderful."

"Will you come around with me tomorrow?"

"Oh yes, yes, if you really want me."

"You made all the difference." Heather's eyes were wide and shining; without knowing how it happened they were holding hands. Their fingers intertwined. Myra had the sense of something under her heart going around and over.

The Final was to take place on Saturday – a thirty-six-hole match. On Friday afternoon, on the seventeenth green, Gerald laid his approach putt dead, and that was that. "But I'm afraid that I won't be able to walk around with you on the great day," said Myra.

"How so?"

"My husband's coming down tonight."

"Doesn't he care for golf?"

"On the contrary, he's really rather good. But it wouldn't be the same with him there."

"I suppose it wouldn't."

"The two of us would be in the way."

"Perhaps."

"But I'll be watching."

"Don't fail to be doing that." Heather paused. "I can't somehow think of you as married."

"You've seen my children."

"I know, but with that Swedish girl it looks as though there were the two of you doing alternate baby-sitting."

Myra laughed. "He's quite a real husband, I assure you."

He looked even more real when he arrived by the late train, yet somehow she did not feel that she had particularly missed him. She had been so occupied that she had not fully appreciated that he wasn't there.

He had brought his golf clubs with him. She ought not to have been surprised, but in fact she was. "You don't expect me to come down to Sandwich and not play golf, do you?"

"The final of the mixed foursomes is tomorrow," she informed him.

"What difference does that make? They only occupy one half fairway at a time."

"I've been watching the matches all the week. I thought you'd want to."

"What? Watch a game when I can play it? Not at my age."

"You don't mind if I watch, do you?"

"Heavens, no, it'll keep you out of the way."

"Then I'll tell Heather."

"Heather?"

"Mrs. Bennett."

"Of course, yes, I'd forgotten."

"I'll telephone her now."

She was smoking. She hesitated then out of mischief left the smouldering cigarette in the ashtray. She called Heather

153

from the bedroom. "It's all right," she said. "Victor wants to play himself tomorrow, so I'll be there."

"Oh, wonderful." There was in her voice a note of genuine relief. "It'll make such a difference. You can't think what a difference you have made to me this week."

I believe I really have, thought Myra.

She returned to the sitting room to find that the cigarette had been stamped out as she had known it would be. She assumed a look of guilt. "I'm sorry," she said. "I get into bad habits when I'm alone."

"It's a revolting habit, you know I think it is."

"You look annoyed."

"I am annoyed."

She laughed. "Almost as annoyed as you were when that girl friend of yours got drunk at parties?"

He started, fixed her with a puzzled look, which changed to one of conspiratorial amusement. "That's a fine parallel," he said. "Yes, just about as much annoyed.. You'd better be on your guard or there'll be trouble." She chuckled. Now she knew what to do if she was in the mood.

Victor looked at her thoughtfully. "Why," he asked, "did you call up Mrs. Bennett?"

"To tell her that you were going to play golf and that I was free to watch the final."

"Have you been watching all these matches?"

"Yes."

"You've never taken the slightest interest in golf before."

"Nobody's ever encouraged me to take an interest in it."

"Oh come now, wait." He paused. "Have you fallen in love with Gerald Armitage?"

Her heart bounded. Victor jealous! Nothing in years had built her up as much. "What could make you think that?" she asked.

"I can't see any other reason why a woman like yourself should gallery a succession of matches of a game in which up to now she has not evinced the slightest interest."

She chuckled inwardly. This was one of the very best moments of her life, that Victor, her self-complacent husband, should have doubts ... She saw in a flash all the possibilities it opened. But she saw also the dangers that were incident to those possibilities. This was not the right moment to exacer-

154

bate an irritation; this was the moment to renew his confidence in himself, to build him up. Why not, now and again, tell a man the truth? Keep a man guessing, so the textbooks said. Wasn't that a tart's philosophy, not a wife's? Victor had a whisky and soda at his side. She had not sat down since her return from telephoning. She walked across to Victor. She raised her hand, she laid it on his cheek. "Do you think, my silly sweet, that any woman who has a husband like you, particularly such a you as she has found over the last few months, could be bothered with a golf-course glamour boy?" She drew her hand in a slow caress along his cheek. "Bring that drink into the next room," she said. "I think that for you four nights away from me is at least one too many."

They breakfasted in their suite with the children and the *au pair girl*. It was gay and cosy and the sun streamed across the table.

"I've fixed up with the secretary for a game this morning. But I might as well go around with you in the afternoon," he said. "I might learn something after all."

At lunchtime the game was all square. "How important is all this for Gerald Armitage?" Myra asked.

"In what way how important?"

"If he stops winning tournaments, will he cease to be of value to his wine firm?"

Victor shrugged. "It's hard to say. It is important for a firm like Gerald's to have as their representative someone who is in the public eye; therefore in ten years' time, or even in five years' time, when Gerald has ceased to be in the news, they'll want someone to take his place. But if he has been an efficient salesman for them while he was making the headlines, they'll keep him on. They're a generous firm; they can afford to be."

"Heather says that athletes who get jobs as wine salesmen don't often keep them."

"That's because so many of them start to drink too much. When they don't have to keep fit for the big events, they've every temptation after all. Their business is booze and they do their business over booze."

"Heather's very gloomy about his future. She thinks that in five or ten years' time he'll be unemployed and unemployable."

155

Victor smiled. "That's partly guilt. She's afraid that she's ruining his life because she can't marry him. It's partly self-importance. She likes to think a man is being ruined on her account."

"You don't like her, do you?"

"I don't feel much either way. I hardly know her. This is first time that I've really met her."

"She's attractive, don't you think?"

"She's photogenic, but that isn't the same thing."

"How so?"

"I don't feel any warmth."

"Oh."

To Myra, Heather was aglow with friendliness. She had seldom felt so at one with anyone. Perhaps after that unlucky marriage, and then with Gerald's being the kind of man he was, she was on her guard with men.

"I guess that Heather has given so much to Gerald that she hasn't much to spare for anybody else," he said.

Myra did not answer. That only showed how little Victor knew about Heather, or about Gerald for that matter.

"And you really want to gallery that match this afternoon?" he said.

"I'd like to, yes."

"You've certainly become an addict. I think that you'll have to start taking lessons when we get back to London."

She began to think so herself during the afternoon. Walking around with Victor was altogether different from walking around with Heather. During those earlier matches, she had identified herself with Heather. She had seen the game from the inside, or rather through Heather's eyes, and as she had scarcely ever talked to Heather, had been far from appreciating, ignorant of the game as she was, what was really happening. With Victor it was different. As they were apart from the players, they could talk without fear of interrupting them. Victor could explain the strategy and tactics of the game. Perhaps it would be a good idea if she took up golf. It would be an added thing for them to share. There was no reason why she shouldn't be quite good. She would not be so tied to the nursery now. She had resented having to go around with Victor instead of Heather, but as it turned out she found herself enjoying herself rather more. And it was good, very good, at

156

the end when the match had been won at the thirty-fourth
hole, to have Heather turning round from the tee, looking for
her in the crowd, then pushing her way through to her. It was
a genuine singling of her out.

"Wasn't it wonderful?" Heather said.

"I was praying for you all the time."

"I knew you were. It made all the difference."

Next morning Victor was again out on the links. Heather
was in her room; she had some work, she said, in connection
with the next term's syllabus. Myra, letting Olga go to church,
took the children to the swimming pool. Gerald was there too.
It was so warm as to be almost sultry. After their swim they
set their long chairs side by side under a beach umbrella. She
could watch the children at the shallow end. It was the first
time that she had been cosily alone with Gerald. Now was the
chance to draw him out, to find if he was a possible prey for
her. She had a feeling that he might be.

"Men's friendships are a curious thing," she said.

He raised his eyebrows. "That's a strange way to open a
conversation."

"They're so important to them; and they keep them apart,
in watertight compartments, from their home lives. Yet they're
incomplete."

"Now there you have said a lot. What's put all this into
your mind?"

"I was thinking of you and Victor. Seeing you together,
hearing you talk together, you'd think you were lifelong
friends. You are now, aren't you?"

"Scarcely that. You know how England is. It's so small. We
all know each other, or about each other. Victor and I belong
to the same crowd. We're in the same age group."

"How often would you say you saw each other?"

"Not all that often."

"You wouldn't ever have a lunch together?"

"No, I'd say never."

"If his name came up and he was being discussed, you'd
join in the discussion, wouldn't you?"

"Naturally."

"He's never mentioned you to me."

"Is there any reason why he should?"

157

"And yet you recognised me on the terrace."

"I explained that. I'd seen your photograph when you were engaged. I thought, Lucky Victor."

"Yet you never said to him, 'I'd like to meet this attractive wife of yours.'"

"It's not the kind of thing that Englishmen say to one another."

"You keep your homes, your clubs, your offices quite separate."

"That's so."

"So really none of you knows each other very well.'

"Now we're getting onto something."

"I don't think, for instance, that Victor knows very much about you."

"I wouldn't think so either. But what makes you think he doesn't?"

"The things he said about you."

"What did he say?"

She hesitated before replying. Now was her chance, if she moved cautiously.

"I rang him up that first evening after meeting you," Myra said. "I asked about you; I knew a bit of course, but he filled in the gaps. Then he asked was Mrs. Bennett with you. I said she was, then he asked, 'Is she staying in the same hotel?' That told me how the land lay, or rather how he thought the land lay."

"He imagines that Heather and I are having the romance of the century."

"Yes."

"And that we can't marry because she's married to a Catholic who won't agree to a divorce."

"Yes."

"It's what a lot of people think. It's what most people think, I fancy."

"And it isn't true?"

"What makes you think it isn't true?"

"What Heather told me."

"What did she tell you?"

"That you weren't having an affair at all."

"That's perfectly correct. We aren't, we never have. What else did she say?"

"That's enough, isn't it?"

158

"It may be, but I bet she told you more."

Myra hesitated. She was not going to reveal what Heather had said about Gerald's mother. It might make trouble.

"It's decent of you to be discreet. But there's no need for you to be. I know what she thinks of me, so I'm pretty sure that I know what she told you. She thinks I'm so absorbed in my mother that I can't fall in love with any woman. That *is* what she said, isn't it?"

"It's what she said."

There was a pause. There was a quizzical expression on his face.

"Isn't that true either?" she asked.

He shook his head. "It's no more than what your husband thinks about me. It's Heather's story, though. And quite a lot of people, women mostly, are ready to accept it."

"Don't you mind?"

He shook his head. "On the whole I'm quite glad to have them think it. It's a useful alibi. Not for the fact that I don't happen to like women in that way, but that I don't happen to be neuter. Very far from it. Does that surprise you?"

"Yes."

He laughed. "I suppose I'd better tell you the whole story of my life."

This is just when I should have my tape with me, Myra thought, but even as she thought it, she suspected that this wasn't going to be a confession that would be of any use to her.

Gerald was smiling calmly. "By the time I've finished you may be surprised at my telling you all this, but you're the kind of person to whom I feel I can talk openly, because I believe that you'd respect a confidence. And even if you weren't, I'm not ashamed of what I'm going to tell you, of the explanation that I'm going to give of how I became the man I am. I fancy it's an unusual story, but then we all fancy ourselves unusual. We think we're special and unique. At any rate, here is my story.

"You don't need telling, it's general knowledge of the devious behaviour that goes on between boys in English public schools. If you incarcerate for eight months of the year, in a monastic atmosphere, boys of eighteen who are grown men and boys of thirteen who have only just ceased to be chil-

159

dren, you must expect drama to ensue. Fifty years ago those in authority refused to believe that such things could happen except in a bad house, in a bad school, in a bad time. Now we've gone to the other extreme. We imagine that everyone in an English public school is indulging in – what shall I say? – classical revels. I fancy that the extent of the problem is as overrated now as it was underrated fifty years ago. I think that actually much less goes on than is supposed; and that, in my opinion, is because there is so little emotional reciprocity. A prefect of seventeen is attracted towards a small boy of thirteen because he is small and weak and pretty, because he is in fact girlish. Now that boy of thirteen, unless he is potentially homosexual – and now and again he is – feels no attraction for the older boy. Because he doesn't and because the elder boy usually has a genuine affection for the younger boy, the relationship remains relatively platonic. There is, naturally, a certain amount of, shall we say, dirtiness between boys in the same age group, but it's something that is casual and unimportant, in which no emotions are involved, which does not go deep, which is quickly outgrown when the boys concerned enter the adult world of women. That is the case ninety-nine times in a hundred. My own case was different. It was the hundredth case: I was involved in a relationship where there was a deep reciprocated emotion. I have never got over it."

He paused. He was still smiling; there was nothing self-pitying in his voice. He was treating as a pleasantry something that was clearly most serious for him.

"He was a year and a half younger than I was. But because I went to school a little early, I was two years his senior on the roster. He was in the choir. At Fernhurst the choir sat in the front of the chapel, on both sides of the aisle, facing one another, at right angles to the main body of the pews. I noticed him right away. For me it was the *coup de foudre*. He was in another house, and at my school, as at most schools for that matter, boys are not encouraged to meet boys in other houses until they are quite senior. There was no chance of my seeing him until he had caught up with me in form and games.

"I made inquiries about him. He was, I learned, bright in class. He was only one form lower than myself. He was clearly going to be something of an athlete. He had come

160

from a preparatory school that played Rugby football, so he had a start on the other new boys. He had made a mark of a kind within two terms. He was tried for the Colts, the under-sixteen side; he didn't get in, but he was given a trial. I thought to myself, In a couple of years we may be in the same sides.

"It was all very distant and romantic, the cherishing of an ideal. At our school, in the terminal roll book, they put against each boy's name the various classes that he attends, so that by finding out which boys in my house were in the same classes that he was, I could work out which classroom he would be in at every hour of the day. We each had a chart which we pinned up in our studies, showing where we would be each hour. I put on my chart in red ink the places where he would be. I would think at the start of one day for instance, I shall be working in my study between ten and twelve. At eleven, when classes change, I shall see him cross the courts between the science laboratories and Mr. Churchill's history hour. It was silly but it was romantic. And it was exciting too, because gradually as one term led to another, he became aware that I was watching him. We could not speak to one another. But we exchanged glances. We smiled at one another. We were conscious of each other. A mutual attraction was building up. We were looking forward to the day when we should both be seniors – we could guess when it would happen. Next autumn, I would think, we shall both be in the football side, we shall both be in the top form – the sixth. Then we shall be able to see each other. Later we should be in the cricket side; do you see the point? As a junior you play only with your own house; as a senior you graduate into an inter-national set, in terms of school life, that is to say. I don't suppose we'd spoken to each other half a dozen times, until the first day of that September term when we both appeared to-gether on the first-fifteen field – it was called 'The Upper'. We looked at each other and we smiled. We both knew what was in the other's mind.

"After the game it was usual to go to the school tuckshop for tea and sausages. Now we could sit at the same table. Our talk was easy and natural; we might have been brought up in the same village all our lives. At the end of tea I said, 'Why don't we go for a walk next Sunday?' It was as easy as all that."

He paused. Myra was reminded of Anna and that other girl at the summer camp.

"We never talked about it," he went on. "'Never seek to tell thy love.' It would have embarrassed us to talk about it. We saw each other when we could. It wasn't easy. A school-boy doesn't have much privacy, and we had to be careful. We visited each other in the holidays, but in term time there were only those Sunday walks and it rained quite often. It was enough though; there was the companionship of the football field. I was scrum half, he was fly half. We understood each other's moves. We had our own sign language. They still say at Fernhurst that we were the finest pair of halves they've had. When the ball came out of the scrum, I'd know exactly where he was; I'd fling the ball out to him, watch him cut through, or open up the threes. Sometimes he'd punt ahead and I'd be there, anticipating. Rugger's a lovely game. It was a miracle for the two of us during the two seasons when we played together. There was the thrill of the game itself, and linked with that there was the oneness that we felt together. It was an extension of our Sunday walks.

"It was the same in the cricket season. I was the steadier bat; but he was the more dashing, the more exuberant. I went in number 4, he came in at 6. I played my innings in terms of his, wearing down the bowling for him, so that he could flog it round the field. Very often we'd be in together. What a good moment that was when the fourth wicket fell and I saw him come down the pavilion steps. There's a wonderful com-radeship about a stand together at the wickets. They used to say in the days of feudal England that village cricket was the cement that held the social structure in its place, that when the squire and the blacksmith had put on twenty runs for the first wicket, they had laid the basis of a friendship that no politician could destroy. We had a number of long partner-ships, he and I. Each batted better when the other was at the opposite end. The way we stole short runs – we never needed the call, we knew when we could steal one. And it wasn't only the cricket and the football. We were in the sixth together. We were discovering English literature. Between fifteen and eighteen one is unearthing a new poet every month. First of all it had been the Romantic revival, Keats, Byron, Shelley, with Browning and Tennyson thrown in; then we were introduced to Swinburne, and the decadents of the nineties; then through Rupert Brooke we went back to Donne and Webster. We were alive, as alert mentally as we were physically. It was the old Greek ideal: the gymnasia of Athens. We were complete as we could never expect to be again. The golden age."

He paused. His voice had taken on a new, a deeper tone. There was no undercurrent of a tremor.

"For eighteen months it was ideal," he said, "and then."

"What happened then?"

"A car skidded."

"Were you with him?"

"No. Sometimes I wish I had been. Provided I could have been killed outright as he was."

"How did you learn?"

"From my father. I can see him walking out of his library into the garden: 'I'm afraid I've bad news. A telegram's come through on the telephone.' Then he told me. A part of my life stopped that morning."

He stopped again. She did not interrupt. She waited for him to continue. "I've never got over it," he said. "Emotionally, I've remained in exactly the same place that I was on that April morning. I've talked to doctors; I've done my best, believe me. They tell me that it's a case of arrested development. If there hadn't been that fatal accident, we'd have gone up to Oxford; our relationship would have changed, would have become a friendship. We'd have picked up girls together, married, gone our separate ways. That would have been the normal development. That is what everybody tells me. But ..." Again he paused. Myra thought, this isn't a time when that tape would have been any use. He hasn't done anything that he's ashamed of; if he is ready to talk like this to me, he must have done the same with quite a number of others. It's not as though we were particularly close. For all I know he may have told his mother. Anyhow, it was time for her to make a contribution to the talk.

"Surely," she said, "you're not telling me that you've remained faithful to a memory for fifteen, seventeen, however many years it is."

He laughed. "Oh heavens, no; but what I have is a fixation as regards physical attraction on the young masculine adolescent. That's what I respond to, and that's the only thing that

I respond to. If I'd outgrown it, as I should have normally, I would, as I said, have gone on to the next course on the menu, but as it was *'coupénet en pleine ardeur,'* to quote Maupassant, I've stayed, immobilised."

"That sounds rather tragic."

"Tragic is too big a word. But it's ... well, perhaps 'awkward' is the right word. Because a very young man only remains attractive for a little while. There's a bloom on him which vanishes quite soon. It's a matter of eighteen months. His features coarsen, he sprouts a beard; his limbs lose their coltish suppleness; he has a masculine odour. A man can fall in love with a girl at fifteen and stay in love with her till she's over fifty. She alters but she doesn't change. But my kind of man cannot stay attracted to an adolescent beyond a certain age. I don't say mine is a common case, but it is not exceptional. There are others like me. And men like me are unable to make a lasting emotional relationship, as quite a number of homosexuals do. We know that it can't last."

"So that you go on being attracted to a succession of young men?"

"That's so."

"Isn't it very dangerous, with the law being the way it is? You can never be protected by that 'consenting adults' clause."

"I have to be very careful, in this country. But not in others, where it's not against the law. In Arab countries, for example, where women are very strictly chaperoned, there's not much alternative for young men. My job lets me travel. I take every opportunity of going to North Africa. I manage."

"I suppose you've taken medical advice?"

"Naturally. I've even tried head-shrinkers, but it didn't do any good. Perhaps I was on my guard with them. I didn't want to have my personality altered. I think that one is wise on a lot of counts not to try to cure one's complexes, but to find out what they are and learn to live with them."

"But you have made experiments with women?"

"Of course. But it didn't work."

"It didn't work at all?"

"Not satisfactorily. I felt disgusted afterwards, and, which is quite illogical, resentful towards the woman."

"Rather like women feel who are made love to by husbands when they are not in the mood."

"I guess it is. I wouldn't know. Anyhow, it's a long time since I've tried."

"Isn't it awkward when they fall in love with you? I'm sure they do."

"My mother's a good alibi."

"Heather's accepted it."

"Yes, but that's quite different. We're simply friends; that's why we are such good partners on the golf course. There hasn't been any suggestion there of funny business."

"But surely, at the beginning, wasn't there?"

He shook his head. "Her marriage put her off men completely."

"How so?"

"You don't know the story?"

"No."

"It was tragic; the story's got around that he was a brute who bullied her. It wasn't that. He wasn't a bad chap, in many ways. But he was a man who should not have ever married. He had syphilis."

"I thought that that kind of thing hadn't happened for fifty years. It sounds like something out of Ibsen."

"It was hereditary. Perhaps he didn't know he had it; or perhaps he thought that as it was hereditary it didn't count. At any rate she got it, without knowing it, of course. Then she became pregnant. The baby was born dead. Perhaps because of the syphilis. I don't know. At any rate she was very ill. It's scarcely surprising that she's through with men."

"Surely she could get a divorce on those grounds?"

"Perhaps. But it isn't so easy to divorce a man who's resolved not to be divorced. As you know, he is a Catholic. Perhaps she doesn't want to be divorced. She doesn't want to have anything more to do with men. And being married to a Catholic is a safeguard."

"Her alibi, like your mother myth."

"Exactly."

"Poor Heather. Poor, poor Heather."

Victor caught the late train after an early supper. He wanted to be at his office fresh next morning. Myra waved him good-bye soon after nine o'clock. I wonder if Heather's on her own, she thought. Gerald was leaving the next morning. Heather was staying on for another week, for the sake of the sand and sun, and a lot of work in connection with her next term's syllabus. Myra called her room. "I was wondering if you were on your own," she said.

"I'm on my own."

"I was wondering if you'd like to have a drink with me."

"I'd like to very much. Downstairs or in your suite?"

"It's cosier in my suite."

Heather was wearing a cerise silk blouse that fitted tightly at the wrist but had loose sleeves. There was a wide bow at her throat. It made her look very collegiate and young; the need to protect and cherish her welled up again in Myra. She was so dear and sweet. It was cruel that fate should have dealt so harshly with her.

"Gerald's bar is much better stocked than mine," said Myra. "But I do have on ice a half bottle of champagne that Victor overlooked."

"I don't think that anything could be nicer than a half bottle of champagne. Golfers don't seem to drink it much. They're thirsty and want beer at lunch. In the evenings they want to be fortified with whisky."

They sat side by side on a Chesterfield. Myra raised her glass and clinked it against Heather's.

"May next term be all that you deserve it to be. I suppose you'll go back there as a conquering heroine."

"Nine out of ten girls don't know I was ever in the thing."

"But your special pets will. I'm sure that you have special pets."

"I have them, yes."

"Pets who think that you are the sun, the moon, the stars and all that revolves in the celestial firmament."

"That's rating it a little high."

"But a lot of the girls do have crushes on you, I suppose."

"You remember how schoolgirls are."

"What effect does it have on you?"

"I do my best to be diplomatic. Not to have favourites, yet not to hurt the feelings of those to whom I am, how shall I put it, rather special."

You are a most dear person, Myra thought. There was a pause. "Was your marriage as appalling as people say it was?"

"I don't know how appalling people say it was."

"I've heard some rather dismal stories."

"What have you heard?"

Myra shrugged. She was not going to let Heather know that she and Gerald had discussed her.

"Victor said that he was a bully."

Heather shook her head. "He was scarcely that. He was insensitive, but brutal, no."

"It wasn't good though."

"It certainly was not."

"Has it left you with a feeling that you've had all you want of men?"

"To put it mildly."

"That's sad, but still . . ." Myra paused. She was in a mischievous, a teasing, mood. At dinner she had shared a bottle of wine with Victor, and the champagne was now sending little ripples of excitement along her nerves. "There are consolations, I suppose."

"Consolations?"

"Substitutes, shall I say?"

"What do you mean by that?"

"Doesn't your heart beat faster when those teenagers who have crushes on you gaze at you dewy-eyed?"

"What a thing to ask. Of course it doesn't."

"Not ever?"

"Never."

"Not even hardly ever?"

They laughed again. Myra was conscious of a mounting tenseness, a quiver of anticipation. But she remembered Naomi's advice. Keep it light. Don't invoke high heaven.

"What about the other mistresses?" she asked.

"What other mistresses?"

"There must be quite a number on your staff."

"Of course."

"How many?"

"Over twenty."

"And most of them unmarried?"

"Nearly all."

"Surely some of them must have looked at you with glowing eyes."

"Why should they? They're grown women."

"What difference does that make? How do you live – each in a separate flat?"

"More like in a college – a central sitting room and reading room and each with her own bed-sitter."

"Haven't any of those twenty colleagues come tapping on your door late at night?"

"I'll say they haven't."

"Not one, not the least littlest one?"

"Not even that."

"I'm astonished."

"Astonished?"

"When I think of the effect you've had on me during these last six days."

It had slipped out, without foreplaning. Ten seconds before, Myra had had no idea that she was on the brink of saying that. For an instant she would have given anything to have it back. Then mentally she shrugged. It was said and that was that. There was no retreat.

Heather stared at her, with astounded eyes. "What are you trying to say?"

Myra laughed. "You don't need to be told that you are extremely photogenic. But that is only where it starts. You have one of the nicest natures that I have ever met. You're a heavenly companion. You're more fun to be with than anyone I know. Every day I've found myself liking you more, growing fonder and fonder of you. You're a delight to look at. I love the way you smile, the way you frown when something puzzles you; I love your voice, it's a deep contralto, and all the tones that come into it. Then in addition to all that – as if that wasn't in itself enough." She hesitated. She was almost out of her depth. I could stop now, she thought. It isn't too late yet; it will be in another minute. This is your last chance. But she knew, even as she warned herself, that she had no intention now of drawing back. The thrill of the chase had gripped her.

168

"In addition to all that," she said, "you've got a perfect figure: a rhythm, a harmony of curves; every movement you made on the links was a delight to me – the way your muscles moved under your sweater; your shoulders, your breasts; your legs and hips – every part in harmony with every other part." She paused but this time not in hesitation. She knew precisely what she had to say. She paused, because she wanted to give the greatest dramatic value to it.

"Going around the links day after day, I found it harder and harder to keep my hands off you. Indeed, I had quite often to hold my wrist behind my back in self-defence."

She put down her glass and took Heather's hand. She undid the two buttons of the tight-fitting cuff. She rolled back the silk and stroked her wrist. "Don't look so terrified. I'm not going to try to rape you." She paused. "At least not right away," she added.

Heather laughed at that. Thank heavens, Myra thought, that she can keep it light. But Heather's face wore a dumbfounded look. "I can't believe that you've said what I heard you say."

"I said it right enough."

"I can't believe that you really meant what I feel you did mean."

"I meant it."

"But you're a married woman."

"That makes no difference."

"You and Victor seemed so happy."

"We are. It's a fine marriage."

"If it is, how can you, I mean if a wife is happily married, she doesn't, well, how could she want more?"

"Sometimes she does."

"Only when ... not, I mean, a young couple like you and Victor. You look as though you were in love with one another."

"I think we are."

"Then how can you feel about me like this?"

"It's completely different."

We're going round in circles, Myra thought. I must get this straightened out. She said, "Have you never been made love to by a woman?"

"No."

"You've missed a lot. You'll realise when you are just how
169

different it is. There are things that only a woman can know about another woman, exactly in the same way that there are certain things which a woman needs that she can only get from a man – a man and a woman complement each other. I don't know exactly what went wrong with your marriage, but you said your husband was insensitive. That's why I thought you might find consolation with a woman, because insensitive is exactly what she wouldn't be."

"Did you really believe I had . . . with a woman, I mean?"

For a moment Myra hesitated, wondering whether to tell the truth or whether to excuse herself on the grounds that she had felt sure that an attractive grass widow, who has been put off men, who was a schoolmistress and a successful one, would almost certainly have accepted the substitute of another woman. That answer would provide an explanation that might serve an immediate purpose, but if you once started lying, you could not stop; one lie led to another. And she wanted to tell Heather the truth. She shook her head. "I was fairly certain that you'd never had an affair with a woman, but I thought that you'd be much happier if you did."

"You're quite right on the first count. How did you know?"

"It's one of the things that you can always tell. Women who like women recognise each other. I imagine that it's the same with men."

"Why do you think I should be happier if I was involved with a woman?"

"Because, darling, you're being wasted while you're not."

She was still holding Heather's hand. She stroked the thin bones of her under-wrist, kneading the soft flesh with her thumb. "You are so young. You are so warm. You shouldn't imprison yourself. Don't let your emotions shrivel; let them flower and blossom. Reread Shakespeare's sonnets. They provide a parallel. They're urging a girl to marry so that her looks shall be handed on to another generation. Your case is different, but there is a parallel. It's an argument against waste, against shutting away your beauty. And there is this too, remember; people who restrain themselves when they are young become bitter and hard and harsh when they grow old. They never mellow. It would be terrible if that should happen to you."

She spoke slowly, soothingly, wooingly. She knew what she

was doing. Heather had been exposed to a considerable shock. She must be cajoled back into a sense of safety. There was no hurry. A whole week ahead of them. Play it lightly. Play it slow, with calculated caution. And all the time the champagne was sending its message along their nerves, relaxing tension, making the blood beat faster.

At length the last sip had been taken. Heather rose. "Time for me to pack up," she said. "It's been a strange, strange evening."

Myra stood up too. She was a couple of inches taller than Heather. She stepped towards her. She raised her arms and took Heather's face between her hands. How soft and cool her cheeks were. She raised Heather's face and tilted it, then gently, slowly, she set her mouth on hers, letting it linger there, letting her lips part, letting the tip of her tongue play on Heather's lips, insinuatingly, urging a breach, beseechingly, until at last in their turn they opened, and for a moment the tip of Heather's tongue touched hers. With her fingertips, Myra was conscious of Heather's trembling. I believe, she thought, it's the first time she's co-operated in a kiss.

I've got to have her! Like a caged panther Myra paced her bedroom. Her heart was pounding. There was a thirst in her that must be slaked. The fever of the pursuit inflamed her, the urge to make a convert, to fill the role of the initiator, to join the select ranks of those able to meet the Naomis of the world on equal terms, to be a member of their inner lodge.

How soft and cool those cheeks had been; how hotly they had flushed; that timid, emboldened tongue. To lead this exquisite creature into all the byways and paths of pleasure, the creeks and crevices of delight. How she would respond; how she would become transformed, transfigured. If I looked a different woman to Anna, how will *she* look to me. I must. I've got to.

Yet even as she argued her own case, the indignant voice of outraged conscience was raised in accusation. You can't do this, not to a girl like Heather. What a base betrayal, to hand her over to these blackmailers, these drug addicts; for that's what you're going to do. You know you are. You're going to fit up that gadget in her room. She's exactly the right person for their needs. She'd do anything to avoid having that tape

171

handed over to her college. She'll collect the drugs all right. Then she'll recruit another courier. And how will she think of you, do you suppose? What contempt she'll feel for you. What a low creature you have become. It's not too late. You could still tell Victor. It might spoil your marriage and his career, but what is that compared with the ruining of this poor girl's life? Don't you despise yourself? You should.

The voice of her conscience and the voice of her blood thundered against each other. Was she really ruining Heather? Had Naomi ruined her? Had she not once felt grateful to Naomi, for opening to her a world of new sensations and, incidentally, revivifying her marriage? Ah, but that had been before she had learned the second part of the price demanded of her: the recruitment of this second courier. What would Heather think of her when she found that out? Well, when it came to that, what did she herself think of Naomi, now that she knew the whole story, that she could put herself in Naomi's place? Poor Naomi, what a bad time she has had. Wasn't that how she felt for Naomi? Why should Heather feel any differently from her?

Wasn't that, in the last analysis, what hard experience taught you, sympathy for others? "Suffering with" was the correct translation of that word. You couldn't judge people if you understood why they had behaved in such a way. If her own actions were set down in black and white and put before a jury, she would be condemned as somebody beyond redemption. Yet that was not how she felt about herself. One thing had led to another. She was in a mess and must get out of it. Here was a heaven-sent opportunity. Why argue with herself? Either she ruined Victor's career or got some confession on the tape. Why not Heather? Why not in heaven's name? It had been done to her.

At the same time she pictured self-accusingly the look that would come into Heather's face when this wretched pimp of a man arrived with his miserable box and began to play back to her a record of the most private moments of her life. Oh damn, oh damn. If only she and Heather could enjoy to their heart's content the enshrined week that lay ahead.

Myra had practically a full week at her disposal – she was due to return to London on Saturday. That gave her five

172

nights. She remembered Naomi's discussion of that South African. "He'll probably make his pounce three days before he leaves. Three nights is what you need for that kind of a romance." On that principle, she should try to bring things to a head on Wednesday. That South African. What a long time ago that seemed.

Wednesday; that meant two quiet days. She must be careful not to frighten Heather. She must lull her into calm, get her off her guard, yet at the same time she must whet her curiosity, tantalise her, set her imagination working, implant prurient ideas.

Much of the time they spent by the swimming pool. It was a good place for private talks, as she and Gerald had discovered. Because, at any moment, you were liable to be interrupted, because you were free to take a swim or order a cool drink, you did not have the feeling "We're here for an appointment. We have to break it up in half an hour; we have to compress all we have to say within a certain time, to get the essential said." There was no sense of pressure. The talk drifted from one subject to another, cosy, friendly talk, but always sooner or later swinging back to this one subject, this omnipresent problem.

Heather could not ask too many questions and Myra fed her curiosity. "How did you start?" Heather asked. "How did you find this out about yourself?"

"I found out very early. I think I was lucky. I was only fourteen. I was at a summer school. There was a girl four years older. She looked at me in a funny way. I seemed to guess."

"Weren't you very surprised?"

"Not really. Her being older made it seem all right. It was all so natural. She wasn't embarrassed. Why should I be?"

"And you enjoyed it?"

"You bet I did. You don't know what you've missed."

Myra asked Heather questions too. "You've got to be very careful when you're with your pupils. I see that. But surely when you're with one of the other mistresses, don't you feel attracted, don't you want to touch her?"

"It's something that hasn't occurred to me. I never imagined that I could be that kind of person. I assumed that I should fall in love and marry and have children. I was only twenty when I married. Then . . ."

173

"Tell me about your marriage."

Heather told her.

"Oh, my poor sweet, my darling." She put her hand over Heather's, stroking it.

"After that I found everything to do with sex repugnant. I resented ... Oh, how can I explain? All that part of my anatomy disgusted me."

"So that you never ... After all, most girls experiment with themselves."

"I know they do. I never did; as a schoolgirl, I mean. I thought it would be bad for me on the playing fields, that it would put my eye out. I could wait till marriage. I'd enjoy it more for having waited. I could look forward to it as a reward." She laughed, a bitter little laugh. "A fine reward indeed."

"And since then ... haven't you felt inquisitive, enough anyhow to try?"

"I might have, I suppose, in time, but ... well, I had an odd experience. I was taking a shower. It was one of those gadgets with a long tube. I was spraying myself like crazy – I've always enjoyed showers – when suddenly I began to feel an altogether new sensation. I was standing up. I began to sway, to move my hips, like a hula dancer. My heart began to pound, I wanted to scratch, to scream, and then ... well you don't need telling how I felt ... I slid back into the bath. I lay there gasping. So this is what they talk about, I thought."

"And now you've learned?"

Heather laughed. "I look for bathrooms that have that kind of shower."

"You take them often?"

"As often as I can, when I'm not playing serious golf."

"You must have enjoyed your shower on Saturday after you won the match."

"I'll say I did, a long, long shower."

"I wish I'd been there."

"I wouldn't have had one if you had."

"Don't be so sure. You might have enjoyed it more if I had brandished the spray."

They laughed again. Myra was still managing to keep it light.

"What do you think of when you take these showers?" Myra asked.

"Nothing. Only of how much I'm enjoying it; how long I can make it last."

"When I used to experiment," Myra said, "I'd always think of someone, some special person. I'd hold my pillow in my arms and whisper to it."

"Was it a man or girl you thought of?"

"Depends upon which was most upon my mind. But perhaps," Myra admitted, "it would be hard to think of somebody under a shower." She paused. "Surely," she went on, "you must sometimes have found some woman especially attractive."

"I've had special friends."

"Nobody, though, that you wanted to touch and hold?"

Heather shook her head. "It's never occurred to me to do that kind of thing."

"You've read about it?"

"Naturally."

"But it never occurred to you to connect yourself with anything like that?"

"Never."

"I've an idea that you're going to feel grateful to me one day."

For two days their long colloquy meandered from one confession to another. In a way it did not seem that it was headed anywhere. There was a constant reiteration of earlier-expressed points of view; it was a covering of the same ground, over and over again.

On neither Monday nor Tuesday night did they have a final nightcap in Myra's suite. On Monday they went to a cinema; on Tuesday they stayed in the bar. They did not appear to have made any progress since the Sunday evening when Myra had made her first avowal. No reference had, indeed, been made to that avowal, yet in actual fact Myra had been conducting a subtle courtship. She had insinuated into Heather's mind the idea that she should take the first step that counts. Heather had become accustomed to an idea that on Sunday had appeared to her not only impossible but outrageous. The idea of it had begun to fascinate her.

175

"Do you really think it would make me happy?" she asked Myra.

Myra smiled. "You remember that couplet, 'You will die unless you do / Find a mate to whisper to'; one needs in one's life one friend who is more than a friend. And you need – we all need – love-making in your life. You as much as anyone, you who are so healthy and so human. Every psychologist will tell that. Seventy years ago doctors used to believe that if you couldn't express sex in a normal marital relationship you should sublimate it in work, in athletics, in a career. We know better now. You can't."

Heather sighed. "I envy your having started all this so young. It's late for me."

Myra shook her head.

"Maybe you'll be glad you waited. You didn't eat unripe fruit."

Already Heather had begun to toy with an insidious prospect. That was on Tuesday, over a final drink after dinner. Yes, she had travelled quite a distance, Myra thought. Tomorrow was Wednesday. With three days left: Naomi's programme.

In the morning Heather played a round of golf. But in the afternoon once again the two were lying out in deck chairs by the swimming pool. They had returned to the familiar topic. "Think," Myra was saying, "of the most attractive woman on the staff. Not necessarily the one you like the best – it's funny but sometimes one doesn't terribly like the person one's in love with – no, think of the most attractive one. Now close your eyes. Picture her. Wouldn't you like to hold her in your arms, to caress her, to be caressed by her? Forget this swimming pool. Forget all these people around you. Think of her, think of the two of you together, in the dusk, *'tendrement enlacées'*. Isn't it a pretty picture?"

Heather opened her eyes, blinked, shook her head. "Almost too pretty a picture. But all the same, if I were to . . ."

Myra interrupted her. "Not 'if', 'when' – when you have your first affair."

"Oh, very well then, when ... I shall feel so awkward. I shan't know, in spite of all you've been telling me, I shan't know what to do."

"Don't worry about that." Myra paused. Now, she thought, now's my chance. "Darling, it'll be very simple," she began.

176

"The first time almost certainly it will be the other one who sets the pace, someone who is experienced, who has been watching you for a little while, waiting for you to make a sign, or for you to respond to some sign from her; that's how it was for me. That's how it will be for you. It probably won't happen in your school at all. It'll be somewhere private, a hotel maybe. She'll simply say, 'I'll come to your room tonight, at half past nine.' And soon after quarter-past, you'll be sitting waiting. You'll be happy, tremulously happy. You won't be frightened as a bride is on her first night. You're not going to be assaulted, opened, hurt. It will be rapture, nothing else. You'll watch the minute hand, impatiently. At last you'll see the handle turn. The door will open. You'll see her outlined against the light of the passage. Then the door will close; you'll hear the lock click. She'll be wearing a gown over her pyjamas. She'll stand beside you. She'll rest her hand upon your shoulder. Her fingers will stroke your shoulder. 'I'm going to give you a bath,' she'll say. 'But I've already had a bath,' you'll say. 'I'm going to give you a special bath,' she'll answer.

"She'll cross into the bathroom. You'll hear the splash of water. 'Come,' she'll say. The room will be filled with a rich, heavy smell. She'll have taken off her clothes. She'll lead you by the hand. She'll lift your gown over your head. Her hand will pass over your back in a long, slow caress. There will be a white scum on the top of the water, but underneath it will be blue. 'So that you can't see what I'm doing,' she will say. She'll splash the water over you; then she'll begin to soap you; and her hands will be so slippery and so smooth. You'll feel that you've never had a bath before. The palms of her hands will roll around your breasts. She will lift first one leg out of the water, then the other. Her washing of them will be a slow caress. Her fingers will tantalise you as they draw nearer, nearer. As she dries you, she will hold you close, all the length of your body against hers. 'Now I'm going to massage you,' she will say. She'll lay you on the bed. She'll sprinkle you with powder. She'll start on your back. She will kneel across you. Your hips will feel the softness of her thighs. She will knead your shoulders, your neck, your back. 'And now the front,' she'll say. But now it won't be only her hands and fingers. It will be her lips and tongue. Her kisses will wander over your face, your throat, your knees. She will bite the lobe of your
177

ear gently, then a little harder, till it almost hurts. As her lips move from one breast to the other, her hands will slide over your stomach, and between your legs, dividing, opening, first one finger, then a second. You will writhe and squirm. There will be no hurry. With a man there is that vibrant urgency that has to be assuaged. It's different with a woman. She can prolong, she can renew your pleasure. Her lips move from your breasts; they descend. Her head is between your legs; your thighs feel the softness of her cheeks. Her kisses linger as they approach. Your anticipation mounts. You can scarcely endure the delay. If only she would hurry, hurry. Yet at the same time you are terrified lest it will end, that it won't last forever. And then suddenly the darting tongue is there. And that for a woman is one of the great physical sensations of her life. It is unique, as is the orgasm itself. Till she has appreciated it, she cannot know what it is. And she will remain forever grateful to whomsoever it is, male or female, who is her initiator. There's no reason why it should not be a man. Perhaps it is better for her in the long run if it is, but with a man – this has to be remembered – all the titillations and sidelines of love-making are a prelude for what is for him l'essentiel. With a woman that isn't so; for her the prelude is l'essentiel. That's by the way. It will be for you, that first experience of a darting tongue, the opening of a whole new world. You will sigh and groan. Your fingers will close in her hair. You will feel simultaneously that you are about to die, expire or explode. Yet never have you been more alive; and then when the succession of sighs has at length subsided, her head will be beside yours on the pillows, and in love, in gratitude, you will have an overpowering impulse to repay the gift that has been made to you. You in turn will slide down the bed, lingering, your kisses playing with her breasts, your head between her knees; then your kisses mounting, and maybe you will feel an instant's hesitation, a doubt, almost repugnance, but your sense of gratitude will override it; and when you have overridden it, you will feel – it's impossible to explain precisely what you feel, it's no doubt different for everyone, I can only tell you what it was for me. I had, for the first time, a recognition of what a woman is, of what I as a woman was myself – that lush, odorous dampness, and the vitality that it contained, the nerve cells and the responsiveness. There are bigger moments, but

178

they are different moments. I am not even sure if they are bigger ... but it's unique. ...." She paused. "Don't worry, darling. It'll all be made very easy for you." She swung herself off the chair. "After all that, I'm for a swim," she said. She lowered her hand onto Heather's ankle. She shook it, stroking the fine thin bones. "I'll come to your room tonight," she said, "around nine-thirty."

11

Well, and that's that, she thought. It was Monday morning and she was back in Hampstead. Victor was on his way to Whitehall. The children were learning the alphabet from the *au pair* girls. The tape recorder was safely locked away. It was the first moment of complete peace that she had known for weeks. For better or for worse the thing was settled. It was too late now to consider rights or wrongs. She had behaved no doubt atrociously, but she was in the clear. Never again, she vowed. Never, never again. Though even as she vowed she thought as so often she had thought before, How could I have known? I didn't start it. Where did I go wrong? The telephone bell rang. The voice was familiar, but she couldn't place it.

"It's Gerald Armitage. There's something I want to talk to you about. Could I come out and see you?"

"Of course, yes, when?"

"This afternoon?"

"Fine. When? For tea?"

"Can you make it earlier. You take tea with your children, I remember."

"How about three o'clock?"

"Three o'clock is fine. Oh, and one other thing. I'd rather you didn't mention to Victor that I'm coming out. You'll understand why when I've seen you."

That's curious, she thought – his wanting to come out at all, and then not wanting to have Victor know. If he hadn't poured out his soul by the swimming pool, she'd have thought he had designs on her.

He was wearing a dark blue pin-stripe suit, with a stiff white collar and a Vincent's tie. It was the first time she had seen him in formal day clothes. There was almost a Treasury look about him. He handed her a medium-sized white envelope. "If you'll look at the photographs inside that," he said, "you'll understand."

They were in colour. The first one showed her entering Valentina's boutique in Beirut. Her back was to the camera. The second was rather dim, but it was clear that the same woman who had gone through the door was being given a gift-wrapped package. The third showed her returning to the street, with the package under her arm. It was a very clear photograph.

"Now," he said, "you'll understand how I recognised you right away."

The fourth showed her at the Customs shed. The inspector had lifted the gift-wrapped package from her night bag and was turning it over in his hand. The fifth and last one was of her own street in Hampstead. It showed Mr. Frank coming out of her house, with his plastic briefcase under his arm.

Myra had been exposed to a number of surprises during the last six months. This was the greatest. She stared at Gerald. She could not think what to say.

"Don't be alarmed," he said. "You are not in any trouble."

"Whom do you represent?"

"One of the more secret branches of the C.I.D. One of my jobs is to watch the drug traffic."

"Then why wasn't I arrested at Customs?"

"Because I believed that if we let you free, we should get more evidence against the people who employed you, as indeed we have done. We've been watching Valentina's shop for quite a while. Then when we found out who you were, we watched your house. Frank was a man we'd had our eyes on. Now we knew. We've watched him over the last four months. The net is now ready to close. But there are one or two extra things I need to know, things that you can tell me." He paused. "You may have been surprised at my making you that long confession at the pool the other morning."

"I was."

"I had a purpose. I wanted you to feel completely at your ease with me, so that you would know that I was someone you could not shock. I want you to tell me your whole story, how you got into this in the first place, what they've made you do, what is your position now."

She told it from the very start, omitting nothing; he did not interrupt. But every now and then, in a half pause, he would encourage her with an "Ah yes, I see." Once he said "Now this is very helpful, I'd been wondering that." When she had finished he said, "You've filled in a lot of gaps. This rounds off the story. We can go into action right away."

He paused. "As to the recruitment of this new courier, you've got the tape with you still?"

She had explained that she had carried out her mission, though she had not given Heather's name. Perhaps he had guessed who it was.

"When will you hand it over?"

"I expect him to ring up tomorrow."

"Then what you have to do is this; delay the handing over until Thursday. Then I can make my plans. I'll have him arrested as he leaves your house, with the tape on him."

"What'll happen to the tape?"

"It will be used in evidence. It will be very useful evidence."

"Will the name of the person who is concerned come out in court?"

"No, no. It will be heard in camera."

"She won't have to give evidence?"

"Not any more than you will."

"You mean that she'll never know a tape was taken of her?"

"Never."

Myra closed her eyes. The extent of her relief was the gauge of her previous anxiety. Heather would never know. They could meet again, with no sense of shame, no hatred, no shiver of betrayal. What a reprieve. What luck. What undeserved good luck.

"Does this mean that as far as I'm concerned the case is over, that nothing's going to happen to me, although I've broken the law, though I've smuggled drugs into the country?"

"You'll hear no more of this."

But even now she was incredulous: that she had got off scot free; that Heather would not suffer; that Heather would never know; that she herself had, in this final adding-up, proved to have done no one any harm. No need for a sense of guilt. "It's a lucky break for me," she said.

"I'm not denying that."

"It was lucky that you, and not someone else, was on the case."

"That's possible. Another man might have had you arrested at Customs."

"Was it because I was Victor's wife I wasn't?"

"No. I didn't know then who you were. I simply felt that we hadn't enough evidence to pounce. I wanted to get the big fish too." He paused. "One of the things I like most about this job is the knowing of secrets other people don't."

"Is that what made you take it on?"

"In part."

She looked at him questioningly. She had an idea that he wanted to talk about himself, an indulgence he could not allow himself very often in view of his devious amatory tastes and the secrecy essential to his job.

"Do many people know that you work for the C.I.D.?"

"Only two or three. Half my value lies in their not knowing. My golf and that commission job for the wine boys make a first-class cover."

"Did the C.I.D. fix you up with that?"

"Indirectly. It's not a very serious occupation."

"Heather worries about that. She wonders what's going to happen to you when you stop winning tournaments."

"I know she does. Poor Heather."

"Do you get a kick out of posing as a playboy when you are really a very hard-working, serious-minded man?"

"I must say I do, particularly where my brother is concerned. Have you heard about him?"

"From Heather, just a little."

"What did she say about him – that he's a pompous prig?"

"That's what it amounted to."

Gerald laughed. " I can see her thinking that. He's not too bad a chap but he's, oh, so worthy. The Malvolio type. He thoroughly disapproves of me. Why can't I get myself a solid job? I chuckled to myself when he reads me lectures. He's jealous too, of course. Because on the whole people like me; and I'm in the public eye. Then there's my mother. I'm her favourite. That maddens him, because he does, in point of fact, love her more than I do."

"That surprises me."

182

"Because you are seeing me in terms of what Heather told you, and I am a devoted son to my mother. What is more, I'm an exceedingly good one, perhaps the better for not being too absorbed in her. Where one loves too much one becomes tyrannical, possessive, jealous; one gives so much that one demands an equal return. It's much easier to be kind to somebody one likes. I'm a very, very good son. I make her very happy. I pretend to be dependent on her. She loves that. Sometimes I borrow money from her."

"Money that you don't need."

"Of course. But it makes her so happy to feel I really need her. I'm terribly grateful to her, so abject, and so contrite. I vow I'll never get into debt again. She says, 'There, there, don't worry, darling. What's money for if I can't help my children with it?' I'll bet she never tells my brother. He would get self-righteously indignant. He's so proud of his independence. Always stood on his own feet, paid his own way. I put the money I borrow in trust for his eldest son. I hope my brother outlives me so that he can have the shock of reading of that legacy in my will. Not that it will do me much good on the other side." He chuckled again. "This will make you smile," he said. "I'm quite high up in this job of mine. Last summer they wanted to put me on the Birthday Honours List, an M.B.E. for public services. I would have loved that, just to see the look on my sainted brother's face. But I had to refuse it – for my mother's sake. She'd have felt so cheated if she learned that all the time I'd had a solid job and didn't need her money. She'd be miserable if she couldn't go on thinking of me as the weak and charming little boy who needs her."

"Perhaps in twenty years, when she's no longer here, they might offer you a knighthood."

"They might at that. The spy who came in from the cold, and sat as chairman of the board."

"You'll be able to cock a magnificent snook at your brother when it does. You must get a good deal of inward chuckling in your job."

"I'm going to get a very pleasant chuckle the day after to-morrow when I inform your husband that owing to some very valuable information that we have received from one of our agents we are at last in a position to round up a ring of dope smugglers."

"How on earth will you come to be telling Victor that?"

"He sits on one of our committees. He's the Treasury's representative to see that we don't spend too much."

"This is a day of surprises for me all right."

For a moment she did not speak. She was following a new thread of thought. "He won't of course know who the agent is?"

"Of course not. We never reveal our sources. We simply tell him how much we've spent on them."

"I see." Again she paused. "Where do you hold these meetings? In his office?"

"No, in ours. We have a discreet flat in Knightsbridge. We meet there every other Wednesday."

Knightsbridge. The Brompton Road. It was on a Wednesday that Kitty had called her up. That was how Kitty had come to see Victor from the top of a 14 bus. She burst out laughing. "No, I'm not going to explain," she said. "This is my own, my very private joke." And what a joke it was! None of this need have happened. If she hadn't felt jealous about Victor, she wouldn't have needed sleeping pills. Her doctor would not have recommended her to take that trip to Malta. If she had not gone, she would never have met Naomi. . . . None of this need have happened, none of this would have happened. But if she hadn't gone to Malta ... Was not her marriage better, fuller, because she had been to Malta? Had not she had doors opened for her that she had not known existed? Did she regret that she had been to Malta? ... No, heavens no, she didn't. Now that the consequent penalties had been removed.

"One day I'll tell you why I laughed," she said. "It is a very private joke, but one that ... Well, I think you are the one person in the world who'd see the point of it." She rose. "Is that all?"

"That's all."

She held out her hand. "This has been the most extraordinary afternoon of my whole life." She paused. "I may not ever see you again, but ... I would like to say this: I like you very much."

He smiled. His fingers folded round her hand. "I, too," he said. He turned to leave, then checked. "I've an idea," he said.

"What's that?"

"This recruitment of another courier ... it was very much
184

a secret-service mission. You carried it out extremely well. May I ask you this ... forgive me please if I seem impertinent ... but after all, as that highwayman in *The Beggar's Opera* said, 'We know enough about each other to hang each other.' We've let down our hair. So tell me, this recruitment of a courier, the actual work involved, was it repugnant to you?"

"I must confess it wasn't."

"Then this is what I'm thinking. Somebody like yourself could be of extreme value to the C.I.D. There are a number of chinks we have to fill. I'm wondering whether in extreme circumstances if I found what seemed to me exactly the right assignment for you, you might undertake it."

"It's worth considering."

"If I'm not being indiscreet, it's the feminine angle that appeals to you."

"It certainly does."

"You wouldn't be badly paid for this."

"That's an inducement."

"What I suggest is this – we put you on a retaining fee, and the great advantage of money paid through the secret service is that you don't declare it on your tax return. It's yours and that is that."

"I can see nothing against that."

"And then when a special assignment comes your way, you'll have all expenses met, taxis, cocktails at the Ritz, cosy little luncheons, then an ample bonus; and you would know it was all in a noble cause."

"You can guess what a difference that would make to me."

They both laughed at that. "Still, it is nice to have your conscience clear," he said.

"That's something I've got to learn about."

"I'll put it up at the next meeting; that'll be next Wednesday."

He called her shortly after four. "It's settled," he said. "For the next three years you will be paid twenty-five pounds a month. It will be sent to you in notes in a registered envelope. You are a member of the Ladies Carlton, aren't you? It'll be sent there on the first day of every month. And when you have a special assignment – which I hope you will have quite soon – there'll be an appropriate honorarium."

185

"It all sounds highly satisfactory."

"And your subversive friend is due to call tomorrow?"

"At ten o'clock."

"I'll see that he is properly received."

Victor was back soon after six. He looked as immaculate and unperturbed as he had on that March afternoon when Kitty had seen him in the Brompton Road from the top of a 14 bus – as she would have seen him today had she been on one. "Had a good day?" she asked.

"A day like all my days."

"Nothing special?"

"The daily round, the common task."

Nothing to show that unbeknown to him the family finances had been improved annually by the endowment of three hundred untaxed pounds. How she would chuckle every time she opened that envelope. It gave her a cosy sense of superiority to have a secret from him. It also endeared him to her. "All the same you do look tired. I'll mix the martinis for a change." She put on Sibelius' *Valse Triste*. It was old and it was sentimental. But it had memories for them both. She was in the mood for it. It heightened, stimulated her already fevered mood. How close music brought them, and their shared love of it would hold them when this other immediate bond that held them now had lost its power. But that, thank heaven, was a long way off.

She watched him fondly as she listened. I really love you, she thought, love you as I never thought I could. At the start I didn't know you. I was flattered. I was excited by your being attracted by me. What can he see in me, I'd think. I didn't know you then. But now I do. I love you for your traits and habits; for your formality that I've broken down; for your secretiveness that I've eluded; for the quirks that nobody but me suspects. You're mine and you're staying mine. There's no other woman in your life. I know that now; and there isn't going to be one, because there isn't anything that you could ask from another woman that you can't ask, that you shan't ask, from me. You're mine, you're staying mine.

She drained her cocktail in a quick deep gulp. "I need another," she said, "and so do you. Finish that one off."

The cold bite of the martini fired her blood. An idea oc-

186

curred to her that fired it even more. This might be the night for that. "Yes, you really do look tired. I'm going to give you a hot bath later on," she said.

She poured the blue essence into the steaming water. The scent of it filled the bathroom. "What does that do?" he asked.

"It takes away your aches and pains. In addition you can't see what I'm doing."

"I see."

Her hands moved upwards from his knees. "I had a friend who worked in a hospital. When she was bathing a man who attracted her she would say, 'Would you like me to wash you here?' I am going to wash you here."

It was the first time that she had bathed him. Bathing Heather had been exciting. But bathing Victor was more exciting. The effects were so much more tangible. The result of her efforts showed above the water like a mushroom. He smiled at the sight of it. "The sturdy uncapped hermit."

"That sounds like a quotation."

"It is."

"What from?"

"A poem called 'The Enchantment' that's attributed to Byron."

"I've never heard of it."

"You wouldn't have. It's never appeared in print, as far as I know. It's handed down by word of mouth from one generation of schoolboys to another."

"Did you memorise it?"

"Yes."

"Please," she said.

With his hands clasped behind his head, he proceeded to recite. "I've forgotten the first few lines," he said. "You must imagine the narrator looking through the window of a chalet on a summer's afternoon. This is what he sees:

> A youth and maid were in the room,
> Were each in youth and beauty's bloom.
> She seemed in age about sixteen,
> He full three summers more had seen.
> And from the way they hugged and squeezed
> Each seemed with other highly pleased.

Their garb was very light for she
Was only clad in her chemise,
While he, the youth, did also lack,
All but one garment on his back.
And there the youth and beauteous maid
Still kissed and hugged, and hugged and played.
At length his free hand wandered o'er
The charms beneath the garb she wore.
Till warming more he bade her lift
Up to her slender waist her shift;
The which she did and there displayed
The loveliest limbs that e'er were made
To Lover's kindly eye presented.
But he the youth was not contented,
But bade her straightway cast aside
The garb which did her beauties hide.'

Victor checked, "I never bothered to learn the lines describing her less essential charms, shoulders, breasts, navel, legs. It then goes on:

'All these he saw, but fixed his eyes
Most on the part below the thighs.
The only entrance to her heart
Lay like a rosebud set apart
And this unlike to other girls'
Was yet unhid by shady curls
But by a down as you might find
Upon the peach's luscious rind
And still its coral lips displayed
Undimmed by this capillary shade
A tempting prize, yet which to name
You, dear, would say it were a shame.
But still there's many a blushing miss
Whose fingers try its path to bliss
And in their teens to show their shrine
Will lift waist high their crinoline
For some fair youth to fill with joy
With his easily erected toy
And in return some inches get
Between her open pantallette.

188

But to my tale: the youth was left
Still gazing at the open cleft
To which his fingers soon did fly
And raised his passions there so high
That casting off the garb he wear
He, too, stood naked like the fair.
And with one arm around, intwined
Felt every part, before, behind.
Nor was she idle for her hand
Grasped something that it nearly spanned
And as it rose she took the dart
Which sometimes almost reached her heart;
And when she did her grasp resign
Her fingers opened love's new shrine
To which with meaning full intent
The sturdy uncapped hermit went.
But in the rosy gates he lingers
Detained by her encircling fingers
Till with sensation dear to wives
Deep in the welcoming cavern dives,
And through and through triumphant goes
Right through the centre of the rose
Till with one last convulsive throe,
She feels love's burning lava flow.'

"There are a few more lines, but I never learned them."

"And I suppose you used to recite this to boys you had designs upon, to get them into the right mood?"

"I never thought of that."

"You should have done. It might have been most effective. Byron – didn't he like young sailors?"

"That's what they say nowadays."

Pensively she moved the head of the uncapped hermit above the water. "You remember that novel we both liked, *Consider the Lilies!*"

"Yes, very well."

"You know what was meant by the Italian way."

"Naturally."

A half smile flickered on her lips. "It's something we've never tried, you know."

189

She knelt forward on the carpet, her head pressed against a cushion. She recalled that first night with the secret weapon, when Victor had knelt between her knees, and she had drawn a special thrill out of his subjection to her authority. Here was the process in reverse, in her abject surrendering to his caprice, irrespective of any pleasure that it might bring to her. There was a curious pride in the utterness of her submission, a sense of peace in her discomfort, of superiority in her abasement, of power in her thraldom.

"Well?" she asked.

"Well?"

"Was it all that wonderful?"

"Not all that wonderful."

"But I'm glad we tried; aren't you?"

"Oh yes."

"It may be better a second time, or a third," she added.

An acquired taste. She wondered if she could ever acquire that particular taste of Anna's. Not with Victor. That would lead to jealousy, as Anna had foreseen in her own different case. Nor could she picture it with Heather and some such man, as Anna had described. She could not see herself as an initiator in this issue. It would have to be with somebody like Anna whose special thing it was. Why not after all with Anna? She mustn't lose touch with Anna. Lena would not last forever. She sighed. It was good to know there were experiments ahead. One day soon she would leave a smouldering cigarette: one day, very soon.

There was a ring at the front door. She looked at the clock. Ten. That would be Mr. Frank. She went down to the front door. He was carrying his plastic briefcase.

"All shipshape?" he inquired.

She nodded and led the way upstairs. She had the tape waiting for him on the desk. She handed it across. "You've got my tape?" she asked.

He nodded. "But I'd like to hear some of your tape first. I have to be sure it's what we want."

"It's rather long."

"We'll hear some selected passages."

He started at the beginning. Myra heard herself saying, "I

recognise that you have to be very careful in a school like Annandale."

"Particularly someone like myself, who's the symbol of health and fitness and propriety. If I taught history or modern literature, I wouldn't need to be so strict."

Mr. Frank let the tape run for a couple of minutes, then switched it off. "Excellent, excellent. There's no mistaking who she is. Now let's try a little action."

He ran the tape through quickly; then once again he switched it on. Heather again, but in a very different voice. "Oh yes, oh yes, it's wonderful." Myra closed her eyes. She could feel Heather's fingers in her hair. Once again Mr. Frank let it run for a couple of minutes, then switched it off. "You certainly know your stuff."

God, what a loathsome little man, she thought.

Again he ran the tape through quickly. Then once again there was Heather's voice. "Don't look so sad, darling. It's I who should be sad, not you. I'll be alone: you won't be."

This was the last morning. Heather had come into Myra's suite for breakfast. Myra had wished she wouldn't. There was confusion with the children. There had been no real chance to talk. Her heart was heavy. It was all over now. In an hour's time she would be on her way to London, with the tape tucked in her suitcase. She would never see Heather again. And within two weeks Heather would be hating her, Heather whose eyes were now aglow, whose voice had taken on a deeper, richer tone. "Don't be depressed," Heather was repeating. "We'll be seeing each other again, so soon, so very soon."

The machine clicked off. "No need to hear any more," said Mr. Frank. "You've done a fine, fine job. Here's your own tape. I'll leave the sound-box, as a souvenir. No sore feelings anywhere, I hope."

He fitted the new tape into his briefcase.

"You can find your way out, can't you?" Myra said.

She wanted to watch what happened from the window.

She heard the front door close, not with a slam, but firmly. She watched him step out onto the pavement, look to the left and right, then prepare to cross the street. As he did so she saw a tall, powerful man walk up behind him; from lower down the street another powerful man walked forward; a third tall powerful man began to cross from the other side. The two men on the pavement each took one of his arms; a largish car drew up beside the kerb. Its door was opened by the man who had crossed the street. Mr. Frank was bundled into the car before he could make any move. The third man followed them inside; the car drove off.

It had not taken twenty seconds. That's that, she thought. He's a rat and he deserves it. Then she thought, who am I to call anyone a rat? I might have been arrested at the airport. She shrugged. She turned back into the room, the tape that Mr. Frank had brought lay on the table beside the sound producer. She fitted it in the box and turned it on. She heard her own broken sighs, her gasps. She heard Naomi pleading, "Darling, now you to me, please please." She switched it off. What a lot had happened since that night. She was a different woman. She had discovered tastes, potentialities in herself that she had not suspected. Victor was a new husband. He must be happier in this new avatar.

Should she be ashamed of the woman that she had become, or should she see herself as doing the things, as being the person that forty women in a hundred would do, would want to be, if they had the chance? ... How much fuller her life was now; how much more there was to look forward to. Heather – she would certainly be seeing her again. Not for long probably. Heather would need more than she could give, a woman to whom she could devote herself. "The mate to whisper to." Herself she did not need that. Victor was that for her in a relationship that she could embellish and enrich. But there were delicious bypaths. She was now in receipt annually of three hundred untaxed pounds. What might that not lead her to?

She drew a long, slow breath into her lungs, she thought of Mr. Frank on his way to Wormwood Scrubs. She shrugged. He had been out of luck; but she was in. Someone had to pick up the good hand in every deal.

I'm going to enjoy the next ten years, she thought.